"You will stay in t
Ramiz turned tow
his eyes seeme

"Do you mean I am to stay in a harem?" Celia's eyes widened in shock. Images from *A Thousand and One Nights*, of scantily-clad concubines oiling themselves and lolling about on velvet cushions sprang to her mind. "Your highness, Ramiz, I am flattered that you should consider adding me to your collection of wives, but…"

"My wife! You overestimate your value. A Western woman, even a titled one, could not aspire to such an exalted position. At best perhaps, she could serve as a concubine."

Celia gave an outraged gasp. "You expect me to be your concubine! I absolutely will not! How dare you! How dare you suggest such an outrageous, indecent…"

He moved so suddenly she had no chance of escape. He seemed to uncoil, to pounce, so that one minute she was sitting next to him, the next she was being dragged helplessly to her feet, held in arms so strong it would be pointless to struggle. Tall as she was, Ramiz topped her by several inches. She was pressed against him, thigh to thigh, chest to chest. His breath was on her face. She could smell him, warm and overpoweringly male. She had never been held thus. She had never been so close to a man.

* * *

Innocent in the Sheikh's Harem
Harlequin® Historical #1049—July 2011

Author Note

The Arabian world of the early nineteenth century is (if you'll pardon the pun) very much virgin territory. As for tents, my experience is confined to nights spent under canvas accompanied by those twin stalwarts of the Scottish summer, rain and midges. Not the most romantic and glamorous of backdrops, however breathtaking the scenery.

Then my lovely editor pointed me in the direction of the intrepid Lady Hester Stanhope, and I was instantly captivated by the exotic, intoxicating and above all utterly "other" world in which she had traveled. It made me wonder, what would it be like for a classic English rose to be stranded in such a place, completely overwhelmed by the alien customs and culture, and wholly in the power of the autocratic ruler of the kingdom in which she found herself. Which is exactly the fate that befalls my heroine, Lady Celia, who finds herself in the behind-closed-doors sensual world of the harem, in thrall to an imperious, powerful sheikh who is so revered as to be thought flawless. Could she possibly be the one to capture the heart of this moody and magnificent prince?

I hope you enjoy immersing yourself in the intensely sensual world I have conjured as much as I have enjoyed creating it.

Innocent in the Sheikh's Harem

MARGUERITE KAYE

TORONTO NEW YORK LONDON
AMSTERDAM PARIS SYDNEY HAMBURG
STOCKHOLM ATHENS TOKYO MILAN MADRID
PRAGUE WARSAW BUDAPEST AUCKLAND

Recycling programs
for this product may
not exist in your area.

ISBN-13: 978-0-373-29649-1

INNOCENT IN THE SHEIKH'S HAREM

Copyright © 2010 by Marguerite Kaye

First North American Publication 2011

For questions and comments about the quality of this book
please contact us at Customer_eCare@Harlequin.ca.

www.Harlequin.com

Printed in U.S.A.

For Joan (Johanna), who taught me to read,
inspired me to read lots, and who was there that day
on the beach in Cyprus when Kit and Clarissa
first popped into my head. Thank you, and love.

Chapter One

Summer, 1818

'Oh, George, do come and see!' In her excitement, Lady Celia Cleveden leaned precariously over the side of the dhow in which they had just completed the last leg of their journey down the northern part of the Red Sea. The crew lowered the lateen sail which towered high above their heads and steered the little craft skilfully through the mass of other dhows, feluccas and caiques, all jostling for space in the busy harbour. Celia clung to the low wooden side of the boat with one gloved hand, the other holding her hat firmly in place, watching with wide-eyed wonder as they approached the shore.

She was dressed with her usual elegance in a gown of pale green sprigged muslin, one of several which she had had made especially for the trip, with long sleeves and a high neckline which in London would have been quite out of place but which here, in the East, she had been reliably informed, was absolutely essential. A straw hat with a long veil, also essential, covered her distinctive copper hair, but her tall, slender figure and youthful creamy complexion still attracted much attention from the fishermen, boatmen and passengers of the other craft currently vying for space in the busy port.

'George, come and see,' Celia called over her shoulder to the man sheltering under the scant cover provided by a tattered tented roof over the stern. 'There's a donkey on that boat with a positively outraged expression. He looks exactly like my uncle when a parliamentary vote has gone against him in the House,' she said with amusement.

George Cleveden, her husband of some three months, made no move to join her, and clearly was in no mood to be amused. He too was dressed with his usual elegance, in a cutaway coat of dark blue superfine teamed with a striped waistcoat from which a selection of elegant fobs dangled, and buckskin breeches worn with top boots. Sadly, though his outfit would indeed have been perfect for a coach journey from his mother's house in Bath to his own lodgings in London, or even for the ride from his London lodgings to his small country estate in Richmond, it was very far from ideal for a trip down the Red Sea in the blazing heat of summer. The starched points of his neck cloth had wilted many hours ago. His head ached from the heat of the sun, and there was a very distinctive rim of sweat marking the band of his beaver hat.

George eyed his young bride, looking confoundedly

cool as a cucumber, with something akin to resentment. 'Blast this infernal heat! Do come away from there, Celia, you're making a show of yourself. Remember you are a British diplomat's wife.'

As if she needed reminding! Celia, however, continued to marvel at the spectacle unfolding before her eyes, choosing to ignore her husband. It was something at which she had become surprisingly adept during the short period of their marriage. The wedding had taken place on the very day upon which they had set out for the long journey to Cairo, and George's new diplomatic posting. George, the collected, organised undersecretary who worked for Celia's father, Lord Armstrong, at the Foreign Office, had proved to be a rather less than intrepid traveller. This left Celia, who was no more experienced than he when it came to traversing the globe, to manage as best she could the challenging task of getting them—along with their mountain of baggage— from London to Egypt via Gibraltar, Malta, Athens, and an unplanned stop in Rhodes, when their scheduled ship had failed to arrive, and much of their luggage had disappeared. For this, and for a plethora of other minor mishaps which were the result of Celia's naïve but plucky determination to get them in one piece to their destination, George blamed his wife. Damp sheets or no sheets at all, poor wine and much poorer food, insect bites and insect stings, nausea-inducing pitching seas and seas that were becalmed—George had borne none of these with the equanimity Celia had so much admired in the man she had married.

She put much of it down to the tribulations of travel,

and maintained an optimistic outlook which she had intended to be reassuring, but which seemed to have rather a contrary effect. 'How can you be so damned jaunty?' George had demanded during one particularly uncomfortable crossing, memorable for its weevil-infested ship's biscuits and brandy-infested ship's captain. But what was the point in lying abed and bemoaning one's fate? Far better to be up on deck, watching hopefully for land and admiring a school of porpoises with comically smiling faces swimming alongside them.

But George could not be so easily distracted, and eventually Celia had learned to keep her fascination for all things strange and colourful to herself. Foreign climes, or at least Eastern foreign climes, clearly did not agree with George's constitution. This was rather a pity, since fate had brought them here, to a clime so foreign Celia had never even heard of it and had been forced to ask one of the consuls in Cairo to point it out on a rather large and complicated map kept under lock and key in his office.

'A'Qadiz.' Celia said the word experimentally under her breath. Impossibly exotic, it conjured up visions of closed courtyards and colourful silks, of spices and perfumes, the heat of the desert and something darker and more exciting she could not put into words. She and her next sister, Cassandra, had read the Arabian tales, *One Thousand and One Nights*, in French, sharing an edited version with their three younger sisters, for some of the stories hinted at distinctly decadent pleasures. Now here she was in Arabia, and it looked even more fantastic than she had imagined. Watching from the dhow as the dots on the harbour became people and donkeys and horses and camels, as the distant buzz became a babble of voices, Celia wondered how on earth she would be able to convey to Cassie even a tenth part of what it actually felt like.

If only Cassie were here with her, how much more fun it would be. As quickly as the very unwifely thought flashed through her mind, Celia tried hard to suppress it—an act rather more difficult than it should be, for though she had been married for exactly three months, one week and two days, she did not feel at all like a wife. Or at least not at all as she had expected to feel as a wife.

The match was of her father's making, but at four-and-twenty, and the eldest of five motherless girls—two of whom were already of marriageable age—Celia had seen the sense in his proposal. George Cleveden was Lord Armstrong's protégé. He was well thought of, and great things were expected of him.

'With a hostess like you at his side, he can't fail,' Papa had said bracingly when he'd first put forward the idea. 'You've cut your teeth in diplomatic circles as my hostess, and a damned fine fist you've made of it. You can hold your own with the best of them, my girl, and let's face it, Celia, it's not as if you've your sister's looks. You take after my side rather than your mother's, I'm afraid. You're passable enough, but you'll never be a toast, and it's not as if you're getting any younger.'

Celia bore her father's casual assassination of her appearance with equanimity. She neither resented nor envied Cassie her beauty, and was content to be known as the clever one of the five Armstrong girls. Elegance, wit and charm were her accomplishments—assets which stood her in excellent stead as her father's hostess and which would stand George in equally excellent stead as he rose through the diplomatic ranks, as surely he would if only he managed to shine in this posting. Which of course he would—if only he could accustom himself to being away from England.

George, it seemed, was the type of man who needed the reassurance of the familiar in order to function properly. It had been his idea to postpone the consummation of their vows. 'Until we are settled in Cairo,' he had said on their wedding night. 'There will be enough for us to endure on our journey without having to contend with that as well.'

Even at the time his words had struck her as somewhat ambiguous. Though lacking a mother's guidance, Celia was not entirely unprepared for her marital duties. 'As with so many things in life,' her stately Aunt Sophia had informed her, 'it is an act from which the gentleman derives satisfaction and the lady endures the consequences.' Pressed for practical details, Aunt Sophia had resorted to obscure biblical references, leaving Celia with the vague impression that she was to undergo some sort of stamina test, during which it was vital that she neither move nor complain.

Slightly relieved, though somewhat surprised, given Aunt Sophia's certainty that gentlemen were unfailingly eager to indulge in this one-sided game, Celia had agreed to her husband's proposed abstinence, spending her first night as a married woman alone. However, as the nights passed and George showed no inclination to change his mind, she could not help wondering if she had been wrong—for surely the more one postponed something, the more difficult it became to succeed? And she wanted to succeed as a wife, eventually as a mother too. She liked and admired George. In time she expected to love him, and to be loved in return. But love was built on sharing a life together, and surely sharing a bed must play a part in that? Lying alone in the various bunks, pallets and hammocks which had marked their progress across the globe, Celia had swung between fretting that she should do something about the situation, and convincing herself that George knew best and it would all come right in the end.

But after a week in Cairo, with George restored almost to his pleasant and agreeable self, he had still shown no interest in joining his new wife in her bed. Plucking up all her courage, Celia had tried, extremely reluctantly, with much stumbling, blushing and almost as many vague biblical references as Aunt Sophia, to broach the subject—a particularly difficult task, given her lack of any certain knowledge of what the subject actually entailed.

George had been mortally offended.

He was trying to be considerate, to give her time to adjust to married life.

They barely knew each other.

It was highly unnatural of Celia to show such a morbid interest in these things which all the world knew only women of a certain class enjoyed.

And finally, he was doing her a favour by restraining

himself from imposing what he knew she would find unpleasant upon her, and she had thrown that favour in his face!

Celia had retired, confused, mortified, hurt and a little resentful. Was she so unattractive? Was there something wrong with her? Certainly George had implied that there was.

Or was there something wrong with George? Not her first unwifely thought, but the most shocking. She banished it. Or tried to. In the absence of any other woman to consult—for she could not quite bring herself to confide such intimate matters to the forbidding Lady Wincester, the wife of the Consul General of Cairo—she had resolved to write to Aunt Sophia. But it was such an awesome task, and putting her fears into words seemed to make them more real, and perhaps George was right— it was just a matter of time. So she had instead written colourful descriptions of all she had seen and all she had done, and made no reference at all to the fact that her husband continued to spurn her company after dark.

When this special assignment on which they were now engaged had come up, it had been with immense relief that Celia had turned her attentions to preparations for the trip. She had accompanied George against the express wishes of the Consul General. A'Qadiz was no place for a gently bred woman, apparently, but on this matter George had stood firm, and refused to go without her. Impressed by what he took to be a newlywed husband's devotion to his wife, Lord Wincester had most reluctantly agreed. Under no such illusion, Celia had prepared to resume her role as chief nurse, comforter and courier with an air of sanguinity she'd been very far from feeling.

The scenery through which they had sailed was enchanting. The deep waters were clear enough for her to watch the shoals of rainbow-coloured fish just by hanging over the back of the boat. Reefs with coral all the shades of sunset and sunrise could be seen just below the surface, shimmering like tiny mystical cities teeming with life. Along the shoreline were palm, orange, lemon and fig trees, olive groves and a myriad of plants with scents so heady that it was, as she had said to George at dusk one night, like being inside a huge vat of perfume.

'It's playing havoc with my hay fever,' he'd sniffed, putting paid to the eulogy she had been about to deliver.

The port of A'Qadiz in which they had now arrived looked impossibly crowded, swarming with people swathed in long robes. The women were all veiled, some with light gauze such as Celia's own veil, others draped in heavier material, with only slits for their eyes. A stack of enormous terracotta urns stood on the quayside, waiting to be loaded for transport north. Through the open doors of the warehouses could be glimpsed bales of silks in a rainbow of colours, and hundreds more of the large urns.

As the dhow pulled alongside, it was the noise which struck Celia next. The strange, ululating sound of the Arabic language, with everyone talking and gesturing all at once. The high-pitched braying of donkeys, the rumbling of carts on the rough stony ground, the low-pitched bleating of the camels which reminded Celia of the rumbling noise her father made when he was working up to an important announcement. Picking up her skirts and leaping lightly to the shore, careful to make sure her veil remained in place, she couldn't help thinking that the camels themselves, with their thick lips and flaring nostrils, looked rather like Aunt Sophia.

She turned to share this mischievous thought with George, but he was clambering awkwardly to the shore with the assistance of two of the crew, cursing under his breath and frowning heavily in a way that did not bode well for his temper. She made a mental note to share it instead with Cassie, in her next letter.

Rummaging in her reticule for a little bottle of lavender water, Celia tipped a few drops onto her handkerchief and handed it to her husband. 'If you wipe it on your brow it will cool your skin.'

'For God's sake, not now! Are you determined to show me up, Celia?' George batted the scrap of lace away.

It fluttered to the ground, where four semi-naked children contested for the honour of retrieving it and handing it back. Laughing at their antics, Celia thanked them all solemnly in turn. By the time she looked up George was disappearing into the crowd, following the trail of their baggage, which was being carried on the heads of the crew of the dhow, ushered on its way by a man dressed in flowing black robes.

Struggling through the small forest of children's hands clutching at her dress, her gloved hands, her long veil, Celia made slow progress. The colours dazzled her.

In the relentlessly glaring light of the sun, everything seemed brighter, more starkly outlined. Then there were the smells. Sweet perfumes and incense, spices that tickled her nose, the dusty dryness of the heat, the strong musty smell of the camels and donkeys all combined to emphasise the incredible foreignness of the place, the far-awayness, the overwhelmingly exotic feel of it.

Except, she realised, stopping amid her small entourage of children to try and locate the train of her luggage with her husband in its wake, it was really she who was the foreigner here. She could no longer see George. *Had he forgotten all about her?* Panic and a spurt of temper made Celia instinctively push back her veil in order to obtain a better view.

A startled hiss came from the people in her immediate vicinity. The children all turned their heads away, covering their eyes. Fumbling for her veil with shaky fingers, she managed to catch the gauzy material in a hat pin and grew flustered. *Where was George?*

Anxious now for a glimpse of her husband, she cast a frantic look around the crowds. The docks were set into the shade of a low outcrop, and many of the storehouses and animal pens were built into the rock itself. Celia's eyes were drawn to the top of the hill, where a lone figure sat astride a magnificent white horse. A man dressed in traditional robes, and if anything even more magnificent than the beast which bore him.

Outlined against the blazing blue of the azure sky, dazzling in his white robes, he looked like a deity surveying his subjects from the heavens. There was something about him—an aura of authority, a touch-me-not glaze—which dazzled and at the same time made her want to reach out, just to see if he was real. He both compelled and intimidated, like the golden images of the pharaohs she had seen in Cairo. And, like the slaves in the murals she had seen on the walls of the temple the day she had finally persuaded George into taking a sightseeing trip, Celia had an absurd desire to throw herself to her knees at this stranger's feet. He seemed to command adoration.

Where on earth had that come from? Celia gave herself a little mental shake. He was just a man. An extremely striking man, but a mere mortal all the same.

He was dressed entirely in white, save for the gold which edged his *bisht*, the lightweight cloak he wore over the long, loose tunic which all the men here favoured. There was gold too, in the *igal* which held his head-dress in place. The pure white of his *ghutra* fluttered like a summons in the light breeze. It fell in soft folds, and must be made of silk rather than cotton, she noted abstractedly. Underneath it, the man's face showed in stark relief. His skin seemed to gleam, as if the sun had burnished it. It was a strong face, the clean lines of his cheeks, his nose, his jaw, contrasting sharply with the soft, sensual curve of his mouth.

His eyes were heavy-lidded—a little like hers. She could not see their colour, but Celia was suddenly acutely aware that his piercing gaze was trained directly on her. She was not properly veiled. He should not be looking at her thus. Yet he showed no sign of looking away. Heat began to seep through her, starting from somewhere in her stomach. *It was the hot sun!* It must be, for it was most unlike her to feel so unsettled.

'My lady?' Celia turned to find the man who had taken charge of their bags standing before her, his hands pressed respectfully together as if he was praying.

Reminded by his averted eyes to pull her veil back into place, Celia dragged her gaze away from the god on the hilltop and returned the gesture with a slight bow.

'I am Bakri. I have been sent by my master, His Highness the Prince of A'Qadiz, to escort you to his palace. I must apologise. We were not expecting a woman.'

'My husband does not travel well. He needs me to take care of him.'

Bakri raised a brow, but swallowed whatever words he was about to say. 'You must come,' he said instead. 'We must leave soon—before night falls.'

Sheikh Ramiz al-Muhana, Prince of A'Qadiz, watched her go, a frown drawing his dark brows together. The man with the weak face could only be the English diplomat, but what in the name of the gods did he think he was doing, bringing a woman companion? His wife? His mistress? Surely he would not dare?

Ramiz watched as the woman followed Bakri to where the Englishman waited impatiently by the camels and mules which would form their small caravan. She was tall and willowy. In the East, where curves were seen as the apex of womanly beauty, she would be deemed unattractive, but Ramiz, who had spent much of his adult life in the great cities of the West, completing his education and later acting as his father's emissary, was not so biased. She moved with the grace of a dancer. In her pale green dress, with her veil covering her face, she made him think of Guinevere, the queen from Arthurian legend. Regal, ethereal, temptingly untouchable. Definitely not a mistress, he decided, yet she had not the demeanour of a wife either.

Ramiz watched in disgust as her husband chastised her. The Englishman was a fool—the type of man who blamed everyone but himself for his faults. He should not have let her out of his sight. The woman was not responding, but Ramiz could see the tension in her from the way she stood a little straighter. Her cool exterior was belied by that flame of hair which he had glimpsed when she had thrown back her veil. She would be magnificent when angry. Or roused. Despite her married state, Ramiz was certain her passions slumbered still. He wondered what it would take to awaken them.

Her husband was not just a fool, but obviously inept. It was one of the things which Ramiz found incomprehensible—this reticence the English had regarding the arts of love. No wonder so many of their women looked uptight. Like buds frozen into permanent furls by frost, or simply withered through lack of the sun, he thought, as he watched the Englishman struggle to mount one of the camels. The woman was organising the loading of their baggage onto the mules. She made short work of seating herself on the high platform which formed the camel's saddle, arranging her full skirts with elegant modesty, for all the world as if she rode one every day. Unlike her husband, who was clutching nervously at the pommel, making the animal dance playfully, the woman sat with her back straight, holding the reins at precisely the correct angle, swaying in tune to the undulating movement of the beast.

Ramiz cursed under his breath. *What did he think he was doing, looking upon another man's woman in such a way?* Even if the man appeared to be an incompetent fool, honour forbade it. The Englishman was his guest, after all, and here at his invitation.

Ramiz was under no illusions. The English, like the French, were waiting in Cairo like vultures, ready to prey upon any sign of weakness as the Sultan of the once-great Ottoman empire struggled to retain his control over the trade routes. Already the ruthless Mehmet Ali had taken Egypt. A'Qadiz, with its port on the Red Sea, could prove a valuable link to the riches of India. Ramiz was in no doubt about the benefits to his country that playing such a role might bring, but nor was he blind to the disadvantages. Westerners were desperate to plunder the artefacts of the old world, and A'Qadiz was a treasure trove of antiquities. Ramiz had no intention of allowing them to be hauled off and displayed in private museums by greedy aristocrats with no understanding of their provenance or their cultural value, any more than he intended handing control of his country over to some conquering imperialist. As Prince al-Muhana he could trace his lineage back far beyond anything English or French dukes and lords could dream of.

Examine what is said, not he who speaks. His father's words, and wise as ever. The Englishman deserved a fair hearing. Ramiz smiled to himself as he turned his horse away from the harbour. Three days it took to travel across the desert to his palace in the ancient capital city of Balyrma. Three days—in which time he could observe, study and plan.

Six camels and four mules formed their caravan as they wound their way up the hill from the port of A'Qadiz into the desert, for Prince Ramiz had assigned them three guards in addition to Bakri, their guide. The guards were surly men, armed with alarming curved swords at their waists and long slim daggers strapped to their chests, who eyed Celia with something akin to disgust and muttered darkly amongst themselves. Their presence was alarming, rather than reassuring to her. George, too, seemed uncomfortable with them, and stuck close to Bakri at the head of the train.

This part of the desert was much rougher underfoot than Celia had anticipated—not really sand at all, more like hard dried mud covered with rock and dust—and it wasn't flat either. After the first steep climb from the sea, the land continued to rise. In the distance she could see mountains, sharp and craggy, ochre against the startling blue of the sky, which was deepening to a velvety hue as the sun sank. The sense of space, of the desert unfolding for miles, beyond anything she could ever have imagined, was slightly intimidating. Compared to such vastness, she could not but be aware of her own insignificance. She was awestruck, and for a moment completely overwhelmed by the journey they had travelled and the task ahead of them in this land as shrouded in mystery as the people were shrouded in their robes.

However, as the caravan made its way east over the desert plain and she became more accustomed to the terrain as well as to the undulating movement of the camel, Celia's mood slowly lifted. She amused herself by picturing Cassie's face when she read of her account of her ride on the ship of the desert, and revived her flagging optimism by reminding herself of the very high esteem in which George, as a diplomat, was held. This mission would be a success, and when it was, George would stop fretting about his career and turn his mind to making an equal success of his marriage. She was sure of it!

They came to a halt in the shelter of an escarpment, the terracotta-coloured stone glittering with agates, as if it were chipped with diamonds. Above them, the sky was littered with a carpet of stars, not star-shaped at all, but huge round bursts of light. 'You feel as if you could just reach out and touch them,' Celia said to George, as they watched the men put up the tent.

'I'd like to reach out and touch my four-poster just at the minute,' George said sarcastically. 'Doesn't look like very luxurious accommodation, does it?'

In truth, the tent did look more like a lean-to, for it had only three sides, with a curtain placed down the middle to form two rooms. The walls were woven from some sort of wool, Celia thought, feeling the rough texture between her fingers. 'It must be goat's hair, for I don't think they have many sheep here. I'm pretty sure that was goat we had for dinner, too,' she said. 'You should have tried some, George, it was delicious.'

'Barbaric manners—eating with their hands like that. I was surprised at you.'

'It is their custom,' she replied patiently. 'You're supposed to use the bread like a spoon. I simply copied what they did, as *you* must do if you are not to starve. Now, where shall I put this carpet for you?'

'I'll never sleep like this, with the guards snoring their heads off next door,' George grumbled, but he allowed Celia to clear the rocks from a space large enough to accommodate him and very soon, despite his protestations, he was soundly asleep.

Celia sat outside the tent, looking up at the stars for a long time. She was not in the least sleepy. Such a vast space this desert was. Such beauty even in its apparent barrenness. When it rained, Bakri said, it was a carpet of colour. She thought of all the little seeds sleeping just below the surface, ready to burst into life. *Promise is a cloud; fulfilment is rain*, Bakri had said.

She was obviously expected to share the same room as George, but she couldn't bear the idea of their first night together to be *this* night, even if her husband was fully dressed and already sleeping. Celia took her carpet and found herself a quiet spot a short distance away, tucked up behind a large boulder. 'Promise is a cloud; fulfilment is rain,' she murmured to herself. Perhaps that was how she should think of her marriage. Not barren, just waiting for the rain. She fell asleep wondering what form such a rain would take if it were to be powerful enough to fix what she was beginning to think might be unfixable.

Above her, still and silent, Ramiz watched for a long

time over the dark shape of the sleeping Englishwoman who could not bring herself to stay in the tent beside her husband. Then, as the cold of the true night began to descend, he made his way back to his own small camp some short distance away, wrapped himself in his carpet, and settled down to sleep next to his camel.

Chapter Two

They came just before dawn. Celia was awoken by the sound of camel hooves. She sat up, cramped from her sleeping position, and peered out over the rock at the cloud of dust moving frighteningly fast towards the tent. A glint of wicked steel drew her attention. Whoever these men were, they were not friends.

There was still time. A few moments, no more, but enough. She must warn the guard. She must save George. It did not occur to Celia that it should be the other way round. She scrambled to her feet, and had taken one step from behind the rock when a large hand covered her mouth and a strong arm circled her waist. She struggled, but the hold on her tightened.

'Keep still and don't scream.'

His voice was low, but the note of command in it was perfectly apparent. Celia obeyed unhesitatingly, too frightened even to register that he spoke English.

The hand was removed from her mouth. She was twisted around to face him, though still held tight in his embrace. 'You!' she exclaimed in astonishment, for it was the man she had seen yesterday on the hill.

'Get back behind the rock. Don't move. No matter what happens, do not come out until I tell you. Do you understand?'

'But my husband…'

'What they will do to him is nothing to what you will suffer if they find you. Now, do as I bid you.'

He was already dragging her back towards her sleeping place. Behind her she could hear shouts. 'Please. Help him—save my husband.'

Ramiz nodded grimly and, wresting a glittering scimitar from its sheath at his waist and a small curved dagger from a silver holder in the same belt, he gave a terrifying cry as he leapt, sure-footed as a lion, over the short distance to the tent, calling out to the three hired guards to come to his aid.

But the guards were nowhere to be seen. Only Bakri stood between the English diplomat, cowering in the far corner of the tent, and his fate. Ramiz cursed furiously and turned his attention to the first of the four men, shouting to Bakri to see if the Englishman had a gun.

Whether he had or not, it was destined never to be used. Ramiz fought viciously, utilising all his skills with the scimitar, slicing it in bold arcs through the air while defending himself with his *khanjar* dagger. It was four to his one. Trapped in the circle of the men, he fought like a dervish, managing a disabling cut in the shoulder to one man before swirling around, his scimitar clanging against that of his enemy with a last-minute defensive move, the strength of which vibrated painfully up his arm.

Two down. Two to go. As Ramiz fought on, sweat and dust obscuring his vision, he became dimly aware of a cry coming from the corner of the tent. Turning towards it, he saw one of his own hired guards raising his dagger over Bakri. 'Help him! In the name of the gods, help him,' he cried out to the Englishman.

It all happened so fast after that. The Englishman moved, but instead of attempting to lend his assistance he pushed past Bakri and his attacker, making for the entrance of the tent. Bakri fell, clutching the dagger which had been plunged deep into his heart. Ramiz abandoned his attempts to slay the other two men and lunged forward. The Englishman was running away. Disgust slowed Ramiz's steps. Even as he reminded himself that the foreign coward was nevertheless his honoured guest, it was too late. One of the invaders raised his scimitar and sliced deep into the Englishman's belly.

A piercing scream rent the air. The woman abandoned her hiding place and, running full tilt towards them, distracted everyone. They would kill her as they had killed her husband. He realised it was what they had come for, these men of Malik, the ruler of the neighbouring principality, for it could only be he who would have contemplated such a dastardly plot. Fuelled by fury, Ramiz launched himself at the two men. They had already reached the woman, yanking her hair back and pressing a lethal dagger to her throat. A well-aimed kick sent the first one flying, unconscious, his dagger soaring through the air in the opposite direction. The sight of Ramiz, his face taut with rage, his scimitar arching down towards his head, sent the other man prostrate to the ground in the time-old attitude of abasement.

'Please, Lord. Please, Your Highness, I beg of you to spare me,' the man muttered, over and over.

Ramiz yanked him up by the hair. 'You have a message for me from your prince?'

'Please, do not. I beg of you. I...'

Ramiz twisted his hold, making the man scream. 'What does Malik have to say?'

'To invite strangers into our house is to risk disaster.'

Ramiz dropped his hold and turned the man onto his back with the toe of his boot. 'Tell Malik that I invite who I choose into my house. Tell Malik he will live to regret this day's work. Now, go—while you still have your life—and take your sleeping friend with you.'

Needing no further encouragement, the man scurried over to his unconscious comrade and roughly bundled him onto a camel, before mounting one himself and galloping off in a cloud of dust.

Ramiz knelt over the body of the fallen diplomat, but there was nothing he could do. As he got slowly to his feet, the Englishwoman staggered towards him. Instinctively Ramiz stood in front of the body, shielding it from her gaze.

'George?' Her voice was no more than a whisper.

Ramiz shook his head. 'It is best you don't look.'

'The guards?'

'Traitors.'

'And Bakri?'

Ramiz shook his head again. Bakri, who had been his servant since he was a boy, was dead. He swallowed hard.

'You saved my life. I'm sorry I didn't listen to you. But I heard George, you see. My husband. I thought— I thought…' Celia began to shake. Her knees seemed to be turning to jelly. The ground was moving. 'I'm a widow,' she said, a touch of hysteria in her voice. 'I'm a widow, and I've never really been a wife.' As she began to fall, Ramiz caught her in his arms. The feel of them, securing her to the solid, reassuring bulk of his body, was the last thing Celia remembered.

She was climbing through a tunnel. Slowly up through the thick darkness she went, fighting the urge to curl up and stay where she was, safe, unnoticed. A slit of light lay ahead. She was afraid to reach it. Something horrible waited for her there.

'George!' She sat up with a start. 'George!' Celia struggled to her feet, clutching her head as the ground rolled and tipped like the deck of a ship in a storm. She was in the tent. *How had she got there?* It didn't matter. She staggered out into the open air.

The blaze of the sun dazzled her eyes, temporarily blinding her. When her vision cleared, she clutched at the tent rope for support. The blood had dried dark on the ground, and she remembered, in a rush, what had happened. The men arriving in a cloud of dust like something from the Bible. The man from yesterday. *Who*

was he? And what was he doing here? Then the fighting.
The cries. And George running. Running away. Even
though he had a gun. Even though he used to practice
shooting at Manson's every week. He had been running
away. He hadn't even looked for her.

*No! She mustn't think that way. He had just pan-
icked, he would have come back for her.*

A clunking sound coming from the back of the tent
distracted her. Celia made her way cautiously, already
knowing in her heart what she would find. Sure enough,
the stranger was there, his gold-edged cloak discarded
on a rock. His headdress was tied back from his face,
which glistened with sweat from his exertions. He was
smoothing sand over a distinctive mound of desert earth.
He must have found a shovel with the supplies their
traitorous guards had left when they'd fled.

He was facing away from her. The thin white of
his tunic clung to his back with sweat, outlining the
breadth of his shoulders. He looked strong. A capable
man. Capable of saving her life. A man who knew how
to take care of things. Who didn't run away. *Stop!*

He put down the shovel and wiped the sweat from his
brow. She must have moved, or made a noise, or maybe
he just sensed her, for he turned around. 'You should
stay in the tent, out of the sun.'

He spoke English with an accent, his voice curling
round the words like a husky caress. His eyes were a
strange colour, like bronze tinged with gold, the irises
dark. He walked with a fluid grace. Celia could not
imagine that such a man was regularly employed in
manual labour. It struck her then that she was quite alone

with him, and she shivered. *Fear?* Yes, but not as much as there should be. She was too shocked, too numb to feel anything much at the moment.

He stopped just in front of her, was watching her with concern. She didn't like the way he looked at her. It made her feel weak. She didn't like feeling weak. She was normally the one who took care of things. Celia straightened her back, tilting her head up to meet the stranger's eyes, forgetting all about protocol and hats and veils.

'Who are you?' Her voice came out with only the tiniest of wobbles.

'Sheikh Ramiz al-Muhana,' he said, bowing before her with a hint of a smile, lending a fleeting softness to the hard, rocky planes of his face. It lightened his eyes to amber, as if the sun shone from them. Everything about him gleamed. She remembered thinking yesterday of the ancient pharaohs. He had that air about him. Of command.

'Sheikh Ramiz...' Celia repeated stupidly, then realisation dawned. 'You mean Prince Ramiz of A'Qadiz?'

He nodded.

'We were on our way to visit you in Balyrma. George is—was...' She drew a shaky breath, determined not to lose control. 'I don't understand. What are you doing here? What happened this morning? Who were those men? Why did they attack us?'

Her voice rose with each question. Her face was pale. Her eyes, with their heavy lids which gave her that sensual, sleepy look, were dark with a fear she was determined not to show. She had courage, this English-woman, unlike her coward of a husband. 'Later. First you must say your farewells, then we will leave this place.'

'Farewells?'

Her lip was beginning to tremble, but she clenched it firmly between her teeth. Big eyes—the green of moss or unpolished jade, he thought—turned pleadingly towards him. Ramiz took Celia's arm and gently led her towards the graves.

Two graves, Celia noticed. And another two at a distance. Prince Ramiz had obviously laboured long and hard as she lay unconscious. Such labour had spared her much. She could not but be grateful.

They stood together, she and the Prince of A'Qadiz, in silent contemplation. Sadness welled up inside Celia. Poor George. A tear splashed down her cheek, then another. 'I'm so sorry,' she whispered. 'I'm so sorry.'

They should never have married. George hadn't really wanted a wife, and she—she'd wanted more from her husband than he'd been prepared to give. It was as well he had not, for were she standing here a real wife, with three months of real marriage behind her, the pain would be unendurable.

Overcome with remorse, Celia clenched her eyes tight shut and prayed hard for the husband she knew now she could never have loved, no matter how hard she'd tried. 'I'm sorry,' she whispered again.

'He is at peace now. He walks with his god.' Ramiz broke the silence. 'As does Bakri, who was my servant, and my brother's, and my father's before that.'

Celia roused herself from the stupor which threatened to envelop her. 'I'm sorry—I didn't realise. It must be a great blow for you to lose him.'

'He died an honourable death.' Ramiz closed his eyes and spoke a prayer in his native language. His voice was low, and the strange words had a simple beauty in their cadence that soothed. 'Now, go back to the tent. I will finish here.'

An honourable death. The unspoken criticism hung like a weight from Celia's heart as she made her way slowly back to the tent. Though common sense told her she could not have saved George, that to have disobeyed Ramiz when he'd told her to hide would almost certainly have resulted in her own death, it did not prevent her from being racked with guilt for having survived.

George was dead. She was a widow. George was dead—and in such a horrible way that it was as if she had dreamt it, or imagined it as a tale from *One Thousand and One Nights*. If only it had been. If only she could wake up.

But she could not. All she could do was behave with what dignity she could muster. With the dignity her father and Aunt Sophia would expect of her. With the dignity which others would expect of George's wife, a representative of His Majesty's government, she reminded herself strictly.

Thus, when Ramiz joined her half an hour later, though she longed to sink onto the carpeted floor, to curl up under the comfort of a blanket and cry, Celia forced herself to her feet. 'I must beg your pardon, Your Highness, if I have offended you by appearing rude,' she said, turning towards Ramiz, remembering belatedly to avert her eyes from his face. 'I must thank you for saving my life, and for the trouble you took with—with my husband.' She swept him a deep curtsy. 'I realise I haven't even introduced myself. I am Lady Celia Cleveden.'

'I think we are long past the need for such formalities,' Ramiz replied. 'Come, we must leave this place if we are to find another shelter before dark. I don't want to risk spending the night here.'

'But what about—? We can't just…'

'There is nothing more we can do. I have already formed the animals into a caravan,' Ramiz said impatiently.

She had not the will to argue. Questions tussled for prominence in her mind, but she had not the strength to form them. And she had absolutely no desire at all to remain here, in the presence of the dead, at the scene of such horror, so she followed the Prince obediently to where her camel was tethered, and when it dropped to its knees at Ramiz's barked command Celia climbed wearily onto the high wooden platform which served as a saddle. Vaguely she noticed that the beast Prince Ramiz mounted was as white as his horse yesterday had been. That its saddle cloth was silk, intricately embroidered with gold, and that the tack was similarly intricately tasselled and trimmed with threads of gold.

He mounted with the ease of long practice, and took up the halters of the leading camel in the caravan, as well as a halter attached to Celia's own camel. Under any other circumstances she would have been furious to have her mount's control taken from her. Now she was simply relieved. It was one less thing to worry about.

They rode for about two hours. When the sun began its spectacularly fast slide down towards the horizon, striping the sky with gold and crimson, they stopped and made camp. Unbelievably, Celia had dozed for part of the way. Distance and rest had already started the healing process. As she fulfilled each of Ramiz's curt instructions her mind sorted and sieved through the events, forming questions which she was determined he would answer.

They sat by a small fire, eating a simple meal which Celia prepared from their supplies. A new moon was rising. *Hilal.* The crescent moon. The sign of new beginnings.

'Do you know what happened this morning? Why it happened, Your Highness?' Celia asked when they had finished their food. 'How did you come to be there?'

'Ramiz. You may call me Ramiz while we are in private. I was following you. I wanted to see what kind of man your government had sent to talk to me. I wanted to run the rule over him before our official meeting. I had not anticipated him bringing his wife. If I had known you were coming I would certainly have made alternative arrangements for your journey to my citadel.'

'Just because I am a woman it does not mean I need to be wrapped in cotton wool. I am perfectly capable of dealing with the hardships of a trip across the desert.'

'From what I saw, you are far more capable than your husband was,' Ramiz said dryly, 'but that is beside the point. In my country we take care of our women. We cherish them, and we put their comfort before our own. Their lives before our own. Unlike your husband.'

Celia shifted uncomfortably on the carpet. The narrow skirts of her robe made kneeling difficult. 'George was just—George was not—he was...'

'Running away,' Ramiz said contemptuously. 'Was he armed?'

'He had a gun,' Celia admitted reluctantly.

'He could have saved himself and the life of my honoured servant.'

'Your Highness—Ramiz—my husband was a good man. It is just that this was all—and the attack—it was terrifying. He acted on—on instinct.'

'A man whose instincts are to abandon his wife in order to save his own skin is not worth saving. Nature has bestowed upon women their beauty for man to appreciate. To man has been granted the strength to provide and protect them. To break such rules is to go against the natural way of things, the formula civilisations such as mine have been following very successfully for many thousands of years. Your husband was a coward and therefore not, in my eyes, worthy to be called a man. I am sorry to be so harsh, but I speak only the truth.'

Though all her instincts told her to defend George, Celia found she could not. To a man like Ramiz, what George had done was indefensible. And in a small corner of her own mind she agreed. She turned her attention to obtaining answers to the rest of the questions she knew would be asked of her when she returned to Cairo. Nothing could bring George back, but she could brief the Consul General, provide at least some information about this principality of which they knew next to nothing. In a tiny way it would mean that George had not died in vain. 'You knew the men who attacked us today, didn't you?' she asked. 'Who were they?'

Ramiz threw his head back to look up at the stars, suspended like lanterns so close above them. 'Until two years ago my elder brother Asad was the ruler of A'Qadiz. This kingdom and those surrounding it are lands of many tribes, many factions, and my brother embroiled us in many battles. He believed that the sword was mightier than the tongue. It was to cost him his life.'

'What happened to him?'

Ramiz shook his head slowly. 'He was killed in a pointless, ultimately futile skirmish. I don't share his philosophy. I believe most men are reasonable, and reasonable men want peace. Peace is what I have been working tirelessly to achieve, but not all my neighbours agree with me. Nor do all accept my strategy of negotiating with foreign powers such as the British. Today was a warning, and I must act swiftly or everything I have begun to achieve will crumble into dust. It is unfortunate that you have been caught up in this, but there is nothing I can do about it for now. It is another two days' journey to Balyrma. We must start at first light.'

'Balyrma!' Celia exclaimed. 'But surely—I mean, I had assumed you would take me back to Cairo.'

'There can be no question of that. I must return home urgently.'

'Can you not provide me with another escort?'

Ramiz indicated with two spread arms the vast empty expanse of the desert night. 'You think I have magic powers? You think I can summon an escort for you by sheer force of will?'

'I'm afraid I was not briefed, and my husband chose not to share the details of this mission with me. I can be of little use to you in that regard.'

'It is of no matter. It would not be appropriate to hold such discussions with a woman in any event,' Ramiz said dismissively.

She already knew that. George had said as much, and it wasn't really so very different from the way things were back home in England. 'If that is the case, surely it would make more sense for me to go back to Egypt. It is but a day's travel to the port and...'

'I have spoken. You would do well to remember that in this country my word is law.'

Celia was taken aback by the abrupt change of tone. Ramiz had removed his headdress. His hair was black, surprisingly close cut, emphasising the shape of his head, the strength in his neck and shoulders. Now he ran his fingers through it, making a small lick stand up endearingly on his forehead, and Celia realised he was younger than she had thought, perhaps only two or three and thirty. But his looks belied his maturity. He spoke with the voice of authority, the voice of a man used to being obeyed without question. A man, she reminded herself, who held the power of life and death over her.

Celia, however, was not a woman to whom unquestioning obedience came naturally. 'Is it because of the attack this morning?' she asked carefully. 'Are you worried they may return?' She had not thought of this until now—how vulnerable they were, only the two of them. Nervously, she peered out into the inky black of the desert, but she could see nothing beyond the vague contours of the hills.

She was immensely relieved when Ramiz shook his head decidedly. 'They would not dare return now they know of my presence here.' His mouth thinned. 'It is a stain on my honour, and on that of A'Qadiz, that they came at all.'

'You saved my life.' Without thinking, Celia laid her hand over his. 'You could not have known that your own men would turn traitor.'

Her hand was cool. Her fingers were long, that same lovely creamy colour as her face. Women with such colouring so often turned an ugly red in the sun, or freckled, yet she looked to be flawless. Ramiz wondered how flawless. Then he reminded himself that he should not be wondering. He removed her hand deliberately. 'You will come to Balyrma with me, and that is an end to it.'

'For how long?'

Ramiz shrugged. 'Until I decide what is to be done with you.'

Celia frowned. It seemed she had no option. Would it not be best to accept her fate rather than estrange her host by arguing? Though she did not know the details of George's mission, she knew much depended upon it. In any case, even if she was granted her wish to return to Cairo immediately, as George's widow she would not be permitted to stay. She would be sent home. Was that what she really wanted? The answer to that question was obvious.

'Where will I stay in Balyrma?'

'In the palace, as my guest.'

'I don't think that would be good idea,' Celia said uncertainly. 'As an unaccompanied woman it would not be appropriate for me to stay in your palace, especially as you are clearly going to be occupied by urgent matters of state.'

Ramiz laughed harshly. 'You may talk like a man, but you are a woman, are you not, Lady Celia? You need not worry about your virtue. You will be housed in the women's quarters, to which no man but me is permitted entry.' He turned towards her. In the firelight, his eyes seemed to glow like amber.

'Do you mean I am to stay in a harem?' Celia's eyes widened in shock. Images from *One Thousand and One Nights*, of scantily clad concubines oiling themselves and lolling about on velvet cushions sprang to her mind. 'You expect me to form part of your harem? You're not serious. You can't be serious.' Her voice had a panicky edge to it. 'I am not—you expect me to…'

It was that word—*harem*. Ramiz saw immediately what she was thinking. He had encountered the same misunderstanding time and again during his travels as his father's emissary. Europeans imagined a harem to be some sort of exclusive bordello. It angered him to have such inaccurate assumptions made, so he no longer tried to explain. If their fevered imaginations wanted to conjure up scores of nubile women in a perpetual state of arousal waiting for their lord and master to take them to his bed, let them!

'The harem is the place for women in the palace, so that is where you will stay.'

'Your Highness—Ramiz—I am flattered that you should consider adding me to your collection of wives, but...'

'My wife! You over-estimate your value. A sheikh may only marry an Arab princess of royal blood. It is the custom. A Western woman, even a titled one, could not aspire to such an exalted position. At best perhaps she could serve as a concubine.'

Celia gave an outraged gasp. 'You expect me to be your concubine? I absolutely will not! How dare you? How dare you suggest such an outrageous, indecent...?'

He moved so suddenly she had no chance of escape. He seemed to uncoil, to pounce, so that one minute she was sitting next to him, the next she was being dragged helplessly to her feet, held in arms so strong it would be pointless to struggle. Tall as she was, Ramiz topped her by several inches. She was pressed against him, thigh to thigh, chest to chest. His breath was on her face. She could smell him, warm and overpoweringly male. She had never been held thus. She had never been so close to a man before. Not like this, held in such a way as to make her unbearably conscious of her own powerlessness. She should be afraid, and she was, but she was also—something else.

'What do you think you're doing?' Her voice was annoyingly breathless. 'Let me go.'

'You think me a savage, don't you, Lady Celia?' Ramiz said, his voice low and tight with anger.

'I do not! You are obviously educated, your English is flawless, and...'

His grip on her tightened. 'You think the ability to speak a simple language like yours is a measure of being civilised? I also speak French, Greek, German, Italian and at least four variations of my own language. Does that make me more civilised than you—or less? I have travelled widely too, Lady Celia,' Ramiz said with a vicious look. 'Far more widely than you or your pathetic husband. But still all of that means nothing to you, does it? Because I respect the traditions of my own country, and those traditions include keeping a harem. So I can never be anything other than a savage in your eyes, can I?'

Her temper, rarely roused, saved Celia from fear. 'I don't for one moment think of you as a savage! Your country is older by far than mine. I would not be so arrogant. I think it is you who are the one making assumptions about me.'

He had thought her slender, but even through the ridiculous constraints of her English corsetry he could feel her curves. The swell of her breasts pressed against his chest. The dip of her waist made the gentle undulation of her bottom even sweeter. She smelled of lavender and soap, and faintly of that enticing tang of female. The idea of her as his concubine, thrown at her out of anger, was shockingly appealing. Such a vision it commanded, of her creamy skin spread delectably before him, of her delightful mouth at his command, of her long fingers touching him, doing his bidding. Of her submission. He wanted her. Badly. Blood rushed to his groin, making him hard.

Celia struggled to free herself. 'I won't be your— your love-slave, no matter what you do to me. Anyway, they're bound to come looking for me when they hear nothing from George, and if they find me in your harem—'

'Enough!' Ramiz pushed Celia contemptuously away from him. 'I am a sheikh and a man of honour. I would never take a woman against her will. It is an insult that you think me capable of such an act.'

Realising just how foolishly she had leapt to all the wrong conclusions, Celia felt her cheeks burn. 'I'm— I'm sorry,' she stuttered. 'I'm not thinking straight. It's just, with everything that's happened...' A sudden wave of exhaustion hit her with such violence that she staggered. The horror of the day's events came back to her. George was dead, and she was alone in the desert with a man who seemed to think the world should do his bidding. This world was his world; he had good reason for making such an assumption.

Noticing how pale she had become, Ramiz eased Celia back down onto the carpet by the fire. 'You must rest now. We have a long day's travel ahead of us tomorrow. The camels are an excellent early warning of danger, and I will be here by the fire. You need have no fears.'

In the light of the stars her skin looked translucent and pale as the new moon. Her eyes were glazed, vulnerable, and no wonder. She had been through much today, and endured it with a stoicism and bravery that was impressive. His anger fled like a falcon released from its fetters. Ramiz covered her gently with a blanket, then placed himself at a short distance, laying his scimitar within easy reach, and prepared himself for a long night's vigil. He didn't think the assassins would strike again, but he was taking no chances.

Chapter Three

Celia slept heavily, waking the next morning just before dawn with a thumping headache and a brain which felt as if it was made of cotton rags. Ramiz was already up and about, readying their caravan, and a pot of sweet black coffee was bubbling appetisingly on the embers of the fire.

Ramiz seemed distracted, a heavy frown drawing his dark brows together under his *ghutra*, making him seem both more intimidating and older. As they wended their way inexorably east across the huge stretch of desert, following a trail which to Celia's untutored eyes made only fleeting appearances, she had ample time to observe him. Despite the fierce heat of the sun, which made the horizon flicker hazily and seared relentlessly through her thin dress and the veil which she kept in place to protect her from the dust, Ramiz sat bolt-upright in the saddle, on full alert. One hand sought the constant reassurance of the curved sabre in its silver sheath. His eyes—the only part of his face she could see, for he had pulled his headdress over the rest of his face—were slits of bronze, casting their keen gaze in front, to each side, to the rear of the caravan. On one occasion he stopped, pulling his white camel up so suddenly that the beast seemed to freeze in mid-trot. It would have been comical had it not been frightening. Celia pulled up beside him, peering anxiously where he pointed.

'Something moved,' he whispered, though she could see nothing, and could still see nothing when he relaxed. 'Just a rabbit,' he said, pointing at a tiny dot a few hundred yards away. 'If I had my falcon we could have had it for dinner.'

'Your falcon?'

'The wings for my heart,' Ramiz said. 'And a good provider too, out here.'

'You have an affinity with animals, I think. What happened to your beautiful horse? The one I saw you with the day we landed?'

'Stabled near the port. I think, from the way you hold your seat on a camel, that you like to ride?'

'Very much, and to hunt too. My father owns a string of racehorses and my sisters and I were thrown into the saddle almost before we could walk.'

'You have many sisters?'

'Four. I'm the oldest.'

'And your father? What does he do apart from race horses?'

'He is a statesman. Lord Armstrong—he is quite well-known in diplomatic circles.'

Ramiz's eyebrow lifted. 'You are Lord Armstrong's daughter?'

'You know him?'

'I met him once, in Madrid. He is a very influential man. Your marriage was of his making, then?'

'Why should you think so?' Celia asked, riled by his cool and annoyingly accurate assumption.

'It's obvious, having such a strategist as a father, and with such excellent family contacts—your uncle also serves in the British government, does he not?'

Celia nodded.

'Despite my own poor opinion of your husband, he must have been well thought of, and also very ambitious to have been given and accepted this mission. A most welcome addition to your father's sphere of influence, in other words. He would have been foolish not to recommend the match. Am I correct?'

Put like that, her marriage seemed a very cold affair indeed. But Papa had not put it like that. She could have said no—couldn't she? And George—he'd thought of her as more than some sort of useful social appendage, hadn't he? Celia found herself rather unwilling to answer this question.

'It is true my marriage had my father's approval, but the choice was mine. Just because such things are arranged in your country, you should not assume that we do things the same way.'

She could tell by the way Ramiz's eyes narrowed that she had made a mistake. It was not like her to speak so rashly. In fact she was known for her tact—one of the few virtues which George had openly admired in his wife. But there was something about Sheik Ramiz al-Muhana that put her constantly on the back foot. He was so sure of himself. And unfortunately so often right!

'I think it is you who are making assumptions, Lady Celia,' he said.

He was right. She was wrong. Yet she could not bring herself to apologise. 'Tell me, then, did your own wives have a say in the matter?'

'My wives? How many do you think I have?'

'I don't know, but I do know it is the custom here to have more than one.'

'Another lazy assumption. It may be the custom, but the reality is very much the choice of the individual. Some men have only one wife, others nine or ten—though that is very rare. Men provide their wives with the protection of their own household, they give them children and shelter, an established role. Women have a better life married than single. What is wrong with that?'

'What is *wrong* with it?' Celia bit her lip. She should not comment on things she did not understand, even things that just felt—wrong. Slanting a look at Ramiz from under her lashes, she wondered just for a moment how much of what he was saying he actually meant. The thought came to her that he was teasing, punishing her for her naïvety and a little for her English prejudice—which perhaps she deserved. 'I would not have liked to share my husband with another woman,' she said cautiously.

'I doubt your husband would have had either the capacity or the inclination.'

Once again, although Ramiz's words were shocking, he had merely voiced what Celia herself had begun to question. Entrenched loyalty and guilt, rather than faith in what she was saying, made her leap to George's defence. 'You are quite right, he wouldn't,' Celia said shortly. 'Because unlike you he believed in constancy.'

'He was so constant to you that he left you to die. If you were my wife…'

'I am very glad I am not.'

'If you were, at least you would know what it meant to be a wife.'

Celia bit her lip, torn between the desire to ask Ramiz what he meant and the knowledge that she would not like the answer.

'One of the differences between our cultures,' Ramiz continued, sparing her the indignity of asking him to elaborate, 'is that in mine we appreciate that women as well as men have needs. If you were my wife, they would have been generously satisfied. As George Cleveden's wife…' He shrugged.

She was extremely glad of her veil. Heat flushed Celia's skin, prickling uncomfortably on the back of her neck. *What did he know? How did he know?* Though her curiosity was certainly roused, embarrassment got the better of her. 'In my country, such things are not mentioned.'

'Which is why, in your country, so many women are unhappy,' Ramiz countered.

Were such things discussed in the harem? If that was where she was destined to go—not that she would for a minute actually allow Ramiz to… But if it was where she was going, would she be able to find out from the other women? Another wave of heat spread its fingers over Celia. 'We should not be discussing this,' she said primly.

'Between a man and a woman there is nothing more important to discuss.' Ramiz could see she was mortified, but somehow he couldn't stop himself. There was something about the too-cool Lady Celia that made him want to test her limits. And, though he should definitely not be thinking such thoughts, now that he had, in his imagination, placed her within his harem, he could not stop picturing her there. 'To take pleasure, one has also to give. In order to give, one must have knowledge. If you were to be my concubine,' Ramiz said outrageously, 'then I would first need to understand what gives you pleasure. And you would need to do the same for me.'

'But I am not going to be your concubine,' Celia said, the tension in her voice evident. 'You said so yourself.'

'True. But I wonder, Lady Celia, what bothers you more? The idea of being my concubine or the knowledge that, if you were, you would enjoy it?'

She was nonplussed by this question, as it had never occurred to her to think that this imperious sheikh, who could have any woman he wanted, might actually find her desirable. No one else ever had. Until George had asked her to marry him she had never been kissed. In fact, rather shamefully, no one had ever even tried to kiss her, whereas they seemed never to stop trying to kiss Cassie.

Men wanted to make love to Cassie. They wanted to make conversation with Celia. She was obviously lacking something. She was witty, she could be charming, she was educated and she was good company, but she wasn't desirable. It was not something which had bothered her until recently. Not until George had—or had not! Now, it was a curiously deflating feeling.

Was Ramiz toying with her? Celia peered through her dusty veil, trying to read his face, but with only his eyes visible, and those carefully hooded by his heavy lids, it was impossible. 'I think,' she finally said, after a long silence, 'that I have enough to cope with in real life without indulging in hypothetical and frankly ridiculous speculation.' She couldn't know for sure, but she sensed that he was smiling beneath his headdress. 'Can we change the subject, please? Tell me about Balyrma. There is so little written about your country, I don't know very much about it at all beyond the name.'

They had been in the saddle for most of the day, riding through the heat of noon which, under less pressing circumstances, Ramiz would have avoided. Celia had made no complaint, sitting straight in the saddle, drinking water from the canteen only when it was offered, maintaining by some miracle a cool, collected appearance in clothes more fitted to a stroll in an English garden than a long trek across the merciless heat of the desert. Looking at her now, Ramiz felt a faint twinge of guilt. She might not have loved her husband, and in his view she was well rid of him, but she had endured a hugely traumatic time with remarkable courage, and deserved to be indulged a little.

So he told her of Balyrma, and became so engrossed and passionate when talking of his beloved city and its people, of their ancient traditions and its sometimes violent history, that he barely noticed the miles being eaten up. He discovered in Celia an attentive and intelligent listener, with a wide frame of reference, who surprised him with some of the astute observations she made. She was enthusiastic too, and eager to find links between A'Qadiz and the ancient Egypt of the pharaohs whose tombs she had explored. Her enthusiasm was infectious. In his anxiety to defend a point she disputed, enjoying the cut and thrust of their debate, Ramiz almost forgot she was a woman.

'You may be right about the true purpose of the Sphinx,' Celia said triumphantly, 'but the fact is you will never be able to prove it, for nothing like that was written down.' The sun was sinking. Ahead, she could see what looked like a small copse of trees. Thinking she must be mistaken, Celia pushed back her veil and shaded her eyes with her hand. It certainly looked like greenery.

'It is an oasis,' Ramiz explained, 'where water comes up from the ground and provides succour for plants, animals and weary travellers alike. We will stop here for the night. You will be able to bathe, if you wish.'

'Bathe!' Celia breathed the word ecstatically.

It was the first time Ramiz had seen her smile. It changed her completely, warming her complexion, softening the clean lines of her face with the curve of her full bottom lip, highlighting the slanting shape of her eyes, giving him the most tantalising glimpse of the sensual woman hidden beneath her cool exterior. There was something incredibly alluring about her. Unawakened. He remembered now that it was how she had first struck him. Perhaps it was the implied challenge in that which aroused him. Yet again he reminded himself that he should not be thinking such things.

They had reached the oasis. It was small—a watering place, no more—not big enough to encourage permanent settlement. But it was a well-known stop and Ramiz was surprised to find they were the only ones there. His camel dropped obediently to its knees and he dismounted, going immediately to assist Celia, who clambered stiffly down. Ramiz put his hands around her waist and lifted her clear of the pommel. She was light as a feather. He set her to her feet and reluctantly let her go.

'I will see to the animals. The bathing pool is over there, away from the well.'

Ramiz lifted her portmanteau down from the mule and handed it to her. Needing no further encouragement, Celia headed in the direction he had indicated. Underfoot, the sand of the oasis was much softer than the rough track they had followed, much more like the gently undulating desert she had imagined. The trees she had seen were palms, growing high in clusters by the drinking well, around which also grew little patches of green scrub. The bathing pool was an ellipse of vibrant blue set into the sand, no more than ten feet across, backing into a high wall of rock. Water trickled out from a fissure a couple of feet above the level of the pool. Over the years it had worn a track, so that now it formed a tiny waterfall.

Celia longed to stand beneath it. A quick check assured her that she was screened by the palm trees. In minutes, she had discarded her dusty layers of dress, petticoats, stays and stockings, and stood, for the first time in her adult life, shockingly naked, outdoors. It was a fantastically liberating experience. She stretched her arms above her head, tilting her face to look up at the first twinkle of the stars. A scatter of pins and her hair fell in a heavy sweep down her back.

She stepped into the warm pool. The sand sloped gently down, soft and firm underfoot. The water caressed her skin like velvet. At the deepest point, in the middle, it came up to her waist. She sank down to her knees, sighing with contentment as it worked its balmy magic on her aching limbs and dusty skin, before lying flat on her back, floating, her hair trailing out behind her. She soaped herself thoroughly, then washed her hair, rinsing it under the crystal-clear waterfall, relishing the contrasting icy cold of the water trickling over her shoulders before it merged with the warmer water of the pool. The crescent moon was reflected on the surface. In its pale light her skin seemed milky, other-worldly, as if she were a statue come to life.

She had never really looked at her body before—had taken for granted her unblemished skin, her slim figure, well-suited to the fashion for high-wasted narrow dresses, but otherwise unexceptional. Now, released from the fetters of her corsets and the bounds of polite society, she explored her shape. Standing under the waterfall, she watched the paths each drop made, down her arms to nestle in the crook of her elbow, between the valley of her breasts, along the curve of her ribcage to the dip and swell of her stomach. So familiar, and yet so new. She lay on her back again, floating weightlessly, gazing up at the stars. How would her body look to someone else. Too skinny? Too tall? Too pale? Her breasts were not small, but they were hardly voluptuous. Was this good or bad? What would a man think? Ramiz, for example...

'I was beginning to fear you had drowned.'

Celia started up out of the water, then sank quickly to her knees under it. 'How long have you been there?'

'You looked like Ophelia, with your hair trailing out behind you like that. Only unmistakably alive, I'm relieved to say.'

The look on his face was also unmistakable. He liked what he saw. The knowledge was shocking, but it gave her a little rush of pleasure all the same. Ramiz was barefooted, and without his headdress or his cloak. Even as she noticed this he began to unbuckle the belt around his waist, which held his knife and scimitar. Then he tugged at the little pearl buttons at the neck of his robe, giving her a glimpse of smooth skin, lightly tanned. It was only as he made to pull the *thoub* over his head that Celia realised he intended to join her. 'You can't come in,' she yelped. 'Not while I'm still here.'

'Then come out,' Ramiz said.

'I can't. I haven't anything on.'

'I couldn't help but be aware of that,' he said with a crooked smile. 'I'll look away, I promise.'

Still crouched below the water, Celia considered her options. She didn't even have a towel. The idea of boldly standing up and walking past him naked was horrifying, even if he did keep his eyes closed, but not nearly as alarming as the idea of waiting for him to take off his clothes and join her before she made her escape.

'Celia?'

Ramiz sounded impatient. Bored, even. He had probably seen hundreds of women without their clothes. And she was getting cold. And feeling a little foolish.

'Close your eyes,' she instructed, and as soon as he did so Celia took a deep breath and stood up. Wrapping her arms protectively round herself, she splashed her way out of the pool with as much grace as she could muster, trying to persuade herself that she was fully clothed and not dripping wet and stark naked.

Her clothes were in the shade of the palms to Ramiz's right. She just had to walk past him as quickly as she could. The sand was hot under her feet. She caught her toe on a stone and stumbled, only just retaining her balance. Glancing up she saw that Ramiz had kept his word. His lashes fanned dark on his cheeks. It was the strangest experience, standing there without her clothes, knowing all he had to do was to open his eyes. She felt exposed, and just the tiniest bit excited. Celia paused. What if…? Then she panicked, and headed quickly for the shelter of the palm trees.

He felt rather than heard her hesitate, so intensely conscious was he of her tantalising presence. He didn't need to look. He could imagine her all too clearly as he heard the soft sigh of the water yielding her up, the shiver of the sand as it cradled her feet. Her retreating form, so tall and slender, would glimmer in the moonlight, her hips swaying like a call to pleasure. Her hair, dripping down over her shoulders, would be clinging lovingly to the pouting tips of her breasts. As her footsteps retreated quickly over the sand, he imagined her disappearing into the fringe of palms like a nymph into a forest.

The urge to follow her there, to enter the forbidden garden of such delights, was so strong that Ramiz took a step forward before he managed to stop himself. He opened his eyes. She was safely out of sight. She should be safely out of mind. As the widow of a British diplomat sent to discuss a treaty, and the daughter of an eminent statesman with influence across Europe, she was definitely not for him. Never before had it been so difficult to make his body do his mind's bidding, but he managed it. Honour. His god. He managed it, but only just.

A few yards away Celia dressed hurriedly in a clean nightdress. It was cotton, with long sleeves and a high neck, and in combination with her pantaloons and a shawl was, she decided, perfectly decent for a night in the open—for Ramiz had, to her relief, left the tent behind. She could not bear the thought of sleeping in her stays again, and banished the image of Aunt Sophia's shocked face by reminding herself that Ramiz had already seen her almost nude anyway.

Don't think about that! But she couldn't help it. He found her attractive. There had been no mistaking that look on his face. It was dangerous, not something she had taken into account at all, but it was also exciting.

It was not until she was making her way back across the sand to the fire, carrying her portmanteau, and saw Ramiz standing under the waterfall that she realised something quite astonishing. The attraction was mutual. At least she thought it must be attraction she was feeling—this sort of fizzing in her blood at the sight of him, this little kick of something in her stomach. The way her eyes were drawn to him. She hadn't felt it before. Ever. But she wanted to look. No, more than look—to devour him with her eyes.

He had his back to her, was leaning his hands against the rock and allowing the spray to trickle over his head, to find a path down his shoulders, his spine, to where she could just see the curve of his buttocks emerging from the pool. His skin gleamed, smooth and biscuit-coloured in the moonlight, stretched tight over the bunched muscles of his shoulders. She wondered how it would feel to touch. Then she realised she was spying on him, and decided that she didn't want him to catch her in the act, so she forced herself to walk back to their camp without once looking back.

By the time Ramiz joined her, dressed once more in a *thoub*—a clean one, she noticed—his hair damp, smoothed like a cap sleekly to his skull, Celia had the makings of a meal ready, and a composed expression on her face.

She fell asleep almost as soon as she had eaten, curled up in a blanket by the fire. She slept deeply at first, but then the dreams came. Strange dreams, in which she chased George through labyrinthine buildings, up stairs with no end, through rooms whose walls suddenly closed in on her, across endless passageways with too many doors. And always he was behind the one she couldn't open, or had only just closed. It was George, she knew it was George, but in the way of dreams he took many forms. All of them aloof from her. All of them despising her. In her dream she grew smaller. Frailer. More frantic with every attempt to find him, until finally she opened a door which proved to be in the outside wall of a high tower and she fell, fell, fell, waking with a startled cry just before she landed.

Strong arms held her when she was about to sit up in fright. A hand smoothed the tangle of her hair back from her face. 'A dream. It was just a dream.' A voice, soothing as the softest of cashmere in her ear. 'Go back to sleep, Celia. You're safe now.'

'I tried,' she mumbled. 'I really tried.' Her cheek rested on something hard and warm and infinitely comforting. Vaguely, she registered a slow, regular bump. Like a heart beating. 'Safe,' she mumbled.

A kiss on her brow. A fluttering kiss, cool lips. 'Safe,' the voice said, pulling her closer.

The nightmare faded into the distance, like a black beast retreating with its tail between its legs. She knew it wouldn't dare come back. Celia slept the rest of the night dreamlessly.

She woke feeling much refreshed. Curled up under her blanket by the fire, she could see by the sky that it was not yet morning. The air was cool on her face. She had been dreaming of George. It came back to her now—the running, the never quite catching. She tried to picture her husband, but his image was blurry, like an old painting covered with the patina of age. The months of her marriage felt unreal, like a spell from which she had been freed, a play she had not meant to attend. Just as she had never quite seen herself as a wife, now she could not believe in herself as a widow. She was just Celia, neither Armstrong nor Cleveden, for none of these names meant anything here. Here she was alone in this desert wilderness, her fate in the hands of the man who lay sleeping on the other side of the fire. She was free to be whoever it was she chose to be, and no one in the real world would ever know. It was an intoxicating feeling.

As she crept carefully past Ramiz, heading for the washing pool with her clothes, she remembered something else. Could it really have been Ramiz who had held her so gently? It seemed so improbable. She must have imagined it. If she had cried out, which she thought she must have, it seemed much more likely that he would have woken her and bade her be quiet. But the arms that had held her had seemed so real, and she had felt so incredibly safe enfolded in them. Was Sheikh Ramiz al-Muhana capable of such tenderness?

Returning properly dressed, complete with the stays whose constraints she was starting to loathe, and a fresh pair of silk stockings she wished fervently to do without, Celia decided simply to pretend that nothing had happened and set about making morning coffee while

Ramiz refilled their canteens. When he asked her how she had slept, she told him very well, and no more was said.

She had expected Balyrma to be a walled city, perhaps built into the mountains which were rising like huge sand dunes in the distance, but as Celia looked down on the capital of A'Qadiz from the vantage point to which Ramiz had led them, her first impression was of lush green, so vibrant and vivid that it looked as if the city had been mistakenly painted into the middle of a desert canvas. It was much larger than she had expected too. A patchwork of fields were laid out, stretching across the plain on either side of the well-formed track they were following, neatly bordered with what looked like cypress trees.

'The mountains on either side protect us from the worst of the sun in the summer, and they provide the water which makes all this possible,' Ramiz explained. 'If you look closely, you can also see that they protect us from invasion. See the little turret there?'

Celia peered in the direction he pointed. 'Are you under threat of invasion?'

'Not for more than five hundred years,' Ramiz said proudly, 'but it is a wise man who is vigilant. There are many who envy us our wealth, and some who would mistake my own desire for ongoing peace as a weakness. As you saw to your cost.'

They made their way with their caravan strung out behind them along the increasingly wide road towards the city. With her veil firmly in place, Celia rode behind

Ramiz, and had ample opportunity to observe how he was received by his people. She knew he was a prince, of course, but over the last two days she had put his status to the back of her mind. It was impossible to do so now, as every one of the multitude of people with their mules, camels, horses and trundling carts who passed them on the approach to the city fell to their knees in front of Ramiz, uttering prayers and good wishes, keeping their heads bowed.

Once again Celia thought of the pharaohs, who had taken their status as gods for granted just as Ramiz seemed to be doing. She realised how much latitude he had bestowed upon her, and wondered how many hundreds of social solecisms she had committed. It appalled her, for she was used to thinking of herself as up to snuff on every occasion, and now here she was, entering a magnificent city in the wake of its prince with absolutely no idea how she should behave when she got there. Nerves fluttered like a shoal of tiny creatures in her stomach, making her feel slightly nauseous. She felt an absurdly childish inclination to turn her camel round and flee.

What would her father think of her? Lily-livered, he would say. Highly unusual as the circumstances were, Lord Armstrong would expect his daughter to think and to act like a statesman. Celia sat up straight in the saddle. Whatever lay ahead, she was ready to face it.

What lay ahead was a startlingly beautiful city. Once they had passed through the fields, groves of lemon, orange and fig trees and terraced olive bushes, they entered the city of Balyrma itself. It was walled after all, she realised as they passed through a majestic portal, their path still bordered with devotedly kneeling citizens, into a city straight out of *One Thousand and One Nights*. Terracotta dwellings with slits for windows and turreted roofs, blank walls with keyhole-shaped doors behind which she imagined cloistered courtyards, fountains tinkling at every corner. Through narrow alleyways she caught a glimpse of a souk selling cloth, colours bright as jewels. From another came the heady scent of spices. As they progressed towards the centre of the city the buildings became more ornate; tiled walls patterned with mosaic, elaborate high shutters on the windows worked with intricate patterns of wrought iron.

The palace stood in the exact centre of the town. A high wall, too high to see over, with two beautiful slender towers marking each of the corners. The wall was pristine white, with a flowing border of blue and gold tiles along the middle, leading to the huge central entranceway protected not just by a set of doors of gothic proportions, but also by a grille plated with silver and gold. It was the sort of fairytale palace that normally stood at the end of a drawbridge, Celia wanted to say to Ramiz, remembering just in time not to blurt out her thoughts. But then, as first the gate and then the doors were flung open to receive them, and she caught her first glimpse of the royal palace of Balyrma, Celia lost the ability to speak anyway—for Ramiz's home looked as if it had been conjured up by Scheherazade herself.

Chapter Four

They left the bedraggled caravan of animals and luggage outside. An army of white-robed servants appeared as if from nowhere, it seemed to Celia, and led them down a short covered passageway dotted with mysterious doors, each with a guard armed with a glittering scimitar. The stark white of their robes was relieved only by a discreet embroidered crest depicting a falcon and a new moon, which she had noticed embossed on the entrance gates too, and by the red and white check of their headdresses.

Following in Ramiz's wake, her head respectfully lowered, Celia felt more overwhelmed with every step she took. The huge courtyard they entered was perfectly symmetrical, the pillars and windows and doors which flanked it all mirroring each other, as did the mosaic design in blue and gold which formed the frieze around the walls, continued on the pillars which bounded the open space, and covered the floor of the courtyard itself.

Two fountains played to each other. Risking a fleeting glance up, Celia saw another floor with a colonnaded balcony, and counted another two above that, all glittering white, trimmed with blue and gold.

Ramiz seemed to have forgotten her presence. Engaged deep in conversation with a man whose robes and bearing clearly proclaimed a higher status from the guards, Ramiz himself seemed to have metamorphosed as they entered his domain. His bearing now was remote and autocratic, that of a man who took his power for granted, as he did the obedience of others. She had no idea what he was saying, but even his voice sounded different—short, staccato sentences, none of the soft vowels and curling consonants she had grown used to.

She felt as if she didn't know him. She forced herself to accept that she didn't. What had happened over the last two days had been an oasis, an exotic interlude in the harsh, unyielding desert of reality. This was his real life. Suddenly she was a little afraid.

She hadn't taken his threat to make her his concubine seriously. She hadn't allowed herself to think about his harem. In fact, she had allowed herself to assume that it simply wouldn't happen, that when they arrived here he would change his mind and—and what?

She was alone. Worse, she was a woman alone, which meant she had neither the right nor the power to choose her own destiny. It wasn't a case of being forced to do Ramiz's bidding. She didn't have any other option.

Powerless. The full meaning of the word hit her like a sack of corn swung into her middle, so that she felt her breath whistling out, her stomach clenching. Celia began to panic, her fevered imagination conjuring up all sorts of hideous fates. It would be weeks—months, maybe—before she was missed. She pictured Cassie waiting anxiously every day for a letter which did not come, trying to reassure Caroline and Cordelia and poor little Cressida, and at the same time attempting to persuade Papa to take some sort of action. But what could he do, so far away in London? Nothing. And in the meantime she, Celia, would probably have been cast out into the desert and left to die.

Fortunately at this point Celia's common sense intervened. If Ramiz had wanted her dead he would not have saved her life. If he'd wanted harm to come to her, he'd have left her on her own at the site of the massacre. She couldn't claim to truly know the autocratic Prince standing a few yards away, oblivious to her presence, but she knew enough about the man to believe in his integrity and honour, and she knew enough of his hard-won and volatile peace to understand that he wouldn't risk upsetting the British government by slaughtering the daughter of one of their foremost statesmen. She was acting like a hysterical female when dignity and calm were what was required. She was in a royal palace, for goodness' sake! She was a citizen of one of the world's great powers. Ramiz wouldn't dare lock her in a harem and expect her to do his bidding.

Nodding to herself with renewed resolve, Celia looked up, but Ramiz was gone. She stood quite alone in the courtyard, with only the tinkling fountains for company. She had no idea which of the doorways he had gone through. Though the doors were all open, each was draped in heavy brocade and gauzy lace to keep out the fierce heat of the day. The keyhole-shaped windows of the salons, with their gold-plated iron grilles, stared out blankly at her.

'Hello?' she called out tentatively, feeling horribly self-conscious as she listened to her voice echo up through the courtyard. There was no answer. This is ridiculous, she thought, deciding simply to select a doorway and walk through it.

She was picking up her skirts and making for the nearest one when a voice halted her. Two men were approaching. Huge men with bellies so large they looked like cushions, dressed not in robes but in wide black pleated breeches and shiny black boots. Each had a vicious curved dagger held in the sash which marked where the waistband had once been. Under their black turbans each had a black beard and long black moustaches.

Like two of Ali Baba's forty thieves, Celia thought a little hysterically as the men stopped in front of her. Then they bowed, indicating that she follow them, and with her heart in her mouth she did, through a myriad of doors and cool dark passageways, until they came to another large wooden door set in another white-tiled wall. One of the men produced a large key and pulled the door wide. Celia stepped through into a courtyard almost a mirror image of the one she had left. She thought at first she was back where she had started. Then the door behind her closed, leaving the guards on the other side, and she realised where she was.

Just as Ramiz had told her she would be, she was in his harem.

* * *

It was everything she had expected, and yet nothing like it. For a start she was quite alone aside from the two maidservants who tended to her, bringing delicious foods, exotic fruits she had never seen before, fragrant meats cooked in delicious spices, cooling sherbets and tea served sweet and flavoured with mint.

Adila and Fatima were shy at first, giggling over Celia's clothes, astonished at the layers of undergarments she wore, and utterly confounded by her stays. In turn Celia, who allowed her dresser to look after her hair for grand occasions, but otherwise was used to managing for herself, found their care for her embarrassing— waving them away when they first attempted to bathe her, submitting only when she saw that she had offended them.

By nature modest, Celia had never shared such intimacies as bathing, even with her sisters, but within the seclusion of the harem it seemed less shocking, and she very quickly began to enjoy the pampering of baths strewn with rose petals and orange blossom, having oils scented with musk and amber gently massaged into her skin and preparations for her hair and for her face, which left her whole body glowing and more relaxed than she had ever known.

The harem itself covered three floors, its upper terraces reached by tiled staircases which zigzagged up through the towers, marking the four corners of the courtyards. These upper rooms were empty, echoing, as if they had not been used for some time. The lower rooms, which led one into another in a square around the terrace, were opulently decorated, with rich carpets on the floors and low divans draped with lace, velvet and silk, the jewel colours of blue and gold and emerald and crimson reflected in the long mirrors which hung on the walls. The only windows looked out onto the courtyard, and the only exit was the one through which she had entered, but once Celia had recovered from the shock of her incarceration and accepted there was nothing she could do save wait for Ramiz to return, she found it astonishingly easy to surrender to the magical world of the harem. She had nothing to do save surrender her body to the ministering of Adila and Fatima, and surrender her mind to the healing process.

As the days melded one into another Celia quickly lost all track of time, so strangely did the tranquil seclusion of the harem play on her senses. She had never been so much alone, never had so much peace to simply be. As the eldest, and having lost her mother not long after her youngest sister Cressida was born, it was second nature to Celia to put others first, to be always thinking ahead and taking responsibility for what happened next. Indulgence and inactivity such as had now been forced on her were quite alien. Those who knew her as always busy, always planning, managing at least ten things at once, would say without hesitation that such a life as she was now experiencing would have her beside herself with boredom or screaming for release. Celia would have said so herself. But right now it was the antidote she required to recover not just from the trauma of losing her husband, but from the trauma of realising she wished she had never married him in the first place. If Ramiz had intended this as a punishment, he had been mistaken.

Almost without her noticing a full month passed, marked by the changing of the moon, whose growth from flickering crescent to glowing whole reflected the healing process taking place in Celia herself.

Then, just as she was beginning to wonder if she would be left forgotten here for ever, and her temper was beginning to recover enough to resent Ramiz's extended and unexplained absence, the man himself appeared without warning.

It was evening. Dinner had arrived—a much more elaborate meal than usual, which required an additional servant to bring it. Out of habit Celia was dressed in an evening gown after the daily ritual of her bath and massage. She stared in consternation at the plethora of little dishes in their gold salvers, wondrously appetising but far too much for just one, set out on a low table in the largest of the salons, around which banks of tasselled and embroidered cushions were strewn.

'I can't eat all this,' she said helplessly to Adila, miming that they should take some of it back, but the maid only smiled behind her hand and backed out, shaking her head.

The door to the outside world opened. Not just the usual tiny crack, barely enough to allow the staff to slip in and out, it was flung wide open. Ramiz strode in, resplendent in a robe of opulent red.

She had forgotten how incredibly handsome he was. She had forgotten how tall he was too. He looked a little tired, though, with a tiny fan of lines crinkling around his eyes. He wore no headdress, no belt, and his full robe was more like a caftan with wide sleeves, flowing loosely down to his feet which were clad in slippers of soft leather studded with jewels. The robe was open at the neck, but for all his dress was obviously informal he looked even more regal, more intimidating than she remembered.

She was nervous. Her mouth was dry. Her heart was bumping a fraction too hard against her breast. Celia dropped a curtsy. 'Your Highness.'

'Ramiz,' he said. 'While we are alone, I am Ramiz.'

Alone. She decided not to think about that. Having imagined this moment many times over the last few days, she decided to act as if it were any other social occasion, and to treat Ramiz as if he were an honoured guest and she the hostess. And not, definitely not, worry about being alone with him in his harem.

'Are you hungry? Dinner is here. I wondered why there was so much of it. Now I see you were expected.'

'You would have preferred some warning?' Ramiz asked, picking up immediately on her unspoken criticism.

'It is your palace. It is not for me to dictate where you are, and when,' Celia said tactfully, preceding him into the salon in which the food was laid out, waiting until he had disposed himself gracefully on a large cushion before she sat down opposite him.

'I've been away. I've only just got back,' Ramiz explained unexpectedly. 'I told you I had urgent business to attend to.' He lifted the cover from a dish of partridges stuffed with dates and pine nuts and sniffed appreciatively.

'You mean only just got back as in today?'

'An hour ago.'

Celia was flattered, and then alarmed, and then nervous again. She poured Ramiz a glass of pale green sherbet and pushed a selection of dishes towards him. 'May I ask if your business was successful?' she said. 'I presume it was to do with the other prince—Malik, I think his name was?'

Ramiz looked surprised. 'Yes.'

'Did you—were you—did you have to fight with him?'

'Not this time.'

'What, then?'

'You really want to know?'

Celia nodded. 'I really do.'

It was not the custom to discuss such matters with a woman. It was not in his nature to discuss such matters with anyone. But it had been a difficult few days, and there was something about this woman which encouraged the sharing of confidences. 'My council all urged swift and brutal retribution—as usual, since I inherited most of them from my brother.'

'But you ignored them?'

'Yes. I don't want to follow that path until there are no other options left.'

'So tell me—what did you do? How do you go about negotiating a deal with a man who wields power through fear? Come to that, how do you set about persuading your own people to accept such an alien approach?'

Ramiz smiled. 'You forget I am a prince too. I don't have to persuade my people of anything. They do as I bid.'

'Yes, that's what you say, but I'll wager that you try all the same,' Celia said, with a perception which surprised him. 'You don't really want to rule in splendid isolation, do you?'

'Splendid isolation? That is exactly how it feels sometimes. You can have no idea how wearing it is, trying to break the ingrained prejudice of years,' Ramiz said wearily. 'Sometimes I think— But that is another matter. With Prince Malik...'

He went on to tell her about the events of the last few days, spurred on by her intelligent interest into revealing far more of his innermost thoughts than he had ever done. It was a relief to unburden himself, and refreshing too, for this woman who talked and thought like a man had a knack for encouraging without toadying, and her shocking lack of deference lent her opinions a credibility he would not otherwise have conceded.

By the time the meal was over the weight of responsibility which was beginning to feel like a sack upon his back had eased a little for the first time since he had so unexpectedly come to power. This woman understood the cares of governing. She would have made an excellent diplomatic wife. George Cleveden had chosen well. But George Cleveden was dead, and Ramiz could not regret it, for the woman who was now his widow deserved better. Much better. Not that it was any of his business.

'Are you comfortable here in my harem?' Ramiz

settled himself back against the cushions. The lamps with their coloured glass shades reflected the light in rainbow patterns onto the mirrors and the tiled white of the salon.

Celia thought she recognised that teasing note in his voice, but she could not be sure. 'Extremely,' she said cautiously. 'Your servants have looked after me very well, but I was surprised to find myself the only occupant.'

'I moved my brother's wives and children to their own palace. Those who wished were returned to their families.'

'And you haven't had time to—to stock up on wives for yourself?'

Ramiz burst out laughing. 'That's one way of putting it.'

'You led me to believe you had many wives.'

'No, you made that assumption yourself.'

Celia bit her lip. 'I suppose you get tired of people like me making such assumptions. You wanted to teach me a lesson, didn't you?'

Ramiz held up his hands. 'I confess. Tell me, what did you expect when you came here? A scene from *One Thousand and One Nights*?'

She blushed. 'Something like that.'

'And now?'

'Now I don't know what to think,' she said, opting for honesty. 'In one way, there's something almost liberating in being so cut off from the world and unable to do anything about it. I feel rested. Cured. Better. I've never had so much time to think. It's like I've been able to sort out my mind, make sense of things.'

'You had problems in your marriage, I think?'

After so many days of silence, so many hours spent scrutinising and questioning, it was a huge relief to speak her thoughts. 'I wasn't exactly unhappy, but I think I would have become so, and I know George already was.' A tear trembled on her lashes. Celia brushed it away. 'He was—he did not want—I think he wanted a companion rather than a wife. How did you guess?' She had not meant to ask, but here in the tranquil security of the harem, with the soft light casting ghostly shadows onto the walls, such an intimate topic seemed natural.

He had been conversing with her like a man, admiring her intelligence and strong opinions. Now he saw in that look stripped of its poise, in the vulnerable trembling of her lip, that she was all woman. He remembered her body, glinting pale and alluring in the moonlight by the oasis—an image which had crept unbidden into his dreams these last five nights, so unwanted, so dishonourable that he had banished its memory in the daylight. Now here it was again, and here in the rooms of the palace set aside for sensual pleasure, rooms he had never himself used, his resistance was beginning to falter.

He wanted her. There was every reason for him to deny himself, but he had done so much denying since his brother died he was sick of it. He wanted her. He wanted to teach her. He wanted her to know pleasure. And he wanted her knowing to be his doing.

Ramiz got to his feet. 'I guessed because you have the look of a woman starved of attention. Come with me,' he said, reaching out a hand to pull her to her feet, placing a finger over her mouth to stop her speaking. He led her out of the salon to the courtyard, where the fountains made their sweet music in the jasmine-scented air. 'Look up there.' The deep sapphire of the night sky was framed high above their heads. 'In my culture, we believe that love has wings—wings which can take you all the way up there to the stars, where the heavenly pleasures of the body are worshipped. It is a voluptuous journey. A journey which leaves its mark upon a woman in her eyes, in the way she walks, the way she learns to nourish and to relish her body, knowing that it is a temple of delights. I look at you and I see a woman who has not yet learned to fly. I look at you and I want to help you experience what it feels like to soar in the high clouds.'

His voice shivered seductively in her ear. They were standing by the fountain, his hands on her arms, stroking feathery light up and down her bare skin. She could feel the brush of velvet from his sleeves. He smelt of lemon-scented soap and night-scented man. She pictured herself flying. His presence, the scent of him, the feel of him, the husky sound of him, gave her a fleeting image of what that might be like. Of what he might do to her to make it happen.

She wanted it. Whatever it was, she wanted it, and she knew she would never find a more able tutor. His confidence was intoxicating. His aura of power equally so. His casual mastery, which could intimidate and anger, was here, under the secret stars fascinating, beguiling, and incredibly persuasive.

'Don't you want to know what it's like to fly, Celia?'

Ramiz spoke into her ear. His lips whispered over her skin.

'I don't know if I can,' she said, which was the truth.

His laugh, like a throaty purr, so filled with assurance, made her stomach clench in anticipation. 'Trust me—you can.'

His tongue traced the shell of her ear. His fingers trailed up her arms to the nape of her neck, circling delightful spirals which whirled little pulses into life. Her heart was beating fast. Faster. She was hot and cold all at the same time. His mouth traced the line of her jaw, and she ached, ached for him to kiss her lips, but instead he moved down her throat. His velvet-soft mouth gave kisses that made her arch back in his arms like a bow, so that she could see the sky now, the stars glinting and beckoning and calling to her as his mouth reached the hollow of her neck, and her skin seemed to reach out to greet him, wanting more than the flickering kisses he gave her.

'Ramiz,' Celia whispered, 'Ramiz, please…I want to.'

He scooped her up into his arms, heading for the nearest salon, which happened to be the one in which she slept. The low divan, with its scattering of pillows and silk covers, took up centre place in the room. It was the strangest bed she had ever encountered, for it was round, with neither head nor footboard. Ramiz set her to her feet before it, gazing deep into her eyes, his own glowing amber in the shadowed light with something fierce she didn't recognise and wasn't sure she liked.

She lowered her lids, but he tilted her chin up, forcing her to look at him again. 'You must not be ashamed of your body; you must learn to enjoy it. That is the first lesson you must learn or you will never leave the ground.'

Then his lips covered hers, fitting so perfectly that she stopped breathing. How could mouths fit like that? But they did. Warmth flooded through her. She stood pliant, unsure what to do, confused by the urgent need to kiss him back, so at odds with what she had been told. Ramiz snaked his arms around her back to pull her close. She could feel the solid hardness of his body pressed into her own softness. She had not thought of herself as soft before. Or curved. She had never encountered such blatant masculinity so close at hand. She was melting, and in the melting she succumbed to temptation and kissed him back.

Her lips were petal-soft against his, beguilingly untutored. Ramiz pressed his mouth against hers, tasting her delicately. He felt rather than heard her sigh. If he had not known better he would have said she had never been kissed. Certainly she had not been taught to kiss back. Her inexperience inflamed him. A primal instinct which surprised him to possess, to own, sent the blood surging to his shaft. His kiss hardened too, his mouth easing hers open, his tongue finding hers, coaxing at first, then forgetting to coax and instead demanding. She tasted of heat and promised ecstasy. An ecstasy he could not wholly indulge.

To give is to receive. Tonight he would give, and the giving would have to suffice. Ramiz tore his mouth away. 'Wait,' he said, breathing heavily. 'Tonight you must allow me to wait upon you.' Then slowly, tantalisingly slowly, he began his controlled onslaught on Celia's senses.

His hands tangled in her hair, pulling out the constraining pins, his fingers combing through the rich copper mass of curls until it was spread over her shoulders, trailing down her back, curling over the pearly white of her bosom. He turned her around to unfasten her dress, his fingers trailing over her skin as he slipped it down over her shoulders to pool at her feet. She could feel his mouth on her neck again, on the knot of her spine. His breath was warm on her skin, but she shivered all the same. He unlaced her stays, pulling her close against him, her back to his chest, her skin against the velvet of his robe. She could feel the hard length of him nestling into the curve of her bottom. So other. So male.

She shivered again, but now she was hot, with fingers of heat creeping surreptitiously over her skin like the fingers of dawn through the mists of morning. Ramiz wrapped his arms around her, pulling her hard against him, nudging his erection into the soft mound of her buttocks. His hands stroked up from her waist to the curves of her breasts, through the soft fabric of her chemise, stroking so that her skin prickled. Her nipples hardened. He weighed her breasts in his hands, his thumbs scraping the tips, making them pucker, making her stomach clench, and between her legs something that felt like another unfurling bud seemed to clench too.

He turned her round, kissing her swiftly on the lips

before he pulled her chemise over her head, leaving her clad only in her lace-trimmed pantaloons, for she had given up on wearing stockings. Instinctively Celia tried to cover herself, but Ramiz pulled her hands away from her breasts. 'How can you expect others to enjoy what you cannot admire yourself?' he said. 'You are beautiful.'

Celia blushed. 'I'm not. I know I'm not. My sister Cassie is beautiful. I'm too thin. I don't—men don't—I'm just not.'

'Look at me.'

She obeyed reluctantly.

Ramiz wound a thick tress of hair around his hands. 'The colour of desire. A reflection of the flames which can burn inside you if only you'll let them.' He cupped her head to look deep into her eyes. 'You have a mouth made to frame kisses. The way your lids hide your eyes, they speak of secrets if only a man knows where to look.' His palms grazed down her shoulders, shaping her breasts. 'Your skin is like alabaster, like cream, to be touched and tasted.' He bent his head and took her nipple between his lips, his tongue flicking over the tip, his mouth sucking slowly, then hard, tugging until she moaned, for it felt as if he had set up a path of flames, like a fuse, burning its way from the painful ache of it down through the pooling heat in her belly towards the curling, tensing heat between her legs.

She fell back onto the divan. Ramiz knelt between her legs, his hands spanning her waist as he kissed her breasts, tugging sensations she had never imagined from her, so that she writhed with them, clutching at the silk of the sheets, then at the velvet of his robe, then at the satin of his hair, wanting more and more of what he gave, at the same time vaguely conscious that this must be wrong—for surely she should not be feeling these things? Surely she should not be wanting in this way, even if she didn't know what it was she wanted? Except to fly, as Ramiz had promised.

He was licking his way down her stomach now, tugging her pantaloons over her legs, gently removing her hands when she would have covered herself, whispering to her in a mixture of his own language and hers that she was beautiful, beautiful, beautiful, until almost she believed him. 'Legs made to wrap themselves around a man,' he said to her as he kissed the crook of her knees, carefully pushing them apart to taste the skin on the inside of her thigh.

She was shocked. She was unbearably tense. She shouldn't be letting him do what he was doing, whatever it was he was doing, but she couldn't bear to stop him because she wanted him to do more of it. And when he did, his mouth just feather-touching the place between her legs where the aching was becoming a pulse, she jerked with both shock and pleasure, relieved that he held her down, released from fighting it when his hands stroked her thighs into position and his tongue eased its way onto her, into her, licking, causing such a fluttering sensation within her that she cried out, because it wasn't too much, it wasn't enough.

She felt them then, her wings budding, like the rippling on a pond when a feather lands. She stilled and shut her eyes tight and then she saw them too, pink-tipped wings, pushing their way out as Ramiz circled his tongue to help them on their way, circling so they could push up more, licking to encourage them, soft so as not to frighten, then harder as her wings grew, and pushed, and trembled with their unfurling, lifting her up so that she gasped with the sudden swoop of them, lifting her up again as they bunched tight, readying themselves. And then with one final burst she toppled, thinking to fall, and her wings opened and she flew, soaring and bucking and diving and swooping and soaring again, crying out with the sheer unexpected delight of it, crying out again until she glided and floated slowly, slowly, sleepily back down to earth, exhausted and sated and filled with the glitter of the stars she had touched.

Past experience had taught him the satisfaction of giving pleasure, but always it had been a prelude to receiving. Now, Ramiz gazed at Celia spread out on the divan before him, her perfect skin flushed with satisfaction, her lips, her nipples, her sex all swollen with his attentions, and felt a new kind of satisfaction. He had done this. He had given her this. Blood surged into his groin, swelling his already hard shaft, though he knew he would do nothing about it. He wanted to, but he did not need to. This was enough—this knowing that he had made his mark, that he had been the first if not to have her, then to pleasure her. He had given her something no one else had. She would not forget him.

As he would not forget this picture she made. Unwilling to tempt his self-control, Ramiz got to his feet and pulled the silk sheet over her. 'Sleep now,' he whispered.

Celia's eyes fluttered open. 'Ramiz, I...'

'Tomorrow we must talk of the future. For the moment, rest,' he said.

Then he was gone. Were it not for the cushions scattered across the floor, the rumpled state of the sheets, the faint tingling she felt all over her body, she could almost have persuaded herself it was a dream.

Chapter Five

Celia awoke the next morning restless and confused, and rather appalled by herself. What she had felt last night had been shocking in many more ways than one. She'd had no idea that women such as herself could experience such raw emotion. Surely it was rather base to have done so? Was not such stuff the domain of courtesans? So she had always believed. Aunt Sophia had said so herself—women endured while men enjoyed. But last night—last night… Celia's face burned at the memory of her own abandonment. Then the heat focused lower as she remembered more.

Stop! She sat up in bed, burying her face in her hands, screwing her eyes tight shut in an effort to obliterate the image of Ramiz like some erotic god in his scarlet robe. It would be scarlet, of course. The colour of sin and shame. What he had done—no! *She had encouraged him. She had to admit it.* Her toes curled into the soft silk of her sheets. She had wanted him. And when he had gone she had wanted him again.

It must be the influence of this place. This harem, these rooms, built as a monument to the pleasures of the flesh. All that bathing and oiling of her body which went on—how could she help it if her mind was filled with indecent thoughts? This was a profane place. What she had experienced was temporal, bounded by the locked door to the rest of the palace, swathed in this secret sanctum by the velvets and silks and lace which screened the doorways, fuelled by her own fevered imaginings from that dratted book, *One Thousand and One Nights*. She was inhabiting a fantasy, that was all. A fantasy in which she might have acted as shamefully as a concubine, but that didn't mean she *was* one. She was still Celia.

Except, she thought, gazing distractedly at herself in the mirror once she had dressed in a white muslin gown trimmed with primrose yellow ribbons, she didn't actually know who Celia was any more. She tried to see herself with fresh eyes. She tried to see the Celia Ramiz saw. Did she look different? She wasn't sure. She felt different—more conscious of her body under the layers of her clothes, of the way the different textures felt against her newly sensitised skin when she walked, sat, stretched. Did she believe herself beautiful? Celia stared. No. Cassie was beautiful.

What, then, did Ramiz see? The beautifying effect of the harem? Perhaps some of its sensuality had rubbed off on her last night, but she could detect no trace of it now. 'What he saw last night, Celia Armstrong, was an available woman,' she said, sticking her tongue out at her reflection, failing to notice that she had reverted to her maiden name, because something else had just occurred to her. If last night had just been about her being available, why had Ramiz not simply taken his own pleasure?

At that precise moment Ramiz was busily engaged in sensitive matters of state, not pleasure. He sighed as he read over the terms of the draft treaty his trusted man of business, Akil, had prepared. Though A'Qadiz was the largest of the principalities involved, and the most powerful, it was a complex and delicate matter, with the disparate customs and rights of so many tribes to take into account.

'Sometimes I can understand my brother's preference for war,' he said, rubbing his tired eyes with the back of his hand. 'At least it is simple.'

Akil, who had known Ramiz since they were childhood friends, smiled thinly. Even in those days Ramiz had been a peacemaker, intervening with their father when his elder brother Asad went too far for their tutor or the families of his bullied victims to turn a blind eye, even if Asad was the royal heir. 'Simple, yes, but not necessarily effective. Don't give up, Ramiz. Your pact with Prince Malik has brought us a huge step forward.'

'If it holds,' Ramiz said wearily. 'What updates do you have regarding the new mines?'

Gold was the main source of A'Qadiz's riches, second only to the plentiful supplies of water which allowed the population not only to live well, but to trade key crops such as dates, figs and lemons. 'Good news,' Akil replied brightly. 'The richest seam yet, and it looks as if your hunch to test for silver to the south has paid off too.'

'Excellent. Let us hope that word of the find does not spread too quickly. For the moment the British and the French are content to bide their time in Egypt, scavenging whatever precious remnants of the past they can lay their hands on. They think us a paltry little country to whom they will throw a few stray crumbs by agreeing to use our port to open up a trade route to the riches of India, but if they find out the extent of the gold and silver we have buried in our land, especially in the mines so near to the coast, they will not be able to resist trying to get their hands on it.'

'The Englishman who was killed—did you find his papers?'

'His name was Cleveden. Yes, I did, but there was nothing in them I didn't already know.'

'What of the woman?' Akil asked diffidently. All of Balyrma had heard of the woman's arrival, but like everyone else he was in the dark as to Ramiz's intentions. Despite their long-standing friendship, Ramiz did not confide in him, nor did he take kindly to having his decisions questioned.

'What of her?' Ramiz asked tersely.

'She is still here, I presume?'

'Of course she is.'

'What do you intend to do with her, may I ask?'

A vision of Celia spread naked on the divan last night flashed into Ramiz's head. He had been unable to sleep for thinking of her, unable to prevent himself from imagining what it would have been like if he had taken her as he had wanted to—plunged his shaft into the soft, sweet depths he had prepared with such delightful relish. What he wanted to do with her was just that.

But, as so often, what he wanted and what he could have were very divergent paths. This time the honourable path was the least palatable. Fortunately he had committed to it before the events of last night. If he had not— But he would not think of that. It was decided.

'I wrote to the British Consul General in Cairo, informing him of what happened,' Ramiz explained. 'I did it as soon as we got here, for I couldn't risk the likes of Malik using it against me by trying to implicate me. I expect they'll send someone to collect her—in fact I'm surprised they haven't done so already. Until then she is safe enough here.'

'In your harem?'

'Of course.'

'Your—until now—empty harem, Ramiz?'

'What is that supposed to mean?'

Akil shook his head. 'You know very well what it means. The Council of Elders have asked me to urge you again to consider their list of suitable wives. It is a year since you came out of mourning for Asad, and they are anxious for your rule to be cemented. Also, the people would welcome a royal wedding. It has been a difficult and unsettling time.'.

'Thanks largely to my brother,' Ramiz said sharply. 'It was Asad, not I, who embroiled us in shedding blood. If it were not for me—'

Akil held up his hand. 'Ramiz, no one knows better than I the pain and hardship of the journey which has brought us to peace, but you must understand the people, the council, they do not have your vision. To them, to fight is to prosper. They have not yet seen the benefits your hard-won peace will bring them.'

Ramiz got to his feet and began to prowl restlessly around the room. Aside from the large mahogany desk at which he had been seated opposite Akil, it was lined with bookcases, all of them full, an eclectic selection of works, from the ancient scriptures of his country to Greek and Latin classics and a wide range of modern French and English literature. Much as he respected his heritage, his travels had taught him to respect the culture of all the great civilisations. If only his people were so open-minded.

'So my taking a wife would make everyone happy, would it, Akil?' Ramiz said, resuming his seat.

'If you were to marry one of the princesses the council have suggested, maybe Prince Malik's daughter, it would cement the peace, make us stronger, and make our people more secure. Even if you chose a princess from one of our own tribes—Sheikh Farid's daughter, for example—it would buy you much support. A royal wedding would go a long way to making your people feel—feel…'

'Spit it out, for the love of the gods,' Ramiz said impatiently.

'It would make them feel more secure, Highness. When you have sons, the dynasty will be settled. Without them there is only your cousin, and he is…'

'Weak.'

'Yes,' Akil agreed with relief.

Ramiz frowned. 'Why just one wife, then? If my marriage would cement the pact with Malik, why not do the same with our other neighbours? Why not two wives, or four, or ten?'

'You jest, I think, Highness.' Akil eyed his friend nervously. He looked calm, but Akil was not fooled. Ramiz drummed his fingers on the blotting pad, his mouth held in much too firm a line. Ramiz preferred to wield words rather than a sword, but when roused he had a temper which put his brother's into the shade as a lion's roar would drown out a kitten.

'You can leave off this "Highness" nonsense, old friend. I know you only use it when you want something.'

Akil smiled. 'Ramiz, listen, the council has compiled a list of ten princesses. I have verified it myself. Each one would make an excellent match. You must marry—you know that—for the sake of A'Qadiz.'

'Everything I do is for the sake of A'Qadiz, it has been so all my life, Akil, *you* know that. I never fail to do my duty.'

Akil nodded. 'But this is a pleasant duty, Ramiz. You are a man. All men need a wife to tend to their needs. The women on the council's list, they are not just princesses, daughters of our neighbouring princes and most influential tribes, they are beautiful virgins. Not such an onerous duty as duties go, is it now?'

Ramiz opened his mouth to speak, then closed it again. What was the point in trying to explain what he didn't really understand himself? Akil spoke good sense, he always did, and he spoke it without all the shilly-shallying and obeisance that the council used. He knew he should marry. He knew his marriage would be first and foremost for the good of his country and his dynasty. It was the way of things, had been the way of things for centuries, but the very idea of entering into such a cold bargain repelled him.

Perhaps Akil was right. Perhaps he had spent too long in the West. But he didn't like the idea of himself as some sort of stud stallion, any more than he liked the idea of his wives as brood mares, vying in his harem for his attentions. He didn't want that. He didn't know what he wanted, but it wasn't that.

Ramiz got to his feet again. 'Put these amendments to the treaty before the council. Tell them I'll consider their list of princesses when it is all signed, and the agreement with the British is settled too.'

Akil smiled and bowed. 'A very wise decision, Highness. Your wisdom is only matched by the magnificence of your...'

'Enough,' Ramiz said wryly. 'Go now, before I change my mind. And have the Englishwoman brought to me.'

Celia followed the servant through a maze of corridors guarded by countless sentries, each wearing a white robe with the new moon and falcon crest. She wore no veil, but kept her eyes on the ground, wondering what on earth Ramiz was going to say to her, wondering how on earth she was going to face him after last night without turning the same colour as the guards' checked *keffiyey* headdresses.

The room she was shown into was a library—the first salon she had seen furnished in a Western manner. Ramiz was sitting behind a large desk made of mahogany inlaid with pearl and teak. He was wearing a robe of dark blue, but no headdress, and rose to greet her when she entered the room.

'*Sabah el kheer,*' Celia pronounced carefully, using one of the phrases she had managed to learn from Fatima.

'Good morning, Lady Celia,' Ramiz said, 'I trust you are well?'

What did he mean by that? 'Yes,' she managed faintly. 'And you, Your Highness?' *Your Highness! After last night!* Celia bit her lip and stared fixedly at the carpet. Silk, it was woven with an intricate pattern of vibrant and beautiful colours. It must have cost a fortune.

'It is Ramiz, and I am very well.'

Celia jumped at the proximity of his voice. He took her hand. How had he moved so quietly? Slippers, she saw, for her eyes were still fixed firmly on the floor.

'I wanted to talk to you. Perhaps you should sit down?'

'Yes.' She allowed herself to be ushered into a chair facing the desk. To her relief Ramiz resumed his seat opposite, putting a solid expanse of inlaid wood between them. 'You have a lot of books,' she said, raising her eyes to cast them around the room.

'I do. You may read any that you wish. I have regular packages sent from London and Paris.'

'Thank you. Although I don't expect I will be here long enough to read many of them.'

Silence ensued. Ramiz drummed his fingers on the blotting pad. Celia risked a glance at him from under her lashes. He was leaning back in his chair, looking quite relaxed, as if last night had not happened. Or perhaps it was because it meant nothing to him. She wondered what the etiquette was for such occasions, but, having no experience of them whatsoever, found herself at a complete loss. She thought of some of the women of the *ton* who were reputed to have *affaires*. She'd always been surprised, for the couples betrayed no sign of affection— except poor Caro Lamb over Lord Byron, of course, but one didn't want to take any leaves out of *her* book!

Perhaps the best thing to do was pretend it hadn't happened after all. Celia sneaked another look at Ramiz, caught his eye unexpectedly and blushed furiously.

'You will be wondering what I intend to do with you,' Ramiz said.

'I beg your pardon?' Now Celia did look up, her eyes flashing outrage.

'I've written to your Consul General,' Ramiz continued blandly, 'to let him know that you're safe.'

'Lord Wincester. Papa was at school with him,' Celia said irrelevently.

Ramiz raised an eyebrow. 'You are well connected indeed.'

'So I'll be going back soon?'

'In a few days, I expect. As soon as they send someone.'

'Oh.' She should be relieved. 'They'll send me back to England.'

'Don't you want to go back? To see your family? I think you mentioned sisters.'

'Yes, naturally I miss them—Cassie in particular. But—oh, it's nothing. Just that I was expecting to be here in the East for a couple of years, that's all. I was looking forward to seeing it, to learning something new, and now I shall have to go home to do—well, I don't actually know what I'll do, to be honest.'

'What did you do before?'

'Playing hostess for Papa took up much of my time. I looked after the London house, of course, and then there were my sisters. But Cassie, the next in age to me, is coming out next Season, under my Aunt Sophia's chaperonage, and now that he has me off his hands Papa intends to marry again, he told me so himself.'

'So you are worried there will be no place for you when you return?'

'A little.' Celia shrugged. 'I'm being selfish, thinking of myself. I like to be busy, you see, and I'm used to taking charge, having done so since our mother died. It would be too awkward to stay at home if Papa has a new wife, I'd be forever treading on her toes without meaning to, and anyway I'll be expected to go into mourning.'

'But you will marry again, surely?' The moment he said it, Ramiz realised he disliked the idea intensely.

Celia pursed her lips. 'I don't think so. I don't think I'm very good at being a wife.'

'Now you are feeling sorry for yourself,' Ramiz said

with a twisted smile. 'You hardly had the chance to find out one way or another.'

'True, but— Oh, never mind my worries. I am very sure they are extremely trivial compared to yours. The main thing is I shall no longer be your problem.'

'No.' Strange as it was, he had not thought of her simply quitting his life. Their paths would be unlikely ever to cross again.

'And in the mean time,' Celia said bracingly, 'if there is anything I can do to help you, or—' She broke off, seeing his sceptical expression. 'You're going to tell me that business is men's work, aren't you?'

'I don't have to now that you've said it for me.'

'Papa said I had a brain worthy of a man. He often talked things over with me—not so much to get my opinion as to clear his own mind. He said it helped.'

'You're suggesting I confide the business of my kingdom in you?'

Celia could not help laughing at the shocked expression on Ramiz's face. 'The very idea of it—a mere woman giving her opinions. Too much time spent in the West, your people would say. It has infected him. We must lock him up until he is cured.'

Her eyes twinkled with merriment. Her smile was infectious. 'I think Akil would agree with you,' Ramiz said.

'Who is Akil?'

'He is what your father would call my under-secretary, I suppose, but Akil is much more than that. We have known one another since childhood. He is my other hand.'

'And what did you say to shock him?'

Ramiz steepled his fingers under his chin, gazing thoughtfully at the woman across the desk. In the bright light of day her hair was a deep copper, burnished with darker shades of chestnut. When she laughed, it accentuated the upward slant of her lids, making it look as if her eyes were smiling. She had dared to tease him and to question him, and now she wanted to advise him, and she seemed completely unaware of all the rules she was breaking by doing so. She talked like a man, with the assurance of one accustomed to being attended to, but she had a way of listening, of making him feel she really heard what he said, that made him want to know what she thought, that took away any element of condescension or patronage.

'Akil wants me to marry.'

'And has he a list of worthy brides lined up?'

'How did you know that?'

Celia shrugged. 'Papa told me they did the same for our Prince of Wales. Not that I'm advocating Prinny's marriage as a good example,' she said hurriedly, thinking of the lengths to which the Regent had gone to have his wife exiled, and the string of high-profile mistresses whom he courted blatantly in her absence.

'Your Prince George is a man who—you will forgive me for saying so—indulges in all the benefits of power while carrying none of its responsibilities,' Ramiz said thoughtfully.

'You are quite right. I would not dream of comparing you to such a man. In fact I think you are rather the opposite, for it seems to me that you put duty before all else. Many people envy princes and kings for having the world at their command, but I've never been one of them. It seems to me that it is rather the opposite.'

'You mean A'Qadiz has me at its command?'

'Yes, that's exactly what I mean. Ruling can be a very lonely business, I imagine. I would think you'd be pleased to have a wife to share it with you.'

'If—when—I take a wife, it will not be to reign by my side. That is not the way here.'

'But surely…' Celia bit her lip, realising she had been on the verge of overstepping the mark. Her previous exposure to royalty had led her to surmise that they were a selfish, conceited and not particularly intelligent race, decorative rather than useful, who relied upon others to actually get things done. Ramiz was different in every way. His authority was so ingrained that he thought nothing of it until it was challenged, but though the power he held was absolute, he wielded it for the general good, rather than for his own. Which did not mean that he took criticism, even well meant criticism, easily. 'I beg your pardon. It is not my business. I have no right to express an opinion.'

'What were you going to say? Go on. I promise I won't call the *siaf*.'

'Siaf?'

Ramiz grinned. 'The executioner.'

'Good God, I sincerely hope not. I'm very attached to my head.'

'It's a very clever head—for a woman.'

'From you, Your Highness, that is a great compliment indeed. If you must know, I was thinking that, since you are a prince and can do no wrong, there is no reason for you to stick to something just because that's how it's always been.'

'Tradition plays a very important part here. It is what binds many of the tribes together.'

'I understand that, and I'm not suggesting you turn A'Qadiz into a miniature England, but there are some things you could do which surely everyone would see were for the greater good. Like having your wife play more than the role of a brood mare.'

The fact that he agreed with her, that her words were almost an exact repetition of his own thoughts, was disconcerting. He wasn't sure that he liked it. 'A woman's first duty is to her children.'

'A wife's first duty is to her husband,' Celia said tartly. 'I fail to see how she can perform that fully when you lock her away from the world in a harem.'

'I've told you before, it is to protect her.' She was right, he knew that, but he didn't like being forced into defending something he had himself criticised. It put him in the wrong. Ramiz was not used to being in the wrong. 'Not all women are as—as *capable* as you, Lady Celia,' he threw at her exasperatedly. 'You forget that a wife's role is also to be a woman. Women, in case you have forgotten, are supposed to be the gentle sex. We have a saying here: a good woman is one who listens with stitched lips.'

'And we have a saying in England. The road to success is more easily travelled with a woman to mark the route!'

Ramiz threw his head back and laughed. 'Admit it—you made that up.'

He looked so much younger when he smiled. 'Yes,' Celia conceded, 'but that doesn't mean it isn't true.'

'I'm afraid it is a road I will have to travel alone, albeit with a few beautiful princesses in tow.' He did not quite manage to keep the bitterness from his voice.

'Why shouldn't you choose a wife you can like— grow to love, even? You're the Prince. You can do as you wish.'

'What I wish just now is to end this topic of discussion.'

'Ramiz, when you said I was a *capable* woman, what did you mean?'

A faint flush, just the tiniest trace of colour, kissed her cheeks. Her heavy lids veiled her eyes. 'You are not submissive. You speak your mind.'

'I thought—at least I used to think—that was a good thing. It's how I've been brought up—to think for myself, but not to…to trample on the opinion of others. I hope I don't do that.'

'That's not what I meant, and you don't. You listen. You're a very good listener.'

'But what did you mean, then? Did you mean that I'm intimidating?'

'Not to me!'

'But I could be to other men?'

He saw it then. She didn't mean other men. She meant one in particular. Her dead husband. 'A man who is threatened by a woman is not worthy of being called a man, Celia,' Ramiz said gently. 'Below the capable veneer you present to the world, you are every inch a woman. Did I not tell you last night? You are beautiful.'

She shivered as Ramiz lifted her hand to his mouth and kissed her palm. It felt shockingly more intimate than being kissed on the back of her hand. His lips were warm. Instinctively her fingers curled, forming a little hollow for him. She felt his tongue licking over the pad of her thumb and closed her eyes as the muscles in her belly clenched in response. 'Am I? Do you really think so?' she said, her voice sounding as if she were parched.

Ramiz laughed huskily, his breath caressing her fingers. 'Did I not prove that to you last night too? The point is not what I think, but what you think. Until you believe in your own beauty you will never be able to enjoy it. And if you can't enjoy it…'

Celia tugged her hand away, blushing furiously. 'That sort of enjoyment is what your women learn in the harem.'

'As you did.'

'We are not in the harem now.'

Ramiz pushed himself back in his chair, running his hand through his close-cropped hair. 'No, we're not. You're right. You may select some books to take back with you. I have more business to attend to.'

'Ramiz?'

'Well?'

'I meant it when I offered to help. If there is anything I can do—I'm used to being busy. Being waited on hand and foot, having nothing more to do than decide which scent to pour into my bath, is all very well for a few days, but—is there nothing?'

'You're bored?'

She nodded.

'Would you like to see the city?'

Celia's eyes lit up. 'I'd love that.'

'I can't spare the time today, and I would not trust you with another escort, but I will take you tomorrow. I could arrange for you to pay a visit to Akil's wife instead, if you wish. Yasmina speaks good English. You will still be spending the day in another harem, of course, but at least it won't be this one.'

Celia smiled with pleasure. 'That would be lovely. Thank you.'

'One last thing. Delightful as it was, last night was a mistake. It won't happen again. Ever.'

He was gone through the heavily draped doorway before she could answer him. Which is just as well, Celia thought, inspecting the shelves of the library, because I have no idea whether that is a good thing or not!

Deciding it was best not to even attempt to make sense of that, she instead busied herself in preparation for her outing to visit Akil's wife. It would be good to spend time with another woman. It would also be good to spend time away from the deeply unsettling presence of one particular man.

Chapter Six

Yasmina, a rather beautiful woman with eyes the colour of bitter chocolate and skin like toasted almonds, welcomed Celia warmly, pouring tea from a silver samovar into delicate crystal glasses in silver holders, speaking in careful English with a slight French accent.

The harem itself was a smaller version of the one occupied by Celia in the royal palace, a series of salons built around a courtyard with a fountain and lemon trees, but there the resemblance ended. The entrance was a gilded gate, not a door, and though it was guarded it was not locked. The rooms themselves were populated with Yasmina and Akil's four children, Yasmina's mother, Akil's widowed sister and her two children.

'I expect you think all harems are full of sultry slave girls,' Yasmina said, offering Celia a selection of delicately sugared pastries stuffed with sultanas and apricots. 'The fact is that most are like this. We all have our own salons, so we can be private when we wish to, but we eat and work together, we read and sew together, and as you can see we don't have to worry about being veiled.'

'But don't you mind being confined to one place like this?'

Yasmina laughed. 'We're not. The gate isn't locked. It's just symbolic. It marks a border that we can cross only if we are covered. You will find it is the same in all households in the city. In the desert it is different. Women can wander more freely with their tribes.'

'The door to the harem at the palace is locked.'

Yasmina nodded. 'That was Ramiz's brother Asad's doing. Are there still eunuchs?'

'Two of them.'

'Akil says that Ramiz doesn't know what to do with them. There used to be about ten, but the rest of them were happy to return to Turkey, where they came from, when Asad died. Akil says that Asad kept slaves there too.' Yasmina pulled her cushion closer to Celia's and lowered her voice conspiratorially. 'Concubines, from the East. They say they knew things which would make a man faint with delight.'

'What sort of things?' Celia asked, as much fascinated as shocked.

Yasmina pouted. 'I don't know. I asked Akil, but he wouldn't tell me. I don't think he knew either, though he wouldn't admit it. You know how men are—they like to think they know everything. Anyway, when Asad died Ramiz sent all the women home with dowries, and the wives went back to their families. We all assumed it was because Ramiz was going to take a wife, but he shows no sign of doing so. You should be honoured. You are the first woman to be permitted to enter Ramiz's harem. You will be the envy of every woman in the region.'

'But it's not like that. There is no question of me becoming…'

'His wife? Goodness, no,' Yasmina said with a shocked gasp. 'Of course not. A woman like you would not be permitted to marry Ramiz.' She placed the large tray with the glasses and samovar out of reach and beckoned to her two youngest children, a boy of three and a girl of two. 'This is my son, Samir, and my daughter, Farida.'

The little girl clung shyly to her mother's arm, but Samir was bolder, and reached out to touch Celia's hair. Smiling, she took him onto her lap and allowed him to play with her pearls, at which point Farida overcame her fear of the strange woman in the funny dress and demanded a turn. Laughing, Celia balanced the two children on her lap and taught them to play a clapping game which she'd used to play with her sisters, after which Samir insisted she accompany them on a grand tour of the courtyard to meet the other children. Rejoining Yasmina half an hour later, Celia was rather tousled, and extremely grateful for the cool drink of sherbet which her hostess handed her.

'You are very good with children,' Yasmina said, taking a sip of her own drink. 'I hope you have the opportunity to have some of your own one day.'

'That's unlikely now. I doubt I will marry again.' Celia bit her lip. 'Yasmina, when you said a woman like me could never marry Ramiz, did you mean because I am from the West?'

'Well, that is certainly an issue—it is expected he will marry a princess of Arabic blood—but it is not the main problem. It is because you were married.'

'But my husband is dead.'

Yasmina looked at her in surprise. 'That is not the point. You are not a virgin. Ramiz is a prince of royal blood. His first wife must be his and only his. His seed must be the only seed planted in her garden.' Celia blushed, but Yasmina continued, seemingly oblivious of having said anything untoward. 'His second wife now, or his third, if *she* were widowed it would not matter so much, but a first wife like me is the most important,' she said proudly. 'It is she who bears the heir. Not that I expect Akil to take another wife. Unless he tires of me—but that would be unlikely, for I am most skilled.'

Celia was fascinated and appalled. 'You mean there are—there are things that women can do to…?'

'Keep her man?' Yasmina nodded, smiling coyly. 'Naturally. One of the advantages of sharing a harem with other women is the sharing of such secrets. Wait here.'

Left alone, Celia cooled her wrists and temples in the fountain. What had possessed her to ask such a thing? To have such an intimate conversation with a woman who was a complete stranger? It was this place—the heat, the exotic strangeness of it all. The way the walls of the harem seemed to tempt curiosity about such sensuous matters out into the open. It was because she wanted to know. Not to experience, just to know. And if she didn't find out here, then she never would.

Yasmina returned with a small parcel wrapped in silk. 'Take these. They are charm pamphlets. You won't be able to read the spells of course, but the pictures explain themselves.'

Celia took the package with some trepidation. She should not even be contemplating looking at such material, but it would be rude to refuse. 'Thank you,' she said. 'Shukran.'

'It is nothing. You must come and say goodbye to the children now. Akil is waiting to escort you back to the palace. I hope you will come again before you go back to England.'

'I would love to. I've had a lovely time here; you are blessed in your family.'

Yasmina smiled. 'I hope you too will be blessed one day.' She pressed her visitor's hand. 'You must not grow too fond of Ramiz, Lady Celia. He is a very attractive man, and he has an air about him, no? Potent, I think that is the word. But he is not for you—and you, I think, are a type who loves only once. Forgive me for speaking so, but I have the gift. I don't think you loved your husband, but I think you could easily love Ramiz if you let yourself. He is well named. Ramiz means honoured and respected. He may indulge himself with you—he is a man and you are a woman—but he would never do anything which goes against the traditions of A'Qadiz. You will be hurt if you expect too much of him. Don't let that happen.'

'You're wrong, Yasmina, I promise you.'

Yasmina shook her head. 'I have the gift. I am never wrong in these matters.'

Celia returned to the palace in a thoughtful mood, having thoroughly enjoyed the time spent with Yasmina and her family. She had been surprised to discover that Yasmina's eldest daughter attended school every day. A different school from her brother, but she was, contrary to what Celia had been told by the Consul in Cairo, receiving an education.

Seeing a harem as a family enclosure rather than a bordello had been a revelation which made her look at Ramiz and his kingdom in a completely new light. Not that she agreed with everything Yasmina had said, mind you. Offering a home to her mother and her sister-in-law was one thing—indeed, it was in many ways exactly as things were done in larger families at home, right down to the disgraced, divorced aunt Celia had discovered lived in seclusion on the second floor of the harem. Every family had its skeletons. But as to Yasmina's acceptance of the possibility of sharing her husband with another woman simply because Akil had grown tired of her—no! Absolutely not. All Celia's instincts rebelled at the very thought. She knew, as everyone did, that the Prince Regent had married twice, though poor Maria Fitzherbert's wedding was not legal. She knew that many couples, Prinny included, tacitly consented to each other's *affaires* once an heir had been secured. She did not approve, though she knew she would be deemed prudish to say so. But the idea of living in apparent harmony with what must surely be one's rivals—no!

'That,' Celia said decisively, 'I could never do. As well put a notice in the *Morning Post* that my husband finds me lacking.'

'*Afwan*, Lady Celia?'

'Nothing, Adila,' Celia said, smiling at the maidservant and shaking her head, realising she had spoken out loud. 'It's nothing.'

They had run her a bath. Wishing to be alone with her thoughts, Celia dismissed Adila and Fatima, insisting that she could undress herself. She had come to enjoy their gentle ministrations, the daily oiling, massage and bathing ritual, and would miss it when she went home.

Home. The word sat like a stone on her chest. She didn't want to go home yet. 'So much more to learn,' she told herself as she stripped off her stockings and unlaced her stays. 'I've hardly seen any of the city.'

She'd never used to talk to herself. It was a habit she'd acquired here from being so much alone, and now it felt quite natural. Draped in a loose silk robe, she padded barefoot through to the bathing room. White-tiled, it was decorated as all the salons, with a blue and gold mosaic frieze, the bath sunk into the floor, surrounded by four pillars, with a small fountain bubbling icy cold water at one end. The walls above the waist-height frieze were covered in tiles like mirrors, and above the bath the ceiling arched dark blue, painted with a galaxy of silver stars.

Celia climbed up the shallow step and sank down into the soothing water. Tonight it was scented with cinnamon and orange blossom. The bath was deep, unlike the copper tub they used at home, and she did not need to hunch up, but lay stretched full-length, her head resting on the tiles, gazing up at the stars twinkling in the ceiling, her mind floating, randomly sifting through images of A'Qadiz like a colourful collage. The sunrise over the mountains of the desert. The way the sand changed colour during the day, from toffee to the creamy yellow of fresh-churned butter, to white-gold. Her first glimpse of Balyrma, the astonishing green of the fields, the jumble of fortress-like houses, the tiled walls with their keyhole-shaped doors, the minarets and the sparkling fountains, like a child's drawing of a fairytale land.

And Ramiz. She could not think of A'Qadiz without Ramiz. Her first glimpse of him at his most god-like, watching her from the hilltop above the port. Ramiz the warrior, his scimitar glinting like a vicious halo above his head. Ramiz the man, naked in the moonlit water of the oasis.

She had never met anyone like him, and was not likely to again. Every time she saw him she learned something new. He was intelligent. Amusing. Sophisticated. Intimidating. Arrogant. Above all fascinating. Last night when he had confided in her she had glimpsed a vulnerability in him, though it had been quickly cloaked. There were layers to him that no one was allowed to see. He kept himself apart, wearing his princely personality like a costume. No doubt about it—he was the very epitome of a magnificent and omnipotent ruler, but she liked the man beneath even more.

Celia smiled softly. His eyes—the way they changed

colour with his moods as the desert sand did with the heat. The way that little lick of hair stood up like a question mark when he'd been running his hands through it. His lids were heavy, the same shape as her own, and, like her, he used them when he didn't want anyone to know what he was thinking. She liked that she knew he was doing it because she did it too.

And his mouth. Celia touched her fingers to her own mouth, remembering. Kisses like honey. Darker kisses—exotic, crimsoning kisses, filled with promise. She closed her eyes. The way his mouth fitted so exactly to hers. The way his tongue and his lips spoke to her without words, telling her what to do now, and next, and next. Her fingers fluttered down her throat to the soft flesh of her breasts. She traced their shape, made liquid by the lapping water of the bath, trying to recapture the magic of Ramiz's touch as he'd cupped them, grazing her nipples as he had with his palm, his thumb—like this. Like this…

Her breath came shallow and quick. Her heart fluttered like a bird against the bars of a cage. Warmth seeped through her, as if her blood was heating, trickling to the place just below her belly, where it built so slowly she barely noticed it. Last night Ramiz had said she was beautiful. He'd made her feel beautiful. The way he'd traced the lines of her body, as if he would sculpt her, or draw her a picture of herself. Below the water line her nipples puckered and hardened, needles of feeling, bursts of intensity, feeding the pooling beat of arousal lower down, as tributaries would feed a river.

Celia moaned softly. She traced the path of feeling

down, cupping the point where it gathered like a delta. Beneath her palm she could feel herself—a tiny flutter like a whispered cry of need. Tentatively she touched it with her fingertip. Her stomach clenched. The thing inside her, like last night, bunched. The river was dammed, readying itself for the wall to burst. She touched herself again and moaned, imagining it was Ramiz, wishing it was Ramiz, aching for it to be Ramiz.

She moaned again, turning her head restlessly on the hard-tiled edge of the bath. Something moved on the periphery of her vision. She snapped her eyes open, and it was as if she had conjured him. He was standing in the doorway of the bathing chamber, frozen to the spot, dressed in a robe of pale blue, his face set into rigid planes.

'I came to find you to talk about tomorrow. I thought you would be having dinner.'

His voice was harsh, as if he were angry. Celia swallowed. She shook her head, licked her lips. Her mouth was dry. She tried to sit up, remembered her nakedness, and slumped back under the water.

She looked like Venus rising from the waves, her glorious hair tumbling down the side of the bath, damp curls clinging lovingly to her face. The flush of arousal coloured her cheeks and darkened her eyes. He had never seen anything so lovely. Never witnessed anything so intimate as the way she touched herself. Never been so aroused.

He should have left, he knew that, but he hadn't been able to tear himself away, and now he was here he could think of nothing, nothing, nothing but finishing her journey, of travelling with her, just this once. His hands stroking her flesh. Her hands, with their long delicate fingers, touching his skin. His mouth on hers. Her breathy moans of pleasure saying *his* name, wanting *his* caress.

Ramiz was beyond resistance. Beyond anything save the need to hold her, to taste her, to take her to the heights of pleasure and this time soar with her. He strode over to the bath, kneeling down on the top step, careless of his silk robe trailing in the puddles of scented water. For a long moment he simply gazed at her, damp and pink and creamy white, the fire of her hair reflected in the fire of her eyes, the sweetness of her breath like a whisper on his cheek.

'Celia.' He pulled her towards him, his hands slipping on her shoulders, feeling the delicate blades sharp beneath her flesh as he wrapped his arm more firmly around her, the long sleeve of his caftan trailing in the water.

'Ramiz.' Sleepy with arousal, the word wrapped itself around him as Celia's arms twined around his neck, and he was lost.

Water slopped wildly over the sides of the bath onto the shallow step, forming pools on the tiled floor as he pulled her up, kissing her wildly. No slow build, no delicate preliminaries, passion burst like a ripe fig as they kissed, hands slipping and gripping and sliding, the silk of his robe clinging to their skin, their lips, their tongues, kissing as if they would meld.

She had no thought of resisting, was too far gone in

her own imagined lovemaking to refuse her dream made flesh and blood in the magnificent form of Ramiz. They were standing together on the tiled floor by the bath, wet skin, fevered lips, kissing and licking, licking and kissing.

'Celia, Celia, Celia.' Ramiz said her name like an incantation, punctuating it with kisses to her lids, her ears, her throat, his hands urgent upon her, raising torrents of feeling where before there had been only feeble tributaries. His mouth found her breast, his lips fastening greedily round her nipple. The delicious tugging produced such a rush of heat that she moaned, slumping in his embrace, arching her back so that her breasts implored him for more. His attentions moved to the other nipple. She moaned again, saying *his* name now, over and over, a plea for completion, of wanting and desperate need.

Her hands plucked at the silk of his robe, wanting to touch flesh. She struggled ineffectually with the buttons at his neck, eager now, desperate for the feel of his flesh upon hers for the first time. She wanted to touch him. To see him. To savour him. She wanted to give him what he was giving her. She wrenched at a button and it flew through the air to land with a click on the tiles.

Ramiz laughed—a low, husky noise which gave her goosebumps. She watched, fascinated, as he yanked the other buttons free and then, taking the neck of his caftan between his hands, simply tore it apart, casting it aside onto the floor to stand naked before her for the first time.

The word *magnificent* did not do his body justice.

Celia gazed at him in awe—the golden skin stretched taut over the muscles of his shoulders and chest, the rippling ridges of his abdomen, like the contours of the desert sands of which he was prince. The sheen of water like a glaze cast each dip and rise into relief. Where she was curved he was sharper lines. Where she was soft he was…

She reached out her hand tentatively. Ramiz took her by the wrist, encouraging her. Where her skin was soft, like cashmere, his was smoother, like silk stretched on a tambour frame. She could feel the hardness of his muscles underneath. Ramiz pulled her closer. He guided her wrist lower. The concave stomach. Down. Her eyes followed the same path. Down. To the curving length of him, solid, intimidatingly large. She could not imagine how—where—surely it would hurt?

'Ramiz, I…'

'Touch me. There is nothing to be frightened of.'

'I'm not frightened.' But she was, just a bit, and her voice gave her away. She was afraid of her ignorance. Afraid of failing. Afraid that Ramiz would find her lacking.

He scooped her up, holding her high against his chest, pushing his way impatiently out of the bathing chamber to the next salon, where he kicked a heap of cushions together onto the carpet and sank down onto them. Satin and silk and velvet—she could feel them all on her back, her bottom, her thighs. Satin and silk and velvet on her mouth as Ramiz kissed her.

'To touch is to learn,' Ramiz whispered, trailing his fingers over her hip.

He leaned over her, his mouth following where his fingers had led, feathering kisses like whispers, speaking softly of the pleasure to come. She felt her skin tighten as her flesh seemed to swell under his caress. He kissed the crease at the top of her thigh, pulling her onto her side, positioning himself opposite her so that they lay like two crescents curved into each other.

Ramiz dipped his hand between her legs, lightly stroking his way through the moist folds of her flesh. 'Touch me, Celia. Do as I do. Make me feel as you do. Like this.' With his other hand he placed hers onto his shaft, wrapping her fingers round its length and gently guiding her. Satin and silk and velvet.

Her touch was entirely inexperienced and entirely delightful. He thought fleetingly of the man who had been her husband, a man who had obviously taken no interest at all in his wife's pleasure, and then he banished the thought, for he did not want to think of Celia as a wife, or having belonged to anyone else. He did not want to think at all, for to do so would be to stop, and he could not stop. Not now.

He slipped his fingers gently inside her, easing into the swelling heat of her, enjoying the way she clenched around him, the little gasp of pleasure emanating from her. 'This is what you are doing to me,' he said. 'When I do this, and you touch me like that, this is what it feels like.' Slowly he pulled out of her clinging moistness, only to ease back in again.

What he was doing was a prelude. Finally she understood. Her own fingers clasped around the part of him which was designed to meld them together. She stroked him, wondering at the slight curve on the satiny skin, at the astonishing hardness of him, tracing a line up to the tip of him, softer, rounded, velvety. He was watching her. She gasped as he pushed his fingers inside her again, closing her eyes at the peculiar smarting of this pleasure, more insistent, the edges rougher than last night. Then he did it again, and she stroked him in the same rhythm, and saw the pleasure she was giving him etched on his face, in the way his eyes darkened, the way he bit his lip to stop himself from crying out.

It was the same for him. It was really the same. What she was feeling—this mounting tension, this jagged excitement, this feeling of wanting it done, over, of wanting it to last for ever, this wanting to soar and wanting to cling—he was feeling it too as she stroked him and he stroked her. Then he slid upwards, touching her where he had touched her yesterday, and she felt herself began to slip, but forced herself to cling on. Her thumb caressed the tip of his shaft, and Ramiz gasped. Inside her, he worked magic of his own. It was like being pushed inexorably towards something deep and dark, and as she stroked him and circled him she could see he felt the same. His eyes were closed. A dark flush stained his cheeks. He gripped his lower lip with his teeth. His breathing was fast, uneven. Like her own. Her heart was thumping. Her body was cold, cold—freezing except for where Ramiz touched her and she touched Ramiz. She felt him thicken in her hand, felt herself swelling under his hand, heard him say her name, like a plea, for the first time asking something of her, but before she had time to wonder what he wanted the jagged swelling pressure in her burst through, like water coursing through a dam, and she cried out. Ramiz cried out too, spilling his pleasure over her hand as she melted into his.

He was right. To give was to receive. More than last night. More than she had thought possible. Enough to make her wonder what *more* would feel like. Enough to make her realise that she should heed Yasmina's warning. This was a fantasy formed in a harem and being played out free from the disapproval of the outside world. Nothing more. It could never—must never—be anything more.

Celia sat up, pulling a tasselled cushion onto her lap to cover herself.

Ramiz opened his eyes, reluctantly pulling himself back down from the heights to which her touch had sent him. He had not meant this to happen. *It should not have happened! What was he thinking?* He got quickly to his feet, pulling his torn robe around him. 'This was a mistake.'

'A mistake?' she repeated stupidly.

'It was wrong,' Ramiz said tersely. At least he had not risked any consequences! At least his sense of honour had not wholly deserted him.

His robe was soaking wet from the bathwater, but he didn't seem to notice. It clung to him, making him look like one of those naked statues, strategically draped for modesty's sake. Feeling at a distinct disadvantage, Celia hugged her cushion defensively. With his clothing, Ramiz had donned his mask. She hardly recognised the man who had moaned his pleasure at her touch only moments before.

'What do you mean, it was a mistake?'

'You are here under my protection. I should not have allowed myself—this should not have happened. No matter how much the provocation,' he added.

'Provocation!' Celia's face burned with a mixture of shame and anger. 'I thought I was alone.'

'This is my harem.' He was being unfair, but it was true in a way. If she had not been—if he had not seen her in the bath like that… 'My harem,' Ramiz repeated firmly. 'I am free to walk in here any time I wish.'

'That's preposterous. It may be your harem, but as you've just pointed out I am a guest here. I am entitled to some privacy.'

'And I am entitled to expect my guests to behave more decorously.'

'You're being quite ridiculous.'

'You call *me* ridiculous? You forget yourself, Lady Celia. You forget who you are talking to.'

She knew he had a temper, but she had not before experienced it. His face was pale with anger, his mouth set in a thin line, his hands clenched at his sides. She had overstepped the mark as far as he was concerned, but as far as she was concerned so had he. Her own formidable temper was normally kept firmly under wraps, but his heady change of mood from euphoria to accusation sent it spinning out of her control before she could rein it in.

Regardless of her naked state, she flung the cushion away and got to her feet, her hair flying out like battle colours behind her. 'I don't care who you are—you are being ridiculous. I was taking a bath in the privacy of a bathing chamber. The fact that it happens to be in your harem is completely irrelevant. It is not my fault that you fell victim to your own base desires. I won't be branded some sort of siren just to satisfy your honour, be you prince, sheikh, or simply a man.'

He flinched as if she had struck him. As she had— with the truth of the matter. He had been unable to control himself. No matter that he had not taken her, he had wanted to. 'You are right.'

Celia's temper fled as quickly as it had arrived. There was an embroidered cover on one of the divans under the window. She snatched it up, wrapping it around her shoulders. 'Ramiz, you were not the only one to lose control,' she said painfully. 'I did not provoke you deliberately, but I didn't stop you either.' She reached out to touch his arm. 'You are not the only one to blame.'

He shrugged himself free of her hand. 'You are a woman. I should not have allowed you to submit.'

'Submit?' Celia stared at him in confusion. 'Why must you persist in the belief that I don't have a mind of my own just because I'm a woman? I make my own choices, even if they do turn out to be foolish ones.'

Ramiz sighed heavily. 'I am pleased you think this way, even if it is misguided. I hope this—this event— will not colour the view of my country that you take back to England.'

Realisation dawned, cold and savage. 'You're worried that I'll make things difficult for you through my father?'

'We are at a delicate stage of negotiations with your people.'

'I won't be crying ravishment, if that's what you're worried about.' She glared at him, determined not to allow the hurt she felt to show.

It was the last thing he'd been thinking of, but it *should* have been the first. He could not forgive himself. He could not allow himself to think about why he had done what he did. Or how Celia felt. And definitely not how he felt. It was a relief at least that his actions had not offended her. He must ensure he gave her no further cause.

'Tomorrow, if you still wish, I will take you out to see something of Balyrma.'

'Is that my compensation for keeping my mouth shut? If so, I'd rather stay here.'

'I thought you wished to see the city. If you have changed your mind…'

'I'm sorry, Ramiz, I shouldn't have said that.' Celia attempted a weak smile. 'All this—everything here—it's all so strange to me. I feel like I'm in a dream half the time. I'd love to see Balyrma, and if you have the time to escort me I'd be honoured. I'm sure I couldn't have a more knowledgeable guide. Akil told me you've written a history of Balyrma's origins.'

Ramiz shrugged. 'It is nothing. The work of an enthusiastic amateur rather than a scholar. I will have you brought to me in the morning.' He turned to leave.

'Ramiz.' Difficult as it was to speak of such things, she could not square it with her conscience to allow him to think he had forced her, any more than she had been able to accept that she had enticed him. 'Ramiz, I meant what I said. It was as much my fault as yours. You are not responsible for my actions, no matter how accustomed you may be to thinking you are.'

'It does you credit that you say so.'

'I say so because it's the truth.'

Ramiz smiled like a god descending from the heavens to join the mere mortals. It transformed him. 'It is not just me who is accustomed to shouldering the blame, is it? I think you must be a very protective sister.' He kissed her cheek. 'You are certainly a most unusual woman.'

Leaving her to ponder the meaning of this rather enigmatic statement, Ramiz left.

Chapter Seven

Next morning Celia dressed for the promised sightseeing trip in a lemon-figured muslin walking dress with a double flounce along the hem, trimmed with knots of gold ribbon. Gold ribbon was also threaded through the high neckline and the edges of the tight-fitting sleeves, which were fastened with a row of tiny pearl buttons. Adila had found a way for her to attach the gauzy veil of blond lace to the back of her head, rather as Spanish ladies wore their mantilla, obviating the need for a hat, much to Celia's relief. She wore the veil back over her hair while still inside the palace, and carried her gloves as she followed in the wake of the guard. Despite giving herself a severe talking to, playing over last night's conversation several times in her head, she was extremely nervous about meeting Ramiz again, and quite unable to decide how she felt about anything that had happened. In fact, in the bright light of day, released from the harem's sultry ambience, she found it difficult to believe it had happened at all!

Ramiz was in his library, dressed all in white as she had first seen him, complete with headdress and cloak. 'In desert prince mode,' Celia muttered to herself as he nodded a distant good morning from behind his desk and turned back to complete his conversation with Akil, leaving her standing like an unwanted caller at the doorway.

Though she herself had come to think of the harem as a separate place, ruled by the senses rather than the mind, and though she herself had made every effort to put last night's events firmly to the back of her mind, Celia couldn't help resenting the fact that Ramiz seemed so successfully to have done the same. She eyed him from beneath her lids as she wandered over to browse the bookshelves. How she envied him his detachment. How she wished she shared it. She wasn't used to this feeling of constantly being on the back foot. The Lady Celia Armstrong she knew was used to feeling in charge. In control. Calm. Cool. Sophisticated. Not like some country miss in her first Season, having constantly to consult a book of etiquette and even then always on the verge of a fatal *faux pas*.

But she was not that Lady Celia Armstrong, and she knew she never would be again. She could not forget what she had experienced in Ramiz's arms, under Ramiz's tutelage, and she was very much afraid that what he had taught her had spoiled her for ever for any other man—as this place, this whole experience of the exotic world of A'Qadiz, would spoil her even for her beloved England, if she let it.

It was a paradox, she thought, picking up a volume bound in soft blue leather which was on the table with a stack of books recently come from England. A paradox, because here in this kingdom, where women were veiled and segregated, where she spent much of her time behind the locked door of a harem guarded by two eunuchs, she had never been so free.

Celia opened the book. *Emma, a Novel in Three Volumes by the Author of Pride and Prejudice.* She'd really enjoyed *Pride and Prejudice*. They had read it together, she and her sisters, assigning themselves roles from the sisters in the story. She had been Elizabeth, of course, and Cassie had been Jane, the beauty of the family. Smiling to herself at the memory of Caroline and Cordelia squabbling over who was to be the flighty Lydia, Celia felt a pang of homesickness. She wondered what they were all doing now. She didn't even know what time it was back home—later or earlier? Was it sunny or raining? It was strawberry season. Cressida loved strawberries, though they brought Caroline out in a rash when she ate too many, as she always did, no matter how many times she was reminded. Cordelia preferred the strawberry jam they all made together from Mama's treasured receipt book. It had become an annual rite, taking over the kitchen for the day, filling the big country house with the sweetly cloying scent of jam as it bubbled in the vast copper pot. Cassie had charge of the receipt book now. It would be up to her to order the extra sugar, to take Celia's role as Jam-Maker-in-Chief, no doubt ceding her own role of Measurer-in-Chief to Caroline. Celia could already imagine the argument that would induce between the youngest two of her sisters. Poor Cassie, whose gentle temperament made her loath to intervene in any dispute, would wring her hands and implore them to share and tell them that one role was just as good as another, and they would ignore her completely, and Caroline would get involved, and without Celia to knock sense into all of them the whole jam-making would turn into a complete fiasco...

'Of course it will not,' she chastised herself. 'I just want to think so because it makes me feel indispensable.'

'What does?'

Celia jumped, dropping volume one of *Emma* on to the thickly carpeted floor—so thickly carpeted she had not heard Ramiz approach. Now he was standing uncomfortably close. Why did she always forget how tall he was, and how very good-looking? She took a step back. 'I beg your pardon?'

'You said, *"I just want to think so because it makes me feel indispensable."*'

'Oh. I must have been talking out loud. I hadn't realised. I was thinking of my sisters. It's nothing.'

'You miss them?'

'Yes, of course I do. Though I'm sure they're all fine without me,' Celia said, surprised to find her voice a bit shaky.

'But there's a part of you which hopes they are not, hmm?'

She smiled, trying surreptitiously to blink away the

tears which had gathered in her eyes. 'I know it's a dreadful thing to think. I'm afraid I must be a very controlling female.'

'It's not surprising. You took on the role of mother to your sisters at a very early age, yes? It is perfectly natural that you should worry about how they are coping without you. It is something mothers do, even when their children have families of their own. A very feminine trait.'

Celia sniffed. 'Thank you. I think that might even qualify as a compliment.'

'If you wish to write to them, I will see your letter is safely delivered.'

'You're very kind.'

'I should have thought of it earlier. Your people will wish to be reassured that you are safe and well. They will not want to take my word for it. You must write tonight.'

'I see.' He wasn't thinking of her, but of his own reputation. Of his country's interests. 'If you are too busy for our outing today, perhaps we should postpone it.'

'There is no need. I have taken care of business for today, and Akil has it all in hand. Besides, I wish you to see something of Balyrma while you are here.'

'So that I can report back on how wonderful it is?'

Ramiz's eyes narrowed. 'Because I think it will interest you. If I was mistaken…'

'No, you're not,' Celia said hastily. 'I do want to see it. I was a bit disconcerted, that was all—seeing this book, if you must know. My sisters and I read another by the same author.'

'*Pride and Prejudice?* I read it myself, and enjoyed it. A very amusing account of your English manners. The author must be a very perceptive man.'

'You think it is written by a man?'

'The wit is acerbic, none of the characters are sympathetic, and there is none of the sentimental romanticism endemic in female writers. Of a certainty it is a man.'

'Of a certainty? If you say it is so, then it must be so, Highness.'

Ramiz looked startled, and then he smiled, showing gleaming white teeth and menacing amber eyes. 'You are learning, Lady Celia. I am granting you the honour of my company without escort and in public. You must treat me with respect and deference in front of my people, for if you do not I will be forced to confine you to the harem for the duration of your stay. I hope I have made myself clear?'

She met his gaze defiantly for all of ten seconds, then surrendered. In truth, when he looked at her like that she had no wish to defy him. And he *was* honouring her with his presence after all, and she *did* want his company, more than she cared to admit to herself. Celia drew her veil over her face, and her gloves over her fingers. 'Yes, Highness,' she said meekly, following in Ramiz's wake as he led the way across the courtyard. Which meant he did not see her pout cheekily at him as they went through the passageway and out of the gate into the city.

The heat was so intense it knocked the breath out of

her—like walking into an oasthouse after the hops had been roasted. In the cool of the palace she had forgotten how fierce the sun could be, even this early in the day.

She had also forgotten the reverence in which Ramiz was held. People dropped to their knees as he passed. They did not look at him, but Celia could feel their eyes on her, curious rather than threatening. She was conscious of how strange she must look in her tight-fitting dress, and acutely aware, as she watched Ramiz nod and smile to his people, of just how big an honour he was actually conferring on her in being her guide for the day.

It was not yet nine o'clock, but Balyrma was a hive of activity. Ramiz led the way through the dusty streets away from the tiled houses and minarets of the more affluent quarter to the more crowded area nearer the city gates. 'I thought you'd like to see the souks,' he said over his shoulder. 'Each sector of the city is named for different artisans, and each has their own market. This alleyway here is populated by leather workers; down here is where the potters are, and the tile-makers. Come closer. I'm getting a sore neck talking to you like this.'

'I thought I was to follow in your wake to show you respect.'

'You can show respect just as well by doing as you are bid.'

Celia caught up with him. 'You have the makings of a frightful tyrant, you know,' she said with a smile. 'Highness,' she added as a deliberate afterthought.

'And *you* have the makings of a most subversive citizen.'

'I'm sorry if I seem flippant sometimes. It's just that you can be rather intimidating, and I'm not used to being intimidated.'

They had stopped momentarily, allowing the small retinue of children they had collected in their wake to swarm around her, reaching out to stroke the fabric of her dress. She smiled at them all abstractedly through her veil.

'They are not used to seeing clothing such as yours.'

'I wish I did not have to wear it. It's completely unsuited to this climate, and I feel as if I'm being baked alive.'

'You should have said so before. We can get you some fabrics at the souk. I will have the maids make up some traditional outfits if you really want to go native.'

'I would *love* to go native.'

'You never look hot. In fact you always look extremely elegant.'

'Thank you.'

'You are welcome. Do not look so sceptical, I mean it,' Ramiz said with a wry smile.

They set off again at a slower pace, stopping off at a stall selling sugared almonds, dried dates, long sticks of some sort of sticky toffee packed with sultanas and raisins, and all sorts of other sweet delights which had the children staring in wide-eyed wonder. Ramiz selected an assortment which he handed out before they moved on, walking companionably side by side, Ramiz having forgotten all about his desire for protocol.

'I don't know what it is about you that makes me speak

my mind,' Celia said thoughtfully as they approached the fabric district. 'I assure you, every time you goad me into saying something outrageous I wish I had bitten my tongue out.'

'Before I have it cut out, you mean,' Ramiz said.

She could tell by the way his eyes gleamed, the way his mouth firmed into an upward curve that wasn't quite a smile, that he was teasing. 'Yasmina told me you rule with a hand of iron in a velvet glove. She also told me one of the first things you did when you came to power was to completely overhaul the legal system. You don't even have an executioner any more, do you?'

'There is no need. When people have enough to eat, somewhere for their family to live, a way to earn a living, they have no need to turn to crime. And when the punishment for transgression is to lose all that— banishment—I find it is incentive enough.'

'That is a very progressive way of thinking. Far more humane than we are in England, where a starving man who steals a sheep to feed his family can be hanged.'

'If you read Scheherazade's stories more closely you would see she shares my views.'

'And your people?' Celia asked.

'Some of the tribes prefer the old ways. For them, violence—wars, punishment, whatever—is a way of life. I spend a lot of my time trying to prevent them overturning my treaties. I am due to visit the head of one of the tribes later this week, as a matter of fact. They occupy land on the border of A'Qadiz, where the oasis is disputed territory. It is supposed to be shared. I will spend two days reminding him of this, and he will spend two days trying to extract as much gold as he can from me as compensation for what he claims to be his exclusive rights.'

'You bribe him not to fight?'

'Don't look so shocked. It's a tactic your government uses all the time. And for me it's cheaper in the long run than allowing him to start a full-scale war.'

'Can't you just have him—this head man—replaced with someone who believes in what you're trying to do?'

Ramiz laughed. 'That really would start a war. Enough of this talk. They are my problems, not yours. Come, the fabric district is just here. Take your time. Choose as much as you like.'

'Oh, but I don't have any money with me.'

'I will pay.'

'Absolutely not. I cannot allow you to buy my clothes. It wouldn't be proper.'

'It would not be proper for me to allow you to pay.'

'Then I won't have anything.'

Ramiz stared at her in consternation. 'You honestly think I am concerned about the price of a few yards of material?'

'It's the principle of it,' Celia said firmly. 'In England only a—a courtesan allows a man who is not her husband to buy her clothes.'

'We are not in England,' Ramiz pointed out. 'In A'Qadiz it is for the master of the harem to provide them. You are in my harem, I will pay for these, and that is an end to it.'

Celia was not at all convinced, but looking at Ramiz's

face, at his mouth setting in a firm line, she decided not to antagonise him further. The day was young, and she wanted to make the most of it. She wanted Ramiz to enjoy himself, and if that meant breaking one of her own rules to keep his dignity intact, then so be it. 'Thank you, Highness,' she said with a graceful curtsy. 'In that case I will be most honoured.'

Ramiz grinned. 'You don't fool me with that meek and mild act. And you can stop calling me Highness. No one can understand what you're saying.'

'Thank you, Ramiz, then. I trust the royal coffers are sufficiently full, for I intend to make the most of these wonderful fabrics.'

If anyone had told him that he could enjoy the experience of shopping for silks in a souk, Ramiz would have laughed in his face. Though he enjoyed looking at a well-dressed woman as much as the next man, he had little interest in what that dress comprised of nor in any of the frills and furbelows which accessorised it. But Celia's child-like enthusiasm was enchanting, and for the next hour he watched entranced as she threw herself with unwonted zeal into the business of choosing colours and textures and trimmings.

Celia, who had never before seen such a display of colourful silks, rich velvets and delicate gauzy fabrics she could not even name, went from stall to stall in the souk with a rapt expression on her face. She removed her gloves to plunge her fingers into the thick nap of a crimson velvet, to rub a shawl of the softest cashmere against her cheek, to stroke silks and satins and fine net and coarse damask, turning the purchase of cloth into a wholly sensual experience she could never have imagined. In her excitement she forgot all about deference and reserve. She forgot to put her gloves back on and she forgot to replace her veil, but she was so charming, able to make her wishes clear despite the language barrier, and careful to praise even the plainest of fabrics displayed to her, equally careful to spread her purchases over as many stalls as possible, that rather than cause offence she was treated with real hospitality and warmth. They drank several glasses of tea, and Ramiz found himself playing second fiddle for the first time since he had come to power.

'Thank you for that,' Celia said to him as they left a shop specialising in *passementerie*—elaborate braiding made from gold and silver thread. 'I hope you weren't bored.'

'It was an education. Have you had enough?'

'More than. Do you have to go back to the palace?'

Ramiz shook his head. 'I have arranged a special treat for you.' He led the way through the maze of alleys and terracotta buildings with their stalls opening out from the ground floors, back to a large square where a palace guard was waiting with two snowy white camels. 'A short ride—half an hour, no more. Can you manage it in that dress?' Ramiz asked when Celia looked at him enquiringly.

'Where are we going?'

He smiled and shook his head. 'It's a surprise.'

They left Balyrma by a different gate than the one through which they had entered the city. This one led through an olive grove to the south, to a narrow track, only just discernible, wending its way towards the mountains. Ramiz told her a little more of Balyrma's history as the camels made their stately way along the path. As before, Celia's intelligent questions and thirst for knowledge made him relax his guard, drawing him out, making him laugh, extracting things from deep in the recesses of his mind—childhood memories and ancient legends he had forgotten until now. He liked her. It was a strange thing to say of a woman, but there it was. She was excellent company and he liked her.

The mountains seemed to rear up out of the sand like a child's model or an artist's impression, without foothills or any other preliminaries, more like monuments than natural phenomena. There was no path that Celia could see, and her heart sank at the thought of having to climb, until she realised that Ramiz was leading them to what looked like a large fissure in the rock. A cave?

It was not a cave but a narrow passageway, curving in an 'S' shape only wide enough to allow them to pass through in single file. Enchanted, Celia saw that the rock was carved with strange symbols, and little niches contained carved idols scattered at regular intervals. Craning her neck, she could just see the sky, the brilliant blue colour of approaching noon, though here between the rocks it felt cool. Then they turned the final bend and she gasped with astonishment, for they were standing in a large open square and before her lay a ruined city, built into the rock itself.

'The ancient city of Katra,' Ramiz said. 'We don't know how old it is exactly, but we estimate about two thousand years.'

The city was compact, and despite its great age in a remarkable state of preservation. 'I've never seen anything so wonderful,' Celia said as she wandered through the buildings. 'It's marvelous. I can't believe I've never even heard of it.'

'That is because we have been at pains to keep its existence a secret,' Ramiz explained. 'It is well known that the British and French stripped Egypt of many of its ancient treasures during the wars with Napoleon, and it is well known that your Consul General continues to send artefacts collected by his friends from all over Egypt and the Levant to his own little museum in England, as Lord Elgin did with the Parthenon marbles. I don't want that happening to Katra.'

'No, and I can see why. It's beautiful, and quite eerie too. I feel as if the people have just stepped out this morning and will come back any time. But if you don't want anyone to know about it, why have you brought me?'

Why? Because it was special, and he wanted to share it with her. He realised he couldn't say that. He knew he shouldn't have thought it. He hadn't until this moment. 'Because to understand Balyrma's history one must understand Katra's. I knew it would interest you.'

'You've no idea how much. It's one of the most marvellous things I've ever seen. Thank you.'

Celia had pushed back her veil again. She smiled up at him, her eyes alight with excitement that made them glitter like diamond-chipped jade. Her mouth made the most delightful curve—soft and full. The taste of her, sweet and flowery, came back to him like a punch in the stomach. Her lips like petals on his own. Blossoming as she had blossomed under his touch. Bloomed. Ripened. *What was he thinking?*

'It is past noon,' Ramiz said brusquely, looking up at the sun high overhead. 'I have arranged for shade and food. This way.'

For a fraction of a second she thought he had been going to kiss her. Her heart had begun to beat hard and fast, changing its tempo so suddenly she felt dizzy. Now he was striding ahead of her to where the camels were tethered, leading the way on foot back through the passageway so quickly she had to run to keep up.

As they emerged into the blaze of the sun she saw that a tent had been set up directly under an overhanging ledge. Like the one they had abandoned in the desert it was a square in shape, constructed from wool woven from camel or goat, supported by large wooden props tied with rope, but there the resemblance ended. Thick-piled carpets covered the sand. The walls were hung with tapestries depicting scenes from ancient mythology. Tasselled cushions embroidered with silks, embellished with seed pearls and semi-precious stones, were strewn across the carpet around a low table, upon which a selection of gold dishes were covered. The appetising aroma of spit-roasted goat filled the air, making Celia's mouth water.

Damask hangings created a small room to one side, where a pitcher of rose-scented water stood on a marble washstand. Celia rinsed the dust and sand from her face and hands, tidying her hair in the gilt mirror which had been thoughtfully provided, before she sat down to eat with Ramiz.

The food was delicate, packed with the exotic flavours she had come to relish. A lime and mint sherbet quenched her thirst. Aside from the usual selection of spiced meats and palate-cleansing fruits there was something called a *pastille*—a parcel of flaky pastry stuffed with pigeon, almonds and dates. Unlike at home, where it was the custom to partake only of those dishes within reach—even if one's favourite dish was at the other end of the table—she had discovered that it was expected of her to try a little of everything here. It was a practice she enjoyed, and she said so to Ramiz.

'Every meal is like a picnic, and if I don't like something I can just leave it because I've only taken a little bit. At home, especially at dinner parties, it is expected that you eat whatever is put on your plate. I can't tell you the number of times I've had to chew my way through a perfectly inedible piece of over-cooked meat or, worse, under-cooked fish.'

'It is your habit to drown everything in sauces, which I don't like,' Ramiz said. 'It makes me wonder why. Is the food so awful that it can't be eaten on its own?'

Celia giggled. 'You're probably right. I'm afraid that cooking is not high on the list of British accomplishments.'

She dipped her hands into a little fingerbowl in which jasmine petals floated. He watched her, thinking again what a strange mix she was. He could not understand his attraction to her. No doubt she was thinking the same thing. He could not understand why she had allowed him such liberties. He was the first to stir her, he knew that. Perhaps that was why she stirred him so?

As now.

He wanted to kiss her. He had to kiss her. Taking her by surprise, he reached down and pulled her to her feet, pressing her close, satisfyingly close, so that he could smell her scent and hear her breathing. He smiled at the look in her big green eyes.

'What are you doing?' Celia said breathlessly, though she knew full well what he was doing, and she knew full well that she wanted him to. His mouth was only inches from hers. His eyes were like cast bronze, glazed with heat. Her heart pounded wildly. Her mouth was dry. She was acutely conscious of him, the strength of him, the power in him coiled tight like a stalking tiger beneath the silk of his robe. To her shame, she could feel a wicked excitement rising, making her nipples peak painfully against her chemise.

Ramiz groaned—a grating sound—as if it were rasped out of him. Then he kissed her. A hungry kiss without restraint. The kiss of a man pushed beyond endurance. A kiss of surrender, an admission of need that shamed him even as it incited him to pursue that need to its conclusion. His wanting was so urgent and so immediate he felt he would explode with it. Blood rushed to his groin, making him so hard he ached with a painfully pulsing urge to cast off all restraints and thrust into her, to take her fast and hard and thoroughly, to mark her for ever as his. Her lips were swollen with his kisses. A long strand of copper hair trailed down her cheek.

'Last night,' he said raggedly, 'why did you not stop me?'

'I should have, but I somehow couldn't.' Celia bit her lip. 'It is the harem. There is something beguiling about it. Unreal. Otherworldly.'

'Unreal.' Ramiz nodded. 'Will you stop me now? Here?'

Celia veiled her eyes with her heavy lids. 'I think I won't have to,' she said eventually.

Ramiz sighed heavily. His smile was crooked. 'A very diplomatic answer.' He released her, tucking her hair back behind her ear and kissing the tip of her nose. 'We should get back.'

Chapter Eight

Peregrine Finchley-Burke was the fourth son of an earl. Peregrine's oldest brother, heir to the Earldom, was currently delighting the ladies of the *ton* with his illustrious person, and endowing the gaming tables at White's club with his father's guineas. Peregrine's second brother had chosen the army. Captain Finchley-Burke of the Thirteenth Hussars had been wounded at Waterloo—a bullet which grazed his cheek, leaving him romantically scarred but otherwise unhurt. Since returning to England he had been assisting his elder brother's attempts to gamble away his inheritance at the tables of White's. Peregrine's third brother was made of much sterner stuff, however. So imbued with moral rectitude was the Very Reverend Archdeacon Finchley-Burke that the Earl himself was wont to question his wife's fidelity on the few occasions when his son blessed him with his presence.

Which left Peregrine to serve his country by way of the East India Company. He had, in fact, been on his way to India when the vagaries of the weather had left him stranded in Lisbon long enough for the ambassador there to persuade him that by travelling to Cairo on his behalf to deliver some urgent papers he would be doing his country a great service. In fact, although the diplomatic bag entrusted to Peregrine *did* contain some documents pertaining to matters of the state, the consignment of port which accompanied it was the real matter of urgency. Of this fact, as of so many others, Peregrine remained in blissful ignorance.

It was serendipitous for the Consul General of Egypt, Lord Wincester, that Peregrine's arrival coincided with the need to send a messenger to A'Qadiz with a response to Sheikh al-Muhana's communication, informing him of the death of George Cleveden and the whereabouts of the Lady Celia, his widow. The Consul General had a small, overworked staff—a fact of which he was constantly reminding the Foreign Office—so the naïve and clearly biddable young gentleman who had just delivered his long-anticipated supplies of port was commandeered to act as emissary—a suggestion which much flattered the aforesaid young gentleman, who blessed his luck and began to dream of a glittering career in the diplomatic corps.

Thus was Peregrine's onward journey to India further postponed, and thus did he arrive, dusty, sunburned, saddle-sore and feeling considerably out of his depth, at the royal palace in Balyrma, in the company of the Prince's own guard.

Ramiz was informed of the arrival of this unexpected guest by Akil, immediately upon his return from Katra. It had been a silent ride back, giving him ample time to try to regret kissing Celia and ample time to wish that he had kissed her more. Assuming that the visitor had come to reclaim her, Ramiz found himself extremely reluctant to let her go—though he knew he should be relieved, and continued to tell himself so as he bathed and changed his robes.

Without success.

Ramiz arrived in the throne room, where it was the custom to receive foreign visitors, in a black mood. He wore a formal robe of dark blue silk, fastened with gold buttons embellished with sapphires. At Akil's insistence he wore a *bisht* over this, the jewelled cloak elaborately embroidered with his falcon and crescent insignia. It was a heavy garment, and consequently uncomfortably warm, as was the headdress and its gold-tasselled *igal*, which Akil had insisted upon too. With the famous Balyrman scimitar weighing down the belt at his waist, and the great seal of A'Qadiz weighing down the middle finger of his right hand, Ramiz strode into the throne room with Akil behind him, breathlessly attempting to keep up while avoiding the royal *bisht* which trailed along the tiles, and completing the briefing he had in turn received from Peregrine's escort, all at the same time.

'So this man Finchley-Burke is basically a junior secretary?' Ramiz said, throwing himself onto the throne. A large gilded and scrolled chair, it sat on a carpeted dais at the top of the room, which was some sixty feet long—a vast tiled space, with an ornate mosaic floor bordered on each side by ten pillars, lit by ten stained-glass windows, but otherwise empty of furnishings, forcing visitors to stand in exposed isolation in front of the seated monarch. 'What do you think, Akil? Are we to be insulted at this minion's lack of status, or impressed by the speed with which they have sent him to us?'

Akil took his place by Ramiz's side. 'I doubt they intend to insult you, Highness.'

'They certainly don't mean to flatter me either,' Ramiz replied acerbically. 'Nor Lady Celia, for that matter. Do they expect me to provide an escort across the desert for her? They take too much for granted!'

'Maybe they don't want her back.'

'What do you mean by that?' Ramiz asked sharply.

'Nothing, Highness. A jest, that's all,' Akil said hurriedly, wondering at his friend's mood.

'If you can't find anything sensible to say you will do better to hold your tongue. Go and fetch the Englishman. I've better things to do than sit and stew in this outfit.'

'Ramiz, is there something wrong?'

'Only that I seem unable to make myself clear today.'

Akil opened his mouth to remonstrate, caught the glitter in Ramiz's eye, and changed his mind.

Ushering the Englishman in from the ante-room where he had been pacing anxiously, Akil could not but feel sorry for him.

'How do I address him?' Peregrine asked, tugging at his sweat-soaked neckcloth.

'Highness. Leave your hat here, and your gloves. You

must not shake hands, only bow like this.' Akil demonstrated gracefully. 'And do not meet his eyes.'

'What about this?' Peregrine said, pulling a sealed letter from the pocket of his cutaway coat. 'It's from the Consul General.'

'You may kneel at the foot of the dais and hold it out to him. Are you ready? Follow me. He is looking forward to meeting you,' Akil said, making a quick apology to the gods for the lie. 'Try not to look so terrified.'

Peregrine swallowed hard. 'Righty-ho.'

Akil rolled his eyes, nodded to the guard, who threw open the double doors to the chamber, and stood back to watch as the Englishman made his scuttling way across the vast tiled expanse of floor towards the throne, with all the enthusiasm of a thief approaching an executioner.

Ramiz stood to receive his visitor. Though his manner was brusque, it was regally so, showing no sign of ill-temper nor any discourtesy. He took the letter, breaking the seal immediately, and quickly skimmed the contents, relaxing visibly as he did so. To Akil's surprise Ramiz then signalled for tea to be brought, and when it came, accompanied by cushions to sit on, he sat beside Peregrine—an honour of which the young man, awkwardly crouching, seemed unaware.

'So, you are not here to escort the Lady Celia back to Cairo?'

Peregrine eyed the sweet tea in its delicate glass with caution. 'No, Your Highness. That is—no. The Consul General extends his most profuse apologies, but he felt it better, in the circumstances, to summon Lady Celia's father to fetch her.'

'It is to my great sorrow that Mr Cleveden died so tragically while on the soil of A'Qadiz. Do you wish to take his body back with you?'

Peregrine looked appalled. 'Good Lord, no. That is—like a soldier, you know—buried where he fell kind of thing.' He took a cautious sip of tea. It was surprisingly refreshing. He took another, and allowed his ample derrière, aching from the wooden camel saddle, to sink a little more comfortably down onto the cushion. 'Didn't know the chap, of course, but gather he was destined for great things.'

A picture of George Cleveden fleeing the attack flashed into Ramiz's mind. 'Indeed,' he said noncommittally.

'Despatch to Lord Armstrong went off in the old urgent bag just as soon as your own letter arrived,' Peregrine said, relaxing further. This prince was turning out to be a very nice chap—not at all the dragon he'd been led to expect. 'Frigate waiting off Alexandria, as a matter of fact. With a fair wind and a bit of luck her family will know she's all right and tight very soon.'

'You are acquainted with Lord Armstrong?'

'Good heavens, no. A bit above my touch. As is Lady Celia, if I'm honest. One of these frightfully clever females—type who has all the inside gen on who's doing what to whom—in a political way, if you know what I mean.' Peregrine tittered, caught Ramiz's stern glare, and lowered his eyes. 'Highness. Your Highness. Beg pardon. Didn't mean to—bit new to all this. Awfully sorry.'

Ramiz got swiftly to his feet. 'You will wish to see her?'

Peregrine, who had been hoping for the offer of some more substantial refreshment than tea before facing the Lady Celia, blinked, tried to get to his feet, slipped, and decided that remaining in obeisance on his knees, while lacking in dignity, was preferable to losing his head.

'Well?' Ramiz demanded impatiently.

'Yes—yes, of course. Highness. Your Highness.'

'Tomorrow, I think,' Ramiz said, much to Peregrine's relief. 'You must be tired after your journey. Akil will show you to the men's quarters now. There is a *hammam* there you can use.'

'*Hammam?*' Peregrine's eyes boggled. He could not decide whether to be honoured or revolted, for in his mind the word conjured up a fat exotic odalisque, rather like his nanny but in scantier clothing. Younger, of course, and he hoped not really too much like old Lalla Hughes who, now he came to think of it, had a bit of a moustache going.

'Steam bath,' Ramiz explained, trying not to smile, for Peregrine's thoughts were written plainly on his blistered countenance.

'Oh. Quite. Excellent…I suppose.'

'We dine late here, when the sun goes down. You will join me, I hope?'

'It will be an honour,' Peregrine said with a brave smile.

'If there's anything else you require, Akil will attend to your needs.' With a dismissive nod, Ramiz made for the doors, leaving Peregrine stranded on his knees on the floor of the vault-like chamber.

Back in the harem, Celia was unaware of the presence of her country's emissary. She lay on her stomach while Fatima rubbed scented oil into her skin. The girl's touch was gentle, but firm, easing the tension from her back and shoulders. Celia allowed her mind to drift, wholly accustomed now to the intimacy of her own nakedness, and to Fatima's capable fingers kneading her muscles. Strange how this could feel so pleasant, yet so impersonal. Strange how her body could react so differently to touch. Not just because of how it was done, but because of who was doing it. If Ramiz and not Fatima was delivering the massage, she would not be feeling so relaxed as to be upon the verge of falling asleep.

And of course as soon as his name popped into her mind, so too did his face, and his scent, and the feel of him, and she was wide awake. What was it about him that so obsessed her? Why Ramiz? Why now, at the age of four-and-twenty, was she being assaulted by these feelings? Such acute awareness of everything? Not just of Ramiz, but of colours and textures and taste. It was such a sensuous world, A'Qadiz, and Ramiz was at its epicentre, the very epitome of sensuality.

She was attracted to him—of that there was no doubt. She liked the way he looked. And the way he walked. And the way he talked. And the way he could be so arrogant one minute and so understanding the next. And the way he looked at her as if he saw something no one else saw. He made her feel beautiful. He said she *was* beautiful, and she believed him.

She was attracted to him, and he was attracted to her—a little. Probably because she was different. Infatuation, that was what it was. She was in thrall to him simply because he had been the first to kiss her. The first to touch her. The first to make her feel—*that!* The thing she couldn't put into words. Ecstasy. Carnal pleasure. *That!* She was beguiled.

But it felt like more than that. Ramiz made her laugh. They liked the same things. He knew things about her that she hadn't even known herself. And she knew him too, in a way others didn't. He'd let her see, even if briefly, how lonely, how isolated he felt.

Unreal. It was all unreal and meant nothing. Could never mean anything. She knew that. *She did.*

She was not an Arabian princess. In the eyes of his people her breeding meant nothing, for the blood which ran in her veins was English. No matter how many things she and Ramiz shared, no matter how similar their outlook on life might be, no matter even that they wanted the same things, she was not of his world and never could be.

Celia allowed herself to be helped from the divan into a warm bath. Sinking down into the fragrant water, she closed her eyes. Enchanted, beguiled, in thrall, under his spell. Whatever she was, it would not last.

In fact, according to Ramiz it was already over. Whatever it was. She wished it was not. She wished he would come to her again. Take her to the secret places he could conjure one more time. Continue with the fantasy for just a little longer, while she was here in his harem, locked away from the real world and the reality of the rather tedious life which awaited her as George's widow back in England.

She wished, though she mocked herself for doing so, that for one night she could live out her Arabian fantasy. Lying alone in the bath, she knew it was a dream. She thought of Ramiz—his kisses, his touch. She thought of him and the wanting came, and in the dark of the night she allowed herself to dream.

When Adila opened the harem door to one of the guards the next morning, Celia assumed Ramiz wished to see her, but the man who awaited her in a formal salon in the main body of the palace was a complete stranger. Dressed in a bottle-green cutaway coat, teamed with a rather alarming waistcoat embroidered with pink roses, he was about her own height, but considerably wider of girth. When he bowed, which he did with surprising grace given his apple shape, his fawn knit pantaloons stretched in a rather distressing manner, so that Celia dropped her own curtsy very rapidly, anxious to have him return to the upright in the hope of preventing what seemed to her an inevitable unravelling.

'Peregrine Finchley-Burke,' the young man said. 'At your service on behalf of His Majesty's government, Lady Celia.'

Realisation dawned. 'You have been sent to escort me home?'

Peregrine frowned. For a moment he could have sworn the lady was disappointed. 'No doubt you're eager to return to the bosom of your family,' he said cautiously.

'Indeed—though I have been very well treated here, I assure you. The palace is most luxurious.'

'Just so…just so.' Peregrine rubbed his hands together. 'Pleased to hear that, because the thing is I'm not actually here to take you back,' he said, flinching away instinctively as he delivered his ill tidings. To his relief, however, the tall, elegant woman in front of him did not break down into immediate hysterics, grab his hand, plea for mercy or even cry out in dismay. Instead her sleepy eyes widened and a smile trembled on her rather full mouth before she lowered her lids again and looked away into the distance, clasping her hands together.

'Not here to take me back?' Celia repeated faintly. 'You mean I am to stay here?'

'For the present. Thing is—dashed awkward all this. Forgot—should have said straight away have to pass on condolences. Terrible thing to happen. Consul General seemed to think very highly of your husband.'

'Thank you. You are very kind.' Celia rummaged for her handkerchief in her reticule and dabbed her eyes.

'And you, Lady Celia, it must have been a bit of an ordeal.'

'I was very fortunate that Sheikh al-Muhana was there,' Celia said with a watery smile. 'He saved my life, you know. Forgive my rudeness, Mr Finchley-Burke, please do sit down. Have you spoken with the Sheikh? How did he react when you informed him that I was to stay here?'

Peregrine waited for Celia to take a seat before he

eased himself onto a divan opposite her. Having spent the previous evening balancing his bulk on a cushion, feeling like a seal stranded by the tide on a rock which was too small, he was relieved to find that he was not expected to conduct this particular interview on the floor. 'The Prince left this morning—visiting some outlying tribes or something. Won't be back for quite a few days, apparently. Said to pass on his *adieu* and hoped you would be comfortable until his return.'

What was that supposed to mean? Celia thought indignantly.

'Seems a decent enough chap,' Peregrine continued with a touch of condescension. 'Bit on his high horse at first, but suppose that was to be expected.'

Celia raised her brows delicately. 'He is Prince of A'Qadiz, and it is likely that he holds the balance of power in at least four of the neighbouring six principalities. He is also extremely intelligent, and wealthy beyond anything you can imagine. You underestimate him at your peril.'

'Oh, I don't, I assure you—not now I've seen the place for myself.'

'Why exactly are you here, Mr Finchley-Burke, if you are not to take me back? It seems very strange that you have come all this way simply to pass on a message.' *And, now she thought about it, if Ramiz was as indifferent to her presence as he wished her to believe, why had he not insisted that she leave with this rotund young man?*

'Thing is, Lord Wincester sent an urgent despatch back to Blighty—to your father. Thought Lord

Armstrong should be the one to come and get you—best person to make the arrangements and what not, and also best person to complete the negotiations with the Prince, you know? Kill two birds with one stone, so to speak.'

'So I am to wait here until my father arrives?'

'Shouldn't be too long,' Peregrine said bracingly. 'Matter of a few weeks at most. Said yourself you're very comfortable here.' Peregrine opened his watch, wound it up, then closed it again. 'London time,' he said, à propos of nothing.

Celia raised her brows. 'Is there something else you wish to say to me, Mr Finchley-Burke?'

'Well.' Peregrine plucked a large kerchief from his pocket and mopped his brow. 'Well... You said it yourself, Lady Celia, this Sheikh al-Muhana could turn out to be quite an important man. A'Qadiz has the only decent port on the Red Sea. If we can do an exclusive deal with him and Mehmet Ali in Egypt it opens up a whole new trade route to India. Takes the journey time down from two years to only three months. Imagine that!' Peregrine eased forward confidentially. 'Thing is, don't want anyone else to steal our thunder, so to speak. Would be nice to know Sheikh al-Muhana isn't talking to the competition. That's where you come in.'

'Me? But Sheikh al-Muhana won't do business with a woman. And besides, I have not been briefed.'

'No, no. Of course not. Already said—your father coming out here provides a perfect opportunity. Obviously an opportunity borne out of tragedy, I hasten to add. Lord Armstrong is a skilled negotiator. If anyone can strike a deal with the Sheikh then he can.'

'So what exactly do you want *me* to do?'

'Ah. The Consul General said you'd understand because you're Lord Armstrong's daughter and you know what's what.'

Celia shook her head in bewilderment. 'Understand *what* is what?'

Peregrine swallowed nervously. 'He expects you to—to use your position to England's advantage.'

'My position!' Celia jumped up from her divan, forcing Peregrine to rise precipitately to his feet—an act which left him breathless and sweating. 'And precisely what position do you and the Consul General assume I occupy?'

'Well, I didn't mean to imply—' Peregrine broke off, blushing to the roots of his hair. 'I'm just supposed to tell you that your father would expect you to keep your eyes and ears open. You know—find out as much as you can of the situation here. Anything—no matter how trivial. We know so little of the man and his country, and you are in a unique position to...' he faltered under Celia's basilisk stare '...to—you know—glean what you can. Lord Wincester said to tell you that at least this way the whole damned mission won't have been a complete waste of time and money. Except,' Peregrine added contritely, 'wasn't supposed to say it in quite that way. Beg pardon.'

Celia dropped back onto the divan. The idea of trying to extract information by subterfuge from Ramiz was repugnant, and she was pretty certain it would also be completely unsuccessful. She doubted very much that he would give away anything he did not want her to know.

On the other hand, he *did* trust her. He had trusted her with the secret of Katra. He had confided in her some of his troubles with regard to his neighbours too—had seemed glad of the opportunity to talk, in fact, within the cloistered confines of the harem.

No, she should not even be giving the idea thought. Even to pass on the little she already knew would be seen by Ramiz as a betrayal.

But if she refused, what would everyone think of her? What harm would it do poor George's memory that his widow had no loyalty to her country? Bad enough that his widow was relieved she was no longer his wife— surely she owed him this much in reparation? And, after all, Ramiz might never know. By the time he found out, if he ever did, she would be safe back in Cairo. In England, even.

'And if I do not agree with Lord Wincester's proposal, what then?' Celia enquired.

Judging by the startled look on Peregrine's face, this was not a possibility which had been considered. 'Why on earth wouldn't you? England, you know—empire and all that,' he said vaguely. He scratched his head. 'I suppose you could come back with me, but I'm not sure Sheikh al-Muhana would be too keen on the idea of you leaving without his say-so. Then there's the guards. You'd be kicking your heels in Cairo until your father arrived, and there's the issue of the treaty—because if you left against the Sheikh's wishes I don't doubt he'd be insulted, and your father would have come all this

way for nothing and—well, you see how it is.' Peregrine
spread his hands in a fatalistic way.

If she left it would ruin things, in other words, Celia
thought. And, actually, the one thing she was sure of
was that she didn't want to leave. She wasn't ready to
say goodbye to A'Qadiz—not yet. Nor to Ramiz.

If she stayed she could agree to what Mr Finchley-
Burke asked of her without actually acting upon it. In
fact, Celia thought brightly, there was no need to make
any decision right now, except to agree in principle to
try and do as she was bid.

'Very well. I will stay until Papa arrives,' Celia
said.

Peregrine executed as dignified a bow as he could
manage. 'Excellent. That is excellent news,' he said
with a relieved smile. 'Have to say didn't at all fancy
having to run the gauntlet of those guards.'

Celia held out her hand. 'Goodbye Mr Finchley-
Burke. And good luck with your posting in India.'

'What shall I tell Lord Wincester?'

'You may tell him that he can rely on me to do the
right thing,' Celia replied. Which she would—whatever
that meant.

Ramiz sent no word to Celia for the duration of his
absence, though she learned from Yasmina that he was
in regular contact with Akil. She spent another enjoyable
day at Yasmina's house, eager to discover for herself
what 'ordinary' life in Balyrma was like. Surprisingly
like life at home was what she found, with much of the
day given over to caring for the children—readying

the bigger ones for school, teaching the smaller ones their letters, managing their meals, sewing their clothes, wiping their tears and telling them stories.

'Before Ramiz came to power, only my oldest son went to school,' Yasmina told Celia as the two women sat companionably embroidering a section each of a large forest scene stretched on a frame, while the younger children took their afternoon nap in a separate salon. 'There were no schools for girls. Most of them could not even read, for their mothers couldn't read so there was no one to teach them.'

'Because of course none of the men would,' Celia said sarcastically.

'Of course not,' Yasmina agreed. 'It is the way of things here, Celia. Things are changing, some things are changing very fast, but we must not let the wind carry us to places we do not want to go. Ramiz knows that.'

'I'm sorry, I didn't mean to sound rude. It is just that things are so different.'

'Just because it is different doesn't make it wrong,' Yasmina reminded her gently. 'There are many ways to skin a rabbit.'

Celia smiled. 'We say that too, only it is a cat, I don't know why. Tell me about the schools. What did Ramiz do?'

'Well, he was very clever. He knew unless they trusted the teachers the women would not allow their girls to attend school, so he brought in a teacher to teach the teachers, not the girls. The men didn't like it at first, and even now there are only three teachers and about a hundred girls, so my older daughter is very lucky to have a place, but it is a start, and Akil said Ramiz has big plans. One day everyone in A'Qadiz will be able to read and write. Of course many of our people think this is madness—they say it will change the old order for ever, because people will lose sight of their place and no one will want to do real work, which is why it is all going so slowly. That and the fact that Ramiz is stretched as thin as the finest lace, which is why Akil says he should take a wife.' Yasmina snipped the vermilion thread she had been using and selected a length of burgundy. 'Talking of Ramiz, did you look at those charm books I gave you?' she asked with a slanting smile.

Celia nodded, concentrating on her stitching. The books were filled with extremely explicit pictures showing men and women engaging in an astonishing variety of acts. 'Some of the things,' she whispered, 'I didn't think were physically possible.'

Yasmina giggled. 'I don't think they are. You are not supposed to take them literally. They are meant to inspire, not to instruct. Have they?'

'Have they what?'

'Inspired you?' Yasmina asked with a sly look. 'Don't pretend you haven't thought about it.'

Celia blushed. 'It just seems wrong to plan such things. Shouldn't they just happen—you know, naturally?'

'Of course—at first,' Yasmina agreed. 'And it certainly does not do for a woman to lead the way. Men like to think they do that. But later, when you know each other well, there is much to be said for something different.'

'Oh, well, then, I don't need to worry about it,' Celia said with relief.

'You and Ramiz have not…?'

'No. And we will not. I can't think why we're talking about this, I was just curious.'

'Curiosity killed the goat.'

'We say that too. Only it's a cat again.'

'Be careful, Celia. Remember what I said.'

'I know. He is not meant for me. As if I could forget it,' Celia muttered. Everyone seemed to have an opinion on the true nature of her relationship with Ramiz except her. And Ramiz, of course, who didn't have an opinion because as far as he was concerned there was no relationship. With a sigh, Celia resumed her sewing.

Chapter Nine

The negotiations had stretched Ramiz's patience to the limit. Twice he had threatened to walk away, relenting only because of his determination not to let one of his own people destroy his hard work through ignorance and greed. An agreement had finally been reached and, following the twelve-hour feast ordered by the tribe's elders to celebrate their concord, Ramiz returned to Balyrma exhausted but well satisfied.

It had been a long few days in more than one way. He had found himself missing Celia. It was always a tedious business dealing with the tribes. They favoured a convoluted, highly formal bargaining process with which he was all too familiar, but he hadn't realised how alone it made him feel until now. It was not just the fact that he was one against many; it was also that, being the Prince, he had to appear inviolable and imperious. It was expected of him. Nothing must touch him, which meant there was no one to take his part except himself.

At night, alone in his tent in the middle of the desert, he'd found himself thinking of Celia. The scent of her, the feel of her petal-soft skin against his own. The taste of her mouth, succulent and honey-sweet. He'd wondered what she was doing. He'd wondered if she thought of him. He had cursed himself for wondering, for wasting precious time on such pointless and frustrating thoughts, though still he had indulged them. He had missed her.

He had not intended to seek her out immediately, but upon his return to the palace on the evening of his sixth day away, dusty and tense from the long ride back, that was what he did—without even stopping to change. She was sitting in the courtyard on a cushion, leaning against the fountain. She had been staring up at the stars framed by the square of the top floor of the building, her head thrown back, her long hair rippling loose down her back. When the door opened she turned, startled. Upon seeing him standing there a hand went to her breast.

For a few seconds she stared at him wordlessly. Her skin was ghostly pale in the twilight, her eyes glittering dark. As she got fluidly to her feet, he saw that she was dressed in clothes made from the materials they had bought at the market. Only a week ago, yet it seemed like months. She wore a long caftan slit to the thigh in mint-green silk. The sleeves and hem were weighted down with silver *passementerie* braiding. Loose *sarwal* pantaloons of a darker green, made of some gauzy material transparent enough for him to see the shape of her legs beneath, fluttered out around her. She was barefooted. She seemed to float rather than walk. Her hair rippled like silk ruffled by a breeze. She looked so different. Exotic. An English rose in an Eastern garden.

Ramiz stood rooted to the spot. He hadn't expected this. Hadn't anticipated the unsettling effect seeing her like this would have on him.

'You're back,' she said, stopping uncertainly before him.

'Only just now. I came to see how you were, since I did not have a chance to see you after the visit from your countryman. I half expected to hear from Akil that you had asked to return to Cairo with Mr Finchley-Burke.'

'Since my father has been summoned to complete the negotiations which brought my husband here in the first place, I thought it best to wait. Would you have allowed me to leave if I had asked it?'

Ramiz raised a brow. 'Is that what you would have preferred?'

Celia laughed. 'I should have known better than to expect a straight answer from such an accomplished statesman as yourself.'

'Or from such an accomplished diplomat's daughter as yourself,' Ramiz rejoined with a smile.

'Did your trip go well? You were away longer than you anticipated.'

Ramiz shrugged. 'It's done.'

'At a cost, I take it?'

Ramiz nodded. 'A cost worth paying, though.'

'Have you eaten?'

'I'm not hungry.'

He looked weary. There were little grooves of tiredness at the corners of his mouth. A frown furrowed his brow. Celia's heart contracted. Now he was back, now her heart was beating out its excitement at his presence, she could admit to herself how much she had missed him. Without thinking she reached out to smooth away the lines on his forehead. His skin was warm, gritty with sand under his headdress.

'You're all dusty,' she said inanely, for suddenly she could think of nothing to say, so overwhelmed was she by his presence.

'I should go and change.'

'Stay a while,' Celia said impulsively. 'Talk to me. I've—it's been lonely here without you.'

'You've missed me?'

There was the tiniest trace of a smile at the corner of his mouth. Celia managed a shrug. 'What do you think of my clothes?' she asked, executing a little twirl.

The soft material clung lovingly to her slender frame, hugging the curve of her breasts, the slope of her bottom. He saw the nakedness of her feet on the tiles, the soft flutter of her hair drifting out behind her as she twirled, heard the swish of her caftan as it floated out from her body then settled back down to caress her thighs. The scent of amber and musk drifted towards him, mingling with the warmer, fragrant smell that was Celia, and the whole combination went intoxicatingly to his head. Ramiz reached out to catch a long tress of hair, wrapping it like a bond of copper silk around his hand, pulling her towards him.

Under the caftan she wore only a wisp of silk. She might as well be naked. They were as close as they could be without touching. Heat rose between them. *Could he feel it too?* There was a smudge of dust on his right cheek. His left hand was wrapped in her hair, tugging her head back. The need to touch him was unbearable. Could he see her heart beating? Could he hear how shallow and fast was her breathing? Why was he here? Did she care as long as he was?

'Did you miss me?' Ramiz asked again.

'Yes,' Celia whispered, for it was the truth. She had missed him enormously. She had spent hours and hours wrestling with her conscience over the Consul General's proposal, concluding time and again only that she must do nothing she would later regret, nothing which would compromise her integrity, nothing she could not undo. Which meant avoiding exactly the sort of situation she was now confronting.

But it was all very well to think such thoughts and to hold such high-minded opinions when alone. In Ramiz's disconcerting presence she had no such control. Her mind—that disciplined, logical part of her which had ruled her life until now—was in real danger of surrendering control to her body. And her body was not slow to take advantage, so that without meaning to, without realising she was doing it, Celia closed the tiny gap between them and tilted her head up and put her arms around him. And that was it. She kissed him. She had to. There was nothing, nothing at all she could do about it, for if she did not kiss him she was afraid she would stop breathing.

And when his lips met hers she stopped breathing anyway, just for a moment, so literally breathtaking was the feel of his mouth and the scent of his skin and the complex magic of his just being there. She murmured his name, she pressed herself into the hard lines of his body, and he groaned. And then he kissed her back—a surprisingly gentle kiss, feathering its way along the line of her lower lip, licking into the corners, then the softness inside. His free hand was stroking the nape of her neck, the hollow of her collarbone, the column of her throat.

Then it was over. Ramiz stepped back. He unwound her hair from his hand. He rubbed his forehead, pushing back his headdress so that it fell to the floor. 'I must go and change,' he said reluctantly. 'I must see Akil.'

'Don't go. Not yet. Stay and talk to me. Please.' Celia held out her hand. His hair was rumpled. Without the frame of his *gutra* his face looked younger, almost vulnerable. Her own needs vanished, superseded by the desire to erase Ramiz's lines of fatigue, to ease the tension she could see in his shoulders, just to have him to herself for a little while.

He hesitated, then allowed her to lead him into one of the salons. She made him tea on the little spirit stove there, taking care with the ritual of measuring the leaves from the enamelled chest into the silver samovar, serving it just as he liked it, with no sugar but lemon and mint. And as Celia busied herself with the tea she talked—of her visit to Yasmina, of the books she had read, of her letter to Cassie. Ramiz listened at first with detachment, simply enjoying the graceful way she went about the small domestic task, the sound of her voice and her gentle wit, and then he was smiling over her description of the play Yasmina's children had put on for her, and making her laugh with his description of the English emissary's falling asleep on the cushions over dinner, relaxed enough to tell her about his trip into the desert.

As before, she listened with understanding—sympathetic without being fawning, contributing her own opinions without being asked, contradicting him without offending. Tea was taken, the lamps were lit, and still they sat on, talking and laughing in unperceived intimacy until Ramiz yawned and stretched and said he should go. They both realised that was the last thing they wanted.

'Five nights on a carpet in someone else's tent,' he said, rolling his shoulders. 'I'd forgotten how uncomfortable it can be.'

'Would you like me to give you a massage?'

Ramiz looked as startled as she herself was, for she hadn't meant to offer—only she hadn't wanted him to go, and she wanted to do something that would preserve this unaccustomed intimacy. 'Do you know how?' he asked.

Celia nodded. 'Fatima has shown me what to do, though I've not really had a chance to practise. I find it helps me sleep. Perhaps it would help you too?'

He doubted Celia's touch would make him sleepy. He knew it was one of the things which breached the boundaries he'd told himself to establish, but then so too was talking to her alone like this. And he *was* tired. And sore. And in no mood for anything other than sleep. Not really.

Ramiz got to his feet. 'Where?' he asked, and when

she indicated they use the large circular divan on which she slept he allowed himself to be led into that salon, watched as she spread a fresh silk sheet over the velvet cover while he pulled off his robe, wrapping his lower half in a linen towel, lying down on his stomach and closing his eyes. A swish of material told him Celia had discarded her caftan. He could smell the orange and amber in the oil as she rubbed it onto her hands. When she leaned over him a long strand of her hair brushed his cheek. She tutted and swept it back. Then she leaned over him again. He could feel the heat emanating from her skin, the feathering of her breath on his. Then he surrendered to the supple kneading of her fingers.

She started at his shoulders, where the tension knotted his muscles together like rope. Carefully at first, her touch experimental, she leaned over, trying to keep the contact to her hands, though the temptation to brush her breasts against him, to prostrate herself on top of him, skin to skin, was strong. His eyes were closed tight. His lashes, sooty and soft, fanned onto his cheeks. His hair grew in a shape like a question mark on the back of his head, tapering down like an arrow to his nape. The veins on his neck stood out, so bunched tight were his shoulders. Celia pressed into them with her spread fingers as Fatima had shown her, rolling her thumbs up his spine, circling back down and round again in a soothing motion, pressing harder as she felt Ramiz relax, kneading him with her palms, concentrating on levelling out the twisting stress, smoothing and kneading, pressing and soothing in a smooth rhythm so that she forgot everything except the feel of her hands on his body.

Breathing a little harder with the effort, she leaned a little closer, and a little closer yet, to get just the right angle—until she was kneeling on the divan beside him, then kneeling between his legs as she worked her way down his back, then over him, so that her breasts brushed his heated skin, slick with the delicately scented oil, and her nipples budded through the thin layer of silk which contained them. Below her, Ramiz kept his eyes tight shut. She could feel the steady rise and fall of his chest. Sleeping? The scent of him, a subtle something, male and other, rose like a whisper of smoke from his skin.

She worked her way down to the base of his spine, pulling away the towel which covered him, waiting for a sign that she should stop which did not come. His buttocks were firm and slightly rounded, his flanks were firm too, with a feathery smattering of black hair, surprisingly soft. The softer flesh at the inside of his thighs was hot. Tender from the time spent in the saddle. Heat. It was not just coming from Ramiz.

A trickle of sweat shivered down between Celia's breasts. Wiping it away, she trailed oil over her own skin. She picked up the bottle to trickle more oil onto her hands. A drop escaped onto Ramiz's shoulders. She leaned over to rub it in. Her breasts pressed into his back, her stomach onto his buttocks. Skin slick with oil. A sensual sliding. She lay motionless, relishing the melding of skin on skin, of heat on heat. Below her, Ramiz lay still as a statue.

She had convinced herself he was asleep. Then, as she

sat up, he turned underneath her, so quickly she would have fallen had he not grasped her by the arms, rolled her with him, so that somehow she was under him and he was on top of her, and he did not look at all as if he had been asleep.

His eyes blazed like molten bronze sparked with gold. A slash of colour highlighted his cheekbones. His chest rose and fell, rose and fell almost as rapidly as her own. She could feel the pounding of his heart. Then he kissed her, wildly and passionately, yanking away the strip of silk which covered her breasts. And then he devoured them.

His mouth was on her nipples, hot on their aching hardness. His hands moulded her breasts, shaping them and stroking them, and his mouth was sucking and nipping, making her writhe and moan, strange little gasping pleas she didn't recognise as she bucked under him. Her own hands were grasping and pulling at him. The hardness of his erection was pressing solid and insistent against her thigh. In minutes, seconds, it would be too late. She knew that absolutely—as she knew absolutely that she would not stop him. She wanted this with an urgency she had not dreamed possible. Something as fundamental as the stars urged her on, made her push against him, arch into him, pluck at him as if she would spread him over her, all the time gasping and moaning his name. His mouth on her nipples forged a burning path of sensation, stirred up a cauldron of heat in her belly, and their oiled skin slid and glided and clung.

Her gauzy pantaloons were pleated into a sash at her waist. Ramiz pulled it open. She struggled free of their constraints with neither shame nor modesty, wanting only to feel him against her, beside her, inside her. They lay facing each other, kissing. Mouths fervent with need, eyes burning with desire, fingers seeking out secret creases, stroking into them, until she felt his hand between her legs, cupping her, stroking her, and the hot surge of wet pulsing need made her clench and clench again as he touched her exactly where she needed him to touch her. No teasing this time, no drawing out, just there, and there, and *there*, reading her wants as she moaned and dug her fingers into his shoulders, and jangled like a puppet on strings which Ramiz pulled, until she felt that plundering, plunging sensation build. She jolted as her climax took over, barely noticing that he had rolled her onto her back, that he was between her legs, pushing them up, angling himself over her until he thrust hard and powerfully into her and she screamed out—not with pleasure but with pain.

Ramiz froze. The expression on his face was ludicrous in its intensity. Sheer disbelief, swiftly followed by horror. As the sharpness of the pain receded, and she realised he was going to pull away, Celia clutched at him. 'No.'

But she could not hold him. He cursed long and viciously in his own language, pushing her hands away and pulling himself from her in one move. He grabbed his robe from the floor and pulled it over his head. There was no mistaking the anger which froze his face into rigid lines. His eyes were cold too, glinting chips of amber. Celia sat up, clutching the sheet around her. Bright beads of blood showed crimson on its pristine white, like berries in snow. Hastily she twisted the sheet, but Ramiz had already seen them. He wrenched it from her grasp, forcing her to scrabble for her caftan to cover her nakedness.

'A sheet any bride would be proud of,' Ramiz said through gritted teeth, holding it up so that the traitorous blood spots could not be avoided. 'But you are not a bride. Why in the name of all the gods did you not tell me? Do you think I would have? Do you think I would have let you—allowed myself—? You don't know what you have done.'

'What I have done?' Celia stood up, glaring at him.

'What *I* have done, then. Something your husband evidently did not!' Ramiz ran his hand through his hair. 'Why didn't you tell me?'

'You didn't ask!' But even as she threw the words at him she knew how unfair they were. The reality of the situation came crashing down like a sudden cloudburst. *What had she done?* 'George didn't want—we didn't— he said it would be easier if we waited until we knew each other better,' she said quietly. 'But we never did.'

'Evidently,' Ramiz said bitterly.

'No.' Celia blinked, determined not to allow the tears which burned her eyes to fall. 'I doubt we ever would have, to be honest. I'm sorry. I'm sorry I didn't tell you. I didn't mean this to happen. I should have stopped you. I'm sorry.'

She brushed the back of her hand across her eyes. The defiant little gesture touched him as tears would not have. 'Celia, did I hurt you?'

She shook her head.

'Are you sure?'

She managed a weak smile. 'Just a little.'

'Next time it won't be so—' Ramiz stopped. There would never be a next time for them. There should not have been a first. He should be thanking the fates that he had managed to stop—that shock had allowed him to stop. Only he didn't feel like thanking the fates. Horrified by his own base desires, by the persistence of his erection, which nudged insistently against his belly, he realized that what he wanted to do was to finish what they had started. To sheath himself in the luscious delight of her, to thrust deeper and deeper, until he spent himself inside her, to claim her as his. As his own. As her first.

No! He could not. He would not. Not even if it meant another would take what rightfully should be his.

No! No! No! He would not think of Celia with another. Looking at her trying so hard not to cry, the flush of passion fading from her cheeks, her mouth bruised with his kisses, the delicate creamy white of her breast showing the imprint of his touch, Ramiz fought the urge to take her in his arms and soothe away the hurt he had caused. The stain on his honour, the tangible evidence of that stain on the sheet he gripped, held him back. 'What have I done?'

'It wasn't just you. It was my fault as much as yours,' Celia said resolutely.

'I have deflowered you. The dishonour!'

'Ramiz, as you have already pointed out, I was married. In the eyes of the world I was already deflowered. There is no dishonour because no one will know.'

'*I* will know!'

'Well, I'm sure you'll learn to live with it.'

'Is that all you can say?'

She bit her lip. What she wanted was to know how it felt to really make love. How it felt to have him move inside her. What she wanted was to complete and to be completed—because that, she realised, was what it was really about. Two people as one. That was what she wanted to say, but she couldn't, because for Ramiz it had clearly been nothing more than the easing of tension. The natural conclusion to her massage.

'I think you should go now,' she said instead, wresting the horrible evidence of her virginity from his hands. 'I think we should agree to forget all about this.'

'Forget?'

'Yes. It's for the best.'

'Is this your famous British stiff upper lip? It doesn't suit you.'

'It's what we British call being practical. You're tired. Exhausted, in fact. Go to bed.'

'But you…'

'I will be fine.'

She was right, but it felt wrong. He didn't want to leave her—which was exactly the reason why he should. Nothing about this was right. Staying would only heap more wrong on wrong.

He didn't like the way she was so determined to take her share of the blame. And he definitely didn't like it that it was she and not he who insisted he go. It was all the wrong way round. Where was the clinging vine? Why must she be so stoically independent? He didn't

like it, but there wasn't a thing he could do about it
either.

Ramiz shrugged. 'Goodnight,' he said coldly. Then
he left without another word.

Alone, Celia picked up his headdress from where
he had dropped it carelessly on the floor. The square of
white silk smelled of him. She clutched it to her chest.
Then she curled up on the divan and gave way to racking
sobs and blinding tears.

Peregrine Finchley-Burke's confidence in the efficien-
cy of the Royal Navy was not displaced. Lord Wincester's despatch reached England less than three weeks
after it had been written. The special courier arrived
mud-spattered, his horse's flanks speckled with foam,
at the country estate of Lord Henry Armstrong just as
its owner was preparing for a long overdue meeting with
his bailiff. The contents of the missive, perused in the
seclusion of his study, were shocking enough to require
sustenance in the form of brandy, despite the early hour.
Throwing back the large snifter, Lord Henry read the
letter for a third time. A frown marred his normally
serene countenance, for the consequences of the matter
were potentially far-reaching. A delicate situation. Very
delicate indeed, he thought, scratching his bald pate. It
was a good thing his sister Sophia was here. He could
trust her to manage the girls. But what to do about it all
was another matter.

'Damn the man,' Lord Henry muttered, staring at
Lord Wincester's signature. 'Bloody fool. Only reason
he's out there is because of that fracas in Lisbon. He

thought it was all hushed up, but *I* know the real story.' He poured himself a second snifter. 'Damn the man,' he said again, more loudly this time. 'And damn George Cleveden too! You'd have thought he'd have more wit than to get himself killed in such a manner.' Lord Henry leaned over to ruffle the fur of his favourite pointer bitch, sitting obediently at his feet. 'Bloody stupid thing to do, if you ask me.' The dog whined. 'You're quite right. Time they were all told,' Lord Henry said, bestowing another affectionate pat upon the animal before he got to his feet and left the library in search of his family.

He entered the blue drawing room to find the collective eyes of his four daughters and sister Sophia upon him. Not for the first time he wondered at his own inability to father a son. Girls were all very well, but he couldn't help thinking five girls excessive. And expensive. 'Well, well, here you all are,' he said, with an air of false bonhomie which he mistakenly imagined would reassure them.

Cassandra, the beauty of the family, had been rather too aptly named, for she had a propensity for prophesying tragedy. She clutched dramatically at her father's coat sleeve, her lovely eyes, the colour of cornflowers, already drowning in tears. 'Papa! It is Celia, isn't it? She is—oh, Papa—tell me she is not—'

'Celia is absolutely fine,' Lord Henry said, detaching her fingers from his coat sleeve. 'It is George, I'm afraid. Dead.'

Cassandra collapsed back into a convenient chair, clutching her breast, her countenance touchingly pale. Caroline gave a little gasp of horror. Cordelia and

Cressida simply stared with mouths wide open at their father. It was left to Lady Sophia to seek clarification. 'May one ask what happened to result in such an unfortunate outcome?' she asked, rummaging in her reticule for the vial of *sal volatile* she kept there for such occasions.

'He was murdered,' Lord Henry replied flatly.

This shocking news gave even the normally redoubtable Lady Sophia pause. Casting a baleful look at the two youngest of her nieces, who had squealed in a most unrefined manner, she thrust the *sal volatile* under Cassie's nose.

'May I?' asked Sophia, holding her hand out imperiously for the despatch which Lord Henry was only too happy to hand over. She read it with close attention, her eyebrows rising fractionally as she digested the content. 'You may leave this to me, Henry,' she said to her brother.

Only too happy to obey, Lord Henry left the room.

'I am sorry to inform you that George has indeed been murdered,' Lady Sophia informed her nieces. 'Brigands. It seems he and Celia were on their way to a place called A'Qadiz, which is somewhere in Arabia, on a special assignment which entailed a journey across the desert. That is where poor George met his fate. He died bravely, serving his country,' she said with an air of assurance and a complete disregard for the truth. 'That fact will, I do most sincerely trust, mitigate the rather vulgar manner in which he was slain.'

'And Celia?' Faced with a genuine crisis, Cassie had abandoned her vapours and, though prettily pale, was composed enough to join her sisters on the sofa, putting a comforting arm around the two youngest. 'What does the despatch say of Celia? I take it she is now under the care of the Consul General? Or perhaps she is already on her way home?' she said hopefully.

'Hmm.' Lady Sophia inspected the lace of her sleeve.

'Aunt?'

'Hmm,' Lady Sophia said again. 'Celia is still in A'Qadiz, I am afraid.'

'What? In the desert?'

'She is apparently resident in the royal palace there. As a guest of a Sheikh al-Muhana. Prince al-Muhana, I should say.'

This information was met with stunned silence. Lady Sophia twitched at her lace.

'Cassie, is Celia being held prisoner?' Cressida's chin wobbled.

'Cassie, will she be locked away and have to tell the Sheikh a story every night to stop her getting her head cut off?' Cordelia, aged twelve, asked. Too late she remembered that Aunt Sophia had forbidden them to read *that* book. Cordelia blushed. Cressida pinched her. Caroline drew her a look.

The ensuing reprimand distracted Cassie temporarily from the question nagging away at her. 'Why has Celia been left alone with Sheikh al-Muhana?' she asked, when order had finally been restored.

'A very pertinent question,' Lady Sophia answered dryly.

'A very pertinent question indeed,' Lord Henry said

as he re-entered the room. 'Wincester is a buffoon and a liability, which is why I'm going out there personally to sort this mess out. Don't worry about your sister's safety in the meantime. No foreign power would dare harm the daughter of a senior British diplomat.'

'Papa, Celia has witnessed the murder of her husband. She has been kidnapped by a man who for all we know could have her under lock and key in his harem,' Cassie said, her voice rising as the full horror of her sister's plight began to sink in.

'Now, now,' Lord Henry said, eyeing his daughter warily, 'no point in letting our imagination run away with us. Celia is a sensible gal, and I'm sure the Prince is an honourable man. I'm sure there's no need to worry on that score.'

'No need to...' Cassie stared at her father in disbelief. 'I take it you *are* going to Egypt at once?'

'Well, of course I am.'

'Then I am coming with you,' Cassie said resolutely.

'Don't be ridiculous, girl.'

'I am coming with you, Father, and nothing you can say will dissuade me. Celia is my beloved sister. Heaven knows what she has gone through—is going through even now,' Cassie said with a shudder. 'She will need me to support her. I am coming with you and that's that.'

'Sophia, can't you talk some sense into the girl? The desert is no place for a young lady of breeding.'

'You might have thought of that before you despatched your other daughter, then,' Lady Sophia said witheringly. 'Cassandra is quite right. Celia will need her sister. And what's more she will need her aunt too. I am also coming with you.'

'Eh?'

'You heard, Henry,' Lady Sophia said, fixing her younger brother with one of her glacial glares. 'Now, since time is of the essence, I will go immediately to attend to my packing. You will summon Bella Frobisher to look after the girls. Since it is your intention that the woman is to be their new stepmother, she might as well make a start in getting to know them. Come, Cassandra. We will leave in an hour, Henry.'

Lord Henry Armstrong was renowned as a tough and unyielding negotiator, who had faced down the most cunning and powerful courtiers in all of Europe, but he was no match for his sister and he knew it. 'As you wish, Sophia,' he said resignedly, before leaving to go in search of the brandy bottle for the second time that morning.

Chapter Ten

Ramiz wandered alone in the gardens of the royal palace. The relatively compact area was divided by a series of covered walkways and winding paths, linked with fountains and small pavilions to give it a sense of space. Watered by an ingenious system of sprinklers fed by underground pipes, it combined the traditional plants of the East, such as fig, oleander and jasmine, with a number of species brought back by Ramiz from his travels. Amongst these were several roses. One of his favourites, the lightly scented pink rose which climbed round the gilded trellis by the fountain where he sat now, had been given to him by the Empress Josephine herself, from her treasured garden at Malmaison. The petals appeared almost white when furled, the pink revealing itself like a blush only when the flowers opened fully.

They made him think of Celia. Three nights had passed since his last visit to the harem, and the only conclusion he had reached was that it was best to keep away from her. He had taken something precious, and there was nothing he could do to recompense her for the loss. What he had done was wrong, without a doubt, and Ramiz was unused to being in the wrong. He had never before been in a position where he could not put a wrong right, and he was wholly unused to the position in which he now found himself—torn between the desire to make amends and the equally strong desire to make proper love to Celia.

That was the most shocking thing of all. He had done wrong, commited a sin of honour, but he was struggling to regret it.

The fact that Celia herself refused to accept his crime didn't help. Why had she not stopped him? Why had she not confessed? Why was she determined to brush it off as something trivial? Didn't it matter to her? What did she want of him? Could it be that she was a pawn in some diplomatic game, ready to cry ravishment in order to gain advantage for her country? But she had already insisted she would *not* cry ravishment, and one of the few things he was certain of was that she did not lie.

So why? The last time he'd asked her, after the visit to Katra, she had blamed it on the harem. *Unreal*, she'd said. As in a fantasy? From the start she'd shown a fascination with the harem, or with her perception of the harem drawn from that set of fairytales *One Thousand and One Nights*. Like her compatriots on the Grand Tour, perhaps she was indulging in a fantasy safe from the prying eyes of her peers. It made sense. It made a lot of sense.

The only way to eliminate temptation is to yield to it. An old saying of his brother's. As the eldest son and his father's heir, Asad had been much indulged. Asad had preferred action to words. 'Women talk, men act,' he'd used to say. 'The sword is the instrument of the Prince. To his subjects falls the task of writing down his words.' Too quick to the flame, their father had always said of Asad, but he'd said it in such a way as to make his pride in his eldest son clear.

If truth be told Ramiz and Asad had rarely seen eye to eye. If truth be told, Ramiz thought wryly, nor had he and his father, but that didn't stop him missing them both. Nearly two years now since Asad was killed, and in that time Ramiz's life had been turned upside down. While he had always felt strongly about what he would do differently were he to become ruler of A'Qadiz, he had never seriously considered it happening. Putting his long-considered policies into action had gone some way to help him through the loss of his last remaining close relative, for his mother had died when Ramiz was a teenager, but it had also prevented him from thinking too much about the loss itself. He missed Asad. Why not admit it? He was lonely. He was a rich prince, with thousands of loyal subjects, and he had everything except someone to confide in.

He hadn't noticed until Celia came along. He'd been too immersed in state policy and state negotiations and state legislation. No time to think about anything other than A'Qadiz. No time to think that maybe he needed something for himself. Someone for himself. Perhaps Akil was right. What he needed was a wife.

But the idea of marrying one of the princesses from Akil's list was even less appealing than ever. Such a wife would be taken for the sake of A'Qadiz. Such a wife would not give him anything other than more responsibility, one more thing to worry about. Such a wife would not be like Celia—would not *be* Celia.

Ramiz growled with exasperation. A whole hour wasted thinking, and he was right back where he started. *The only way to eliminate temptation is to yield to it.* One thing Asad had always been good at was getting to the nub of a problem. Lady Celia, with her copper hair and her creamy skin and her forthright opinions, was in danger of becoming an obsession. If she did not think herself dishonoured, why should he worry about it? Why not indulge her in her Arabian fantasy and at the same time rid himself of his unwelcome obsession?

The problem was he didn't like being thought of as *unreal*. He didn't like the idea of her thinking of him only within the confines of his harem. If he was to be her first lover, he wanted her memory of him to be very real and lasting.

Ramiz looked up at the sky, where the sun was just coming into view on its slow arc over the northern wall of the garden. A slow smile crept over his face. He would bring her into the light of day, away from the shady confines of the harem. Seeing her more clearly would surely speed the cure along.

'You wanted to see me?'

Celia stood before Ramiz, his desk serving as a barrier between them. She wore a caftan of cerulean blue, with slashed sleeves pulled tight at the wrist, over a pair of pleated *sarwal* pantaloons the colour of the night sky. It was the traditional costume of a woman at home, but with her mass of copper hair uncovered and dressed in its usual fashion, piled in a knot on top of her head with wispy strands curling over her cheeks, the simple outfit seemed exotic. A lady dressed in the garb of an odalisque. Though she was draped with propriety from head to foot, the fluttery fabrics drew attention to the softness of her body underneath. He caught a glimpse of her forearm through the slashed sleeves of her tunic. Creamy skin. Ramiz dragged his eyes away. It was only her arm! But already he could feel himself hardening.

'Sit down,' he said, annoyed to find that his voice sounded harsh, while Celia looked composed as she took the chair opposite. 'You are well?' he asked.

'Certainly I am well cared for,' she said carefully.

'What does that mean?'

She raised an eyebrow at the tone of his voice. 'Is there something wrong, Ramiz?'

'That is what I have just asked you.'

Celia clasped her hands in her lap. 'I told you, I am well. In fact I'm so well looked after that I'm in danger of forgetting how to do anything for myself. Adila and Fatima anticipate my every need.'

'You mean to tell me you are bored?'

'I was trying to be tactful about it, but yes. I am not used to having nothing to do save embroider and read.'

'But you have been visiting Yasmina?'

'Yes, where I embroider and play with the children—which is lovely, but…' Celia bit her lip. The last few days, without so much as a glimpse of Ramiz, had given her ample opportunity to try and put her feelings for him into perspective, but it was almost impossible to do that within the confines of the harem, redolent as it was with sensuous overtones, not to mention the scalding memory of their previous fevered couplings. There, she was in thrall to him, obsessed by the feelings he could arouse in her. If only she could see him in more mundane surroundings—or what passed for mundane surroundings, given he was a prince. Then she would be rid of this continuous need to be with him, able to acknowledge that she was lonely, and she was bored, and that her body, having discovered something new and enjoyable, was quite naturally wanting to experience it again. That was all it was. Absolutely nothing else!

'I've been thinking,' Ramiz said, interrupting her musing. 'It would be a good idea for you to see more of A'Qadiz, to learn more of the problems we face—I face—in trying to bring our country into the modern world of the nineteenth century.'

Celia stared at him in astonishment. *Was he a mind-reader?* 'But what about—? You said because I am a woman that…'

Ramiz shrugged. 'If I choose to bend a few traditions, that is up to me. You said so yourself, did you not?'

He smiled. Perfect white teeth. Eyes cold glinting metal. Had he guessed what Lord Wincester had asked her to do? Her stomach clenched at the very idea. But if he knew he would surely not be offering her such an opportunity to observe. Was he testing her? She knew with sudden blinding clarity that it was a test she would not fail. She could not possibly betray this man who had saved her life, made her feel alive for the first time in her life and who clearly trusted her. 'I would love to see more of A'Qadiz,' Celia said excitedly. 'What did you have in mind?'

'A significant number of my people belong to Bedouin tribes. They live in the desert, moving from place to place with their livestock according to the season and their own inclinations. We have a tradition here of allowing them to petition the crown for alms. Three times a year they can come to me and ask for assistance.'

'You give them money?'

'Sometimes. Although more often it is food or animals. Money doesn't mean much to the Bedouins. It's not just that, however. I act as arbitrator in their disputes between families and between tribes. It is an opportunity for me, too, to see how things really are and to assess where I can best help them. You must not be thinking these are simply poor nomads. Some of them are very powerful men. It would not do to offend them.'

'So you go to them rather than ask them to come to you?'

'Exactly. We will be away about a week or so. You will come?'

'I would love to.'

'Good. You may go now. I will see you first thing tomorrow morning. We will start before dawn.'

The caravan which snaked out behind them put the one with which Celia had arrived in Balyrma firmly into the shade. She counted at least twenty guards on camels, and it looked like double that number of servants with mules. Akil took on the role as leader of the train. To Celia's surprise Ramiz insisted she ride ahead with him, mounted on a camel as snowy white as his own, its saddle draped with a bejewelled cloth of crimson damask, silver bells jangling on its reins, which were adorned with golden tassels. Covered by an *abeyah* of gold silk—a long robe with side slits to make riding astride easier—and with her hair and face protected from the sun and prying eyes by a headdress of the same colour, Celia felt like an Arabian princess.

She said so to Ramiz, who laughed and said no one looking at her could ever mistake her for what she was: an English rose disguised as a desert flower. He was in a strange mood. She would almost call it relaxed. They would dispense with the formalities and deference while they were in the desert, he told her. She was to remain by his side at all times. She was to address him as Ramiz. She was free to ask whatever she wished to know. He valued her opinion.

At first she thought he was teasing her, but as they rode through the day she discovered he meant it—telling her unprompted all about the meetings to come, the ritual and the forms, even sketching out the main personalities for her. He was altogether charming, showing a side of himself she had not seen before. As the miles of the desert stretched out behind them he became almost carefree. The tension in his shoulders eased. The lines around his eyes relaxed. The formidable air departed, leaving a stunningly attractive man who was frankly beguiling.

And Celia *was* completely beguiled. Perhaps even mesmerised, for she noticed no one but Ramiz. The caravan might as well not have existed. As far as she was concerned they were alone in the desert, riding forever onwards across the sands under the blazing sun, to a destination which would remain elusive, for to arrive would be to break the spell, and she didn't want that to happen.

But when they arrived at the oasis where they would rest for the night the magical atmosphere continued. Instructing Akil to see to things, Ramiz led Celia away from the braying mules and bleating camels and muttering guards to a secluded part of the oasis, where a small pool lapped around a group of palms. The stars above them were like saucers of beaten silver.

'It's a full moon,' Celia said, sitting down by the edge of the pool and removing her sandals to trail her bare feet in the water.

'*Qamar,*' Ramiz told her, sitting beside her. 'A time for wishes to be granted.'

His thigh was pressing against hers. Her shoulder brushed the top of his arm. Celia circled her ankles in the cool of the water. 'What would you wish for, Ramiz?'

'A starry night. A tent to cover me. A beautiful woman to share it with.'

She tried to laugh, but it sounded more like a choke. 'Well, you've got the first two, at least.'

'No, I have it all.' Ramiz cupped the back of her head, gently turning her towards him. 'See—above us the starry sky. Over there the tent. Beside me a beautiful woman. And I intend you to share it with me, Celia. All of it.'

Before she could ask him what he meant, he kissed her. His kiss made his intentions clear, and as she kissed him back she signified her agreement with no thought of refusal. It was why she was here. In his desert. In his arms. It was why he had brought her, and it was why she had come. It was what she wanted more than anything. She saw that now with a brilliance and clarity to match the very moon suspended above their entwined bodies.

Celia put her arms around Ramiz. She nestled into the familiar stirring scent of him. She parted her lips at his bidding, and kissed him in such a way as he could be under no misapprehensions. She would share the night with him. All of it.

They kissed for long, languorous seconds, their arms entwined, their tongues tangling, their toes touching in the cool of the water. Then Ramiz broke away and got to his feet, pulling her with him. 'You understand?' he said. 'There is no going back from this moment.'

Celia nodded.

'It is what you want?'

'Yes.'

'Though ultimately it can mean nothing?'

She knew that! Why did he have to say it? But she knew that too. Ramiz was a man who liked the rules of any pact clear cut and neatly drawn. 'Yes,' she said again. 'I understand, I assure you.'

He nodded. For one ridiculous moment she thought

he would shake her hand, so formal had he become in that moment, but then she realised he was almost as tense as she was. She followed him back to the camp, where a small village of tents had appeared and fires were burning. The smell of goat and rabbit roasting should have been appetising, but though she was hungry it was not for food.

Two larger tents sat at a distance from the others. Ramiz led her towards one, pulling back the damask cloth which covered the entrance to usher her inside. Celia gave a gasp of amazement. Like the tent in which they'd had lunch the day Ramiz took her to the lost city of Katra, the walls were covered in tapestries and the floor in rich carpets. But this tent was much bigger, the coverings in the soft lamplight richer and more colourful.

'Do you like it?' Ramiz asked, smiling at the look of wonderment on her face.

'It's amazing. Like a mobile palace.'

'I must go and speak to Akil. Make yourself at home. I won't be long.'

Alone, Celia wandered around the tent, running her fingers over the tapestries, curling her toes into the luxurious carpets, stroking silken cushions and rubbing her cheek against velvet throws. A second room was obviously intended as a sleeping area. Here her luggage sat and her dressing case had been placed on a low table, beside which stood a full-length mirror. A smaller room led off from this one, where she was astonished to find a copper bath, already filled with water and scented with petals. Without further ado she stripped her dusty clothes off and sank into the water.

Clean, scented, and dressed in a loose caftan of organdie the colour of the setting sun, Celia returned to the main room. In her absence someone had set out dinner—an array of covered dishes from which delicious smells wafted towards her. She was investigating their contents when Ramiz entered the tent.

Like her, he had bathed and changed. His cropped black hair sat sleek on his head. He wore a robe of his favourite dark blue velvet. Though the tent was large, it seemed suddenly very small. His very presence seemed to fill it. It felt incredibly intimate, much more so than the harem. Against the soft drapes and jewelled colours of the hangings Ramiz looked very male. Very intimidating. Celia was assaulted by a jangle of nerves, taking up residence in her stomach like a cloud of little birds.

'Dinner's arrived,' she said. 'Are you hungry?'

'No,' Ramiz replied baldly.

'Would you like something to drink, then?' She reached for a jug of sherbet.

'No.'

'How is Akil?' Celia asked, realising even as she spoke just how ridiculous was the question.

'Celia, come here.'

She put down the jug, but made no move towards him.

'If you're having second thoughts, now would be a good time to tell me.'

'I'm not.' She adjusted the sleeve of her caftan. 'I'm

just a bit—well, as you know, I've never done this before.'

She tried to smile, but her mouth trembled. Her eyes were mossy green, fixed on him with a combination of appeal and defiance that he found irresistible. Ramiz strode over to her and swept her into his arms. 'There's no need to be nervous. I'll show you.'

He nuzzled the tender skin in the crease behind her earlobe. The scent there was pure Celia. He tasted her with the tip of his tongue. Such a vulnerable spot—the softness of her lobe, the delicate bone of her ear behind it, the endearing little crease they formed together which he licked into. Something clutched at him, piercing its way into his heart like the lethal tip of a dagger. He would remember this always.

'Ramiz?'

'Come.' He took her by the hand and led her through to the sleeping chamber. He dispensed efficiently with Celia's robe, tugging it over her head before she could protest. She stood before him naked, blushing, fighting the urge to cover herself with her hands.

Her eyes betrayed her confusion at his lack of tenderness. His instincts were to be tender. It was what she needed. What she wanted too. But it was not what this was about. It was about finishing what they had started. It was about taking what he needed from her in order to cure himself of her too-tempting presence.

'Lie down.'

She did so without a word. He glanced down at her and caught his breath. She looked like the moon goddess, all creamy flesh and blushing curves, with the dark shadow of curls between her legs, the rosy tips of her nipples, the lush pink of her mouth, the deep copper of her hair spread out behind and over her. 'Beautiful.' The word was drawn from him, harsh and grating. He was hard. More than ready.

Ramiz hauled his robe over his head and stood before her, hugely aroused. Celia stared up at him. Wanting hurtled through her, fierce and hot, made urgent by the undertone of fear she was trying desperately not to acknowledge. He looked so remote. Like a conqueror standing over the vanquished—which was exactly how she felt. Except that the blade which would claim her as his was no scimitar. Her eyes were riveted on the curving length of his erection. It seemed impossible that she could contain such a size.

'Ramiz,' she said, sitting up. She wanted him to kiss her. 'Ramiz...' She held out her hand to him.

He stared at her for a long moment, an expression like pain slanting across his face. Then he was beside her. On top of her. Kissing her. Pressing her down under him, his mouth hard, his hands rough, his manhood insistent between her thighs. She was overwhelmed by the intensity of his passion, but excited by it too, and as he kissed her and touched her she became infected by a carnal need of her own, feverishly stroking and nipping and licking, until she was aware of nothing but skin on skin, heat on heat, the scent of him, the sound of his breathing, harsh, rapid, shallow, the thrumming of her blood raging like a torrent through her veins, the clenching pulse of her muscles hurtling her forward, upwards, mercilessly on to some destination of which she was only vaguely aware.

Ramiz grazed her nipples with his teeth. She dug her nails into his back. He moulded her breasts in his hands. She stroked the taut sloping muscles of his buttocks. His fingers found her entrance and slipped carefully inside. She moaned. He slid over the swollen centre of her, around and over, around and over, so that she could scarcely bear the tightening, clenching, sharpness of her response, resisting it, holding tight to it like a swimmer to a rock. But his fingers stroked and circled remorselessly, and she let go with a cry, arching under his touch, barely aware of him readying her, tugging her to him, until she felt the nudging of his shaft.

She closed her eyes and waited for the thrust and the pain, determined not to cry out, but he entered her so slowly, so carefully, she felt only a sort of unfolding as the aftermath of her climax drew him in. She opened her eyes. Ramiz was watching her, the strain of the care he was taking etched on his face. He pushed further into her and she moaned. He stopped. She reached for him, pulled his face towards her and kissed him deeply, tilting her hips encouragingly, moaning again, with pleasure this time, as he sheathed himself in her slowly, slowly, until she thought he could go no further, pausing, pushing again, waiting until she could not bear the waiting. He withdrew from her slowly, and thrust back into her again, slowly and deliberately, watching her, and she knew that she was going to lose herself again. This time she clung to him, felt the frisson of her muscles on his shaft from base to tip, then tip to base as he pushed back into her. She tilted instinctively, wrapping her legs around his waist, and he pushed higher, harder, making her moan and clutch at his back as the ripple of her climax started to build again, or started to finish, and still he continued to thrust, each plunge more deliberate, higher, until she could feel the tip of him touching some tender spot high inside her and she lost control instantly, crying out. Her surrender acted like a trigger. Ramiz lost control almost as she had, thrusting fast and hard with abandon, until she actually felt him swell before he pulled abruptly from her, spilling hot over her belly before collapsing on top of her, wrapping his arms so tightly round her, kissing her so hard that there was no space at all between them as their skin and mouths clung to each other, because to let go would be to die.

She lay exhausted, saturated with a bone-deep heaviness that pinned her to the bed, feeling weightless, as if she was gliding. As Ramiz's breathing steadied he unwrapped himself from her. As he rolled away from her, Celia felt as if her wings had been clipped, so suddenly did she plunge back down to earth.

'Did I hurt you?'

'No.' She wanted him to hold her again, wanted reassurance, words of endearment, but she knew she could have none of those things, so she lay still, holding herself instead.

'Are you hungry now?'

She was, surprisingly, but it seemed rude to say so.

'I'm starving,' Ramiz said with a grin. 'Come on.'

Before she could move, he scooped her up in his

arms, striding with her held high against his chest to the other room. 'We can't eat like this,' Celia said, for they were both still naked.

Ramiz grinned again. 'Trust me—we can.' He kicked a heap of cushions together on the floor, and picked up the huge silver tray upon which the dishes were held, placing it on the carpet in front of the cushions before sitting down. 'Come here.' He patted a cushion invitingly. When Celia didn't move, hugging her arms around her breasts, he caught her hand and pulled her down beside him, so that she sprawled, half lying, half sitting, on a huge tasselled velvet cushion.

Ramiz lifted the cover from a dish and took out a *pastilla*, breaking it open so that some of the pastry flaked onto Celia's arm. He leaned over her to lick it off. Then he offered her a bite of pastry, licking the crumbs from her lips when she bit, before popping the rest into his own mouth.

A pomegranate salad was flavoured with lime juice and finely chopped onion. He fed her from a silver spoon. The lime gave their kisses a tangy taste which sparkled on their tongues.

Roasted aubergines and sweet peppers drizzled with olive oil were next. The oil dripped over her fingers and Ramiz sucked at them, drawing each one into his mouth and licking it clean before moving to the next.

The juice of a pineapple which had been roasted with sugar and ginger he deliberately allowed to trickle down the valley between her breasts. By this time they had given up all pretence of eating. It was a game of call and response. Where Ramiz led Celia followed, so that what had started as his teasing was in danger of turning into his own undoing.

He feasted on her breasts, tasting pineapple juice and salt and sugar, and underneath the delicious tang of what he had already come to think of as essence of Celia. She lay beneath him, aroused, flushed, her hair tangled, her eyes alight with the passion he knew she could see reflected in his. He had never known this feeling before. He couldn't put a name to it. It was as if she was drawing something out of him, mixing it with something of her own, so that she mingled in his blood, so that he felt mingled in hers. As if he knew her. Was inside her. As if she was inside him somehow.

He fastened his mouth around her nipple and sucked, then tugged, then sucked again, delighting in the way she cleaved to him, the way he could make her arch or jolt or writhe, depending on how soft or hard he licked or sucked or nipped. He sucked again, and cupped his palm over the mound of her curls between her legs. Damp. Hot. He pressed the heel of his hand against her in a little circling motion, felt the responding clenching at the base of his shaft. He wanted her again. Now. Urgently.

He nudged her legs to part them, but Celia resisted. Before he could stop her she had pushed him over onto his back. Before he could resist her she'd dipped her hand into a dish of something and trailed it neatly in a line from the middle of his ribcage. Down. It was cold. Creamy. Yoghurt of some sort, he thought vaguely. Then he stopped thinking as Celia began to lick it, daintily flicking her tongue along the path across his abdomen, dipping into his navel, down to where the path ended, at the point where his hair began to thicken. Ramiz closed his eyes and held his breath. There was a pause, during which he thought he would cry out with frustration, and then her tongue flicked over the tip of his shaft. Stopped. Another flick—a little longer. Another. Down. Down. Down the length of him and then back up, in one fluid movement that made him jolt with pleasure. Blood surged. He felt the tightening in his groin that presaged his climax. Dear heavens, he thought he would die with the pleasure of it. If only she would—now—like—just exactly like that! And like that. And—oh—like that!

'Celia.' She stopped. He didn't want her to stop. Ramiz reached down to grip her by the shoulders. The look of surprise on her face would have been funny if he had been in the mood to be amused. He wasn't. He pulled her down over him. Her knees brushed his shoulders. Her breasts were crushed into his stomach. Her mouth was back where he wanted it. And his was exactly where he wanted it to be too. He put his palms on the delightful swell of her bottom, he put his mouth over the delightful mound of wet curls and tender folds between her legs, and moaned as he tasted her and breathed her and sought out the nub of her. He moaned again as she followed him, reflecting and echoing every lick and stroke, resisting, but only just, the urgent clamouring of his climax until he felt hers, and then he let himself go as she came, and he had never, ever felt anything quite so heady as that feeling of her sweetness in his mouth as he surged and pulsed into hers.

It felt right. Which was absolutely wrong. But for now Ramiz cared for nothing, nothing—at all.

Chapter Eleven

Ramiz did not sleep in her tent but returned to his own. For a long time Celia gazed at her reflection by the light of the lamps. She barely recognised the woman staring back at her from the mirror. Her hair was a tangled mess. Her eyes were huge—a darker green than she had ever seen them. Her bottom lip seemed swollen. Her skin was flushed all over, with the faint marks of Ramiz's fingers on her breasts, a slight bruise on her bottom. Between her thighs she was tender. Under one of her nails was a trace of blood where she had dug her fingers too deep into his back. Something else she couldn't put a name to shone from her face too. A different kind of glow she hadn't experienced before. Sensual, that was what it was, she finally decided. Wanton, even. For the first time since she had arrived in the East she saw the point of the veil. She would certainly not like anyone else to see her like this. They'd know straight away.

Sliding between the silk sheets of the divan, she wondered if Ramiz looked the same. Somehow she doubted it. None of this was new to him. They had done nothing he had not done before, and no doubt he would do it again. The idea of him with another woman made her feel sick.

She must be careful. Though she had pleased him, though he had seemed most reluctant to leave, she must remember it meant nothing to him. And he was just a passing fascination for her. She would do well to remember that, too. It meant nothing. No matter how right it felt, or how amazingly he had made her feel. Ramiz was an oasis of sensuality in the desert of her life.

Celia chuckled at that, for it was the sort of thing Cassie would have said. She wondered if he was sleeping. She wondered if he was thinking about her. Celia drifted into a deep sleep, most certainly thinking about him.

When she awoke, the sun was rising and the caravan was already being prepared to depart. She ate a hurried breakfast alone in her tent, conscious that the men were waiting to take it down. Ramiz was waiting with her camel, anxious to make a start, leaving Akil to lead the caravan which would again follow in their wake.

She expected Ramiz to ignore her. She expected him to be brusque, to have returned to his princely remoteness now he had what he wanted from her, but he surprised her, helping her onto the camel with a smile so warm it might as well have been a kiss. They set out as yesterday, in companionable closeness. If this were not Ramiz she would feel she was being courted. But it *was* Ramiz, and he could never court her.

They made camp that night in the same manner as before, but this time they were not alone. 'Sheikh Farid and his tribe,' Ramiz told Celia, nodding over at the cluster of tents about five hundred yards distant. 'We must pay our respects tonight. Dress up. It is expected.'

'You want me to come with you?'

'If you don't he will be insulted. You think they haven't heard of the mysterious English lady travelling with me?'

She hadn't given it much thought, though she realised now that she should have. 'What will they think of me?'

'I have asked Akil to put out the word that you are here as an emissary of the British Government.'

'A woman! They'll hardly believe that.'

Ramiz shrugged. 'Just another Western quirk—treating a woman as a man. It is why we have separate tents. You would not want them to think you my concubine.'

'No, of course not. I—thank you, Ramiz.'

'It is my own honour as much as yours I must protect. Besides,' he added, acknowledging Akil's summons, 'Sheikh Farid's daughter is one of the princesses on my council's list of brides.'

She had been touched by his care for her reputation. Now she saw it was care for his own, and was angry—not at Ramiz, but at herself for reading something into nothing. Celia made her way to her tent, mortified and fighting a wholly unaccustomed feeling which she realised, as she stepped into her waiting bath, was jealousy. 'Of a woman I have never met,' she muttered in disgust, 'and whom he may not marry in any event.'

The bath calmed her, and the oil she rubbed into her arms and legs afterwards soothed her. She must find out the receipt for it from Fatima. Cassie would like to try it, and she knew they would not be able to buy such a thing at home.

Home! The word startled her. Soon she would be going back to England. Far away from the heat and the smells of this beautiful land, from the contrasts of barren deserts and green oases, from A'Qadiz and its exotic foods and vibrant colours. And far away from Ramiz. She wasn't ready to go, not yet, but, counting up the days, she knew it could not be long before her father arrived in Cairo. 'Home.' She said it out loud, experimentally, but it still didn't work.

She couldn't bear the thought of leaving Ramiz. She couldn't imagine her life without him. 'Because I might as well admit it,' she said to her reflection. 'I'm not just beguiled. I'm not just in thrall to him. I'm in love with him.'

Her reflection smiled. A soft, tender smile, which crept warily across her lips. 'I'm in love with Ramiz.' Her smile spread. Her skin tingled. 'I'm in love with Ramiz. Oh, God, I'm in love with Ramiz.' Celia tottered backwards onto the divan. 'I'm in love with Ramiz, and I'm just about to meet the woman he may well marry.' A hysterical little bubble of laughter escaped her, followed by a large solitary tear which trickled like acid down her cheek.

She was in love! Who'd have thought it? Certainly she'd never considered herself capable of such a thing. Not this kind of love, at any rate. She'd always thought of love as something comfortable, something that grew slowly over time, something stolid, dependable, rather than essential. But this, this thing she called love, was nothing at all like that. It glowed inside her like a living thing, pulsing and throbbing with life, the source of her being rather than a pleasant appendage. The reason for her being. Ramiz completed her. He was the heart which beat in her, the sun around which she revolved.

Celia laughed. Such fancies were the stuff on which Cassie thrived, and she had always mocked them, but now she found they were true. It was all true. She had been waiting to be woken. The way he made her feel, the way only *he* could make her feel, was nothing to do with the harem and everything to do with Ramiz. Her body was in thrall because she was in love. Her body responded to him at some elemental level because it had recognised, long before her mind did, what he meant to her. She loved him.

And Yasmina was right too. She would always love him. She was not the type to love twice. There would never be anyone else. She loved Ramiz. He was the beginning of her story and the end.

Except there could never be a happy ever after.

Fortunately Celia had never allowed herself to hope for one. There would be an end to this, and she would have to cope with it. Cope with it and never allow

Ramiz to know. For if he thought she cared he would feel responsible, and that responsibility would touch his honour and—no, she could not allow that.

Celia dressed with care in a pair of lemon pleated pantaloons bound at the ankles with silver and pearl beading. The same design was embroidered onto the long loose sleeves of her caftan, which was velvet, in her favourite jade green, and on the matching velvet slippers too. Around her neck and wrists she roped her mother's pearls, and there were pearls in her hair too, which she wore up, but with a loose knot over one shoulder.

Passable, she thought, looking at herself again in the mirror. The caftan, which was slashed to the thigh, drew attention to her height, and the length of her legs. The pearls lent their lustre to her skin. Her hair was glossy from the care lavished on it by Adila and Fatima. She looked exotic, she realised. Although the outfit covered more of her than a ballgown, the diaphanous material of the pantaloons, visible through the caftan's vents, made her legs clearly visible. The soft folds of the caftan itself hinted at her uncorseted shape beneath. Celia laughed, wondering what Aunt Sophia would think of her going to pay a visit without her stays!

Ramiz might not love her, but he desired her, and in this outfit even Celia could see that she had a certain allure. Which was consolation enough, she told herself firmly as she left the tent.

Ramiz was conferring with Akil. Dressed in his formal robes, white silk edged with gold, the state scimitar glinting at his waist, he looked every inch the regal prince. He was preoccupied, giving her a cursory glance only as he rapped out instructions to the guards, inspected the gifts which were to be given to Sheikh Farid, and listened impatiently as Akil read through his seemingly endless notes.

The procession they formed to walk the short distance to the Bedouin tents was impressive. Ramiz took the lead, preceded by his Head of Guards, a great hulk of a man whose robes, Celia thought, were large enough to form a tent of their own. She herself followed Ramiz, with Akil behind her, flanked by the remainder of the guards carrying blazing torches to light the way.

Sheikh Farid was a small man of about the same age as Celia's father. He was simply dressed, in a black robe and red-checked headdress, but his womenfolk more than made up for his lack of ostentation. Celia counted six wives, bedecked in so many gold anklets, bracelets, necklaces and earrings that they jangled when they moved. Bedouin women covered their skin with complex ink and henna tattoos—swirling designs encompassing leaves and flowers, mixed in with ancient symbols. Their nails were stained red with henna, and their eyelids stained black at the corners, much in the way the eyes of the pharaohs were painted. They did not wear the veil, and stared with blatant curiosity at Celia, though when she smiled in their direction they giggled and lowered their eyes.

She kept discreetly in the background, under Akil's watchful eye. Though he had said nothing, she was aware that Akil did not approve of her presence here. No doubt he fretted over the propriety of it, and she could not blame him—especially since his suspicions had all too recently been proved correct. He would think her a loose woman. No doubt he would be glad when she was gone, for he could not approve of her relationship with Yasmina. It saddened Celia, and she determined to do all she could to ensure she intruded on official business no more than necessary.

As it turned out, she enjoyed her role as onlooker immensely, for it gave her the opportunity to observe Ramiz the Prince. It was a role he performed with the assurance and dignity she had come to expect of him, but as the ritual of the alms-giving got underway what impressed her most was his complete lack of arrogance. Throughout the long process of receiving each person who wished to make a plea, Ramiz showed only patience and concern. He had that rare ability to talk without talking down, taking time to calm the most nervous of the supplicants or the most aggressive of the litigants, treating the ancients with touching deference, joking with the younger men as a contemporary. Despite the long line of supplicants, there was no sense of hurry. Every case was given due consideration, every decision proclaimed formally to the audience before the next commenced. Not everyone received the outcome they'd hoped for, but all seemed to be treated fairly, and Celia realised that this, and not the sums of money given out in alms, was the point. Prince Ramiz was seen to be fair and just, as well as accessible.

She was impressed and touched—not just by Ramiz's humanity, but by his vision, for he was obviously intent on demonstrating to his people the principles by which he ruled. The principles to which too many other rulers, in Celia's experience, paid merely lip-service. He truly was a remarkable man. She loved him so much.

Humbled, and slightly overcome by the strength of emotion which enveloped her, Celia crept unnoticed from the ceremony. Away from the blaze of the torches which lit Sheikh Farid's tent, the full moon cast a ghostly light across the Bedouin encampment. She wandered a little distance from the tents, absorbed in her thoughts, enjoying the cool of the evening and the scents of the desert which came to life after dark. The vast stretches of sand which surrounded her began to have their usual effect, imbuing her with a strange combination—a sense of her own insignificance and at the same time a feeling of endless possibilities. Desert euphoria, she called it, for it was both exhilarating and chastening, like flying in Signor Lunardi's balloon, which Papa had been fortunate enough to witness on its inaugural flight from Moorfields.

A shuffling sound alerted her to the presence of another person. A glint of steel showed the shadowy figure to be one of Ramiz's guards, no doubt instructed to keep an eye on her. Strange to think that when first they'd met she would have been insulted by this apparent lack of trust. She knew better now, and recognised it for a combination of deeply embedded chivalry and an equally strong duty of care which was an essential part of him. She had come to like it.

Nodding to the guard as she passed, Celia made her way back to the Bedouin camp. The line of people was coming to an end. Fires had sprouted up outside many of the tents, and the smell of cooking filled the air. Women were gathering around the glowing embers, chatting and laughing. A group of semi-naked children were playing a ball game. As Celia stopped to watch, the ball landed at her feet, and before she knew it she was embroiled in the game, whose complex rules were explained with many gestures and much hilarity.

Her regular visits to Yasmina's extended family had given her a smattering of the language, and when the ball game petered out Celia recognised the word for story as the children gathered around her and tugged pleadingly at her caftan. Sitting cross-legged on the sand, surrounded by a circle of expectant faces, she prayed that her enthusiasm and the children's participation would make up for her lack of vocabulary, and launched into one of Samir's favourite stories, which happened to be one of her youngest sister Cressida's too. *Ali Baba and the Forty Thieves.*

'*As-salamu alaykum,*' Ramiz said to the last of the suppliants, a man seeking arbitration over the return of his divorced daughter's dowry. 'Peace be with you.'

'*Wa-alaykum as-salam*, Highness,' the man replied, bowing backwards out of the tent.

Ramiz rubbed his temples and looked around. 'Where is Lady Celia?' he asked Akil sharply.

'She left some time ago.'

Ramiz glared at him. 'I told you to keep watch over her.'

'I did, Highness. A guard is with her.'

Ramiz made to leave.

'Majesty?'

Ramiz eyed the restraining hand on his arm with a cold hauteur which made Akil step hurriedly back. 'Well?'

'I have arranged with Sheikh Farid to have his daughter formally presented to you tomorrow. I apologise if I speak out of turn, but you would do well to leave the Lady Celia to her own devices,' Akil said, blanching at his friend's glacial expression but remaining firm. 'No-one believes this story you have had me put about,' he hissed, ushering Ramiz to one side, away from listening ears and prying glances. 'Anyone with eyes can see what you are to her. She turns to you as a flower does to the sun. And you, Highness, if you are not careful you will fall under the spell she casts. Her father is an influential man. Do you think he will take kindly to having his daughter used as a concubine?'

'How dare you speak to me on such a subject? Just because you are my friend, Akil, do not think I will tolerate interference in my personal life.'

'Ramiz, you are a prince. Unfortunately you do not have a personal life. It is because I am your closest friend that I dare to speak. You think I don't know how tirelessly you have worked in the last two years? You think I don't know how much you have done for A'Qadiz? How much more there is still for you to do? It would be foolish to offer insult to the English over such a trivial matter as a woman, and equally foolish to insult Sheikh Farid, whom you know holds sway over almost all of our Bedouins. Trust me on this matter. Leave that woman alone, or if you must go to her bed at least have the

discretion to do so away from the eyes of those who
hold power.'

There was a long silence. Furious as he was to be
spoken to in such a way, Ramiz was even more furious
at himself. He rubbed his eyes. 'If I have been indiscreet
it shall be remedied, but you are making a camel out of
a flea. Lady Celia is under no illusions about our—our
relationship. She is perfectly well aware of its temporary
nature and will make no trouble.'

'Ramiz, I tell you she is in love with you.'

Ramiz shook his head. 'You are quite wrong. Like all
foreigners she is obsessed with the sensual elements of
our culture, and who can change her, coming as she does
from a people who make a virtue of indifference, who
equate virtue with frigidity and passion with vice? Lady
Celia is indulging her passions safe from the prying eyes
of her compatriots. She is simply taking advantage of
the situation.'

'Is that what you're doing?'

Ramiz clenched his fists. 'You overstep the mark,
Akil. What I am doing is enjoying the company of
one who wants nothing from me except myself. A rare
enough thing since I came to power, you will agree.'

'Ramiz, if it is just a woman you need, you
could—'

'Enough! That is quite enough!' Ignoring the sudden
hush around them, ignoring the guards who had rushed
towards him at the sound of his raised voice, even ignoring Sheikh Farid, who was making his way towards
the commotion, Ramiz gripped Akil by the shoulders.
'She is not *just a woman*! If I *ever* hear you speak so

discourteously of Lady Celia in my presence again, I will have you banished—do you understand?' he said through gritted teeth.

Akil nodded.

'And if I ever hear from Lady Celia that you have treated her in any way disrespectfully, or if I hear from her that you have allowed your wife to see your own prejudices, I will have you banished. Yasmina is Celia's only friend here. It would be a great shame if she were to lose her. Do I make myself understood, Akil?'

White as his master's headdress, Akil nodded again.

Ramiz released him. 'Then let us put this behind us. We go too far back to allow it to come between us.'

Akil straightened the *igal* which held his own headdress in place. 'I hope that is true,' he murmured, but he did so very quietly.

Ramiz's anger had shocked him to the core. For once Akil was certain he knew better than his friend. The sooner Lady Celia was on her way back to Egypt the better, so Ramiz could get on with the serious business of taking a suitable wife.

In search of a little quiet before the feasting began, for it would last much of the night, Ramiz encountered Celia in the centre of a circle of ragged children with rapt expressions on their faces. Taking care to remain out of sight, he watched, fascinated, as she recounted a tale, amused by the clever way she encouraged the children to join in with words and gestures when her own surprisingly large stock of vocabulary failed her.

He hadn't known she could say anything other than good morning and thank you, but she'd picked up a lot more than that in the time she'd been here. From the maids, he presumed. And Yasmina, of course.

Akil's words had angered him, but he knew his friend well enough to understand how strong his feelings must be for him to have spoken in such a way. He was wrong about Celia, though; it was a ridiculous notion to think her in love. Almost as ridiculous as the idea that he, Prince Ramiz al-Muhana of A'Qadiz, could feel such a thing. Princes did not fall in love except in fairytales. English roses did not fall in love with Arabic princes except in fairytales—which was almost certainly how Celia saw it, and exactly what he'd just said to Akil.

He looked at her now, absent-mindedly stroking the hair of the little girl who sat by her side while balancing another on her knee. He'd noticed it the day she'd arrived at the port, and again the day they went to the market in Balyrma—how children were drawn to her, how naturally she talked to them, stooping down to their height, never using that patronising tone with them which so many childless women used. Affinity— that was the word. It must come from looking after her sisters.

Akil worried too much. He was so focused on his great plan to tie up their hard-won peace with a good marriage that he couldn't see clearly. No matter how comfortable Celia might look here, A'Qadiz was not her home. No matter how incredible last night had been, it was just a temporary passion. Like all passions, it would take flight sooner rather than later. Sooner, if he continued to indulge it. She would be gone soon enough. He would do his duty to A'Qadiz, as he had always done his duty. After thirty-five years of doing so he deserved these few days.

The privilege of sitting in Celia's lap was now being disputed by a little boy. Without pausing in her narrative Celia managed to accommodate both children, but it left her no hands free. 'Open sesame!' she declared, but without being able to throw her arms wide the English version of the words fell flat. The children looked puzzled.

'Iftah ya simsim,' Ramiz said, unable to resist joining her, much to the children's awed delight. 'Open sesame,' he said carefully, lifting up a small boy to clear a space by her side.

'Open sesame,' the children repeated gleefully.

'Thank you,' Celia whispered. She smiled at him—a smile he hadn't seen before. Tender. It must be the children. She was thinking of her sisters. Akil was wrong.

Akil was definitely wrong, Ramiz thought again later, much later, as they made their weary procession back to the tents after a long drawn-out dinner. He nodded goodnight to his friend. Akil bowed stiffly and retreated to his own tent without a backwards glance, still piqued by the dressing-down Ramiz had administered.

Celia would be asleep by now. She had eaten separately, with the women, and been escorted back at least an hour ago. Ramiz had intended going straight to his own divan, but Akil's unspoken disapproval and the need to prove him wrong sent him to Celia's tent. If she was asleep he would not wake her.

But she was not asleep. When he pulled back the curtain the lamps were lit in the main room. She was reclining, still dressed in her velvet caftan, on a heap of cushions, reading a book which she put immediately to one side as soon as he appeared in the doorway, holding out her hand invitingly.

Ramiz hesitated. She didn't look any different to him. Beautiful. With more awareness, maybe, in the way she smiled at him—but that was because she was more aware of her body. Of how it could feel. Of what he could do to it. Of what she could do to him. His manhood stirred.

'Celia, you do not—you know this cannot last?'

She lowered her eyes. 'Of course not. Are you come to tell me our fairytale is over already, Ramiz?'

'Fairytale?' he repeated, taken aback by her repetition of the very word he himself had used.

'That is how I think of it. Don't you?'

He took her outstretched hand, allowing himself to be pulled down to join her on the cushions. 'A fairytale? Am I your prince?'

'Yes.'

'Then you must do my bidding,' Ramiz said, pulling the pearl pins from her hair and running his hands through it.

'Your wish is my command, master.'

'Excellent,' Ramiz said, pulling her caftan over her head. He ran his palms down her shoulders, across her breasts, skimming the indent of her waist to rest on the curve of her hips before tugging his own robe over his head. 'Though tonight I think it should be your wish which is my command. What would you like me to do with this?'

Sheikh Farid presented his daughter Juman the next morning. The visit was obviously expected. Watching from the shade of her tent, Celia saw Akil fussing over the positioning of the furnishings in the tent in which Ramiz slept. The whole front of the main room had been lifted up to reveal an interior bigger and much richer than the one she enjoyed. Akil was supervising the placing of a tea service, watching carefully as one of the servants polished the gold samovar to his satisfaction, while Ramiz sat in a corner reading.

Sheikh Farid arrived on horseback—a magnificent and extremely rare black thoroughbred which contrasted perfectly with the grey on which his daughter was mounted. A third horse, another grey, pranced delicately on a leading rein behind them. Even from a distance Celia could see that father and daughter rode well— hardly surprising since she had learned last night that the thoroughbreds, with their distinctively arched necks and high, swishing tails, formed a significant part of Sheikh Farid's livelihood.

The Sheikh's daughter was younger than she had expected—nearer Caroline's age than Cassie's, perhaps only sixteen or seventeen. Though Yasmina had told her that girls married young here in A'Qadiz, Celia could not help thinking that sixteen was far too young for Ramiz. The girl would bore him to death. What on earth were Akil and the council thinking about, suggesting such a baby for a man like Ramiz?

But, watching her spring lithely from the horse, she began to see exactly why this girl had been recommended, and when she was invited to join them for tea in Ramiz's tent her understanding was completed. Juman Farid was extraordinarily beautiful, with ebony hair that shone with health, almond eyes which managed to be both mysterious and seductive, and vermilion lips which no matter how hard Celia stared at them showed not a trace of artifice. She had a figure which was a perfect hourglass too, and not only that she was quite obviously as blue-blooded as the horse which had carried her here. No doubt, Celia thought bitterly to herself, she had a pedigree just as long and impressive, for she was the firstborn of Sheikh Farid's first wife, and even Celia knew how important such precedence was.

Though she was dressed in the traditional *sarwal* trousers and tunic under the *abayah* which had cloaked her upon the horse, Juman's charms were nonetheless subtly on display, for the gauzy gold and crimson chiffon left little to the imagination.

So Celia thought—until she realised what she was thinking and castigated herself for it. She was jealous! It was hardly Juman's fault that she was so attractive and so eminently suitable a princess for Prince Ramiz. It was not as if she was behaving with anything other than perfect propriety either. Juman spoke only when spoken to, insisted that Celia pour the tea, and kept her eyes discreetly lowered. Only when Sheikh Farid suggested she show Ramiz the horse they had brought for him to try out did she leap up excitedly and clap her hands, her enthusiasm shining through in a way so entirely genuine that Celia was mortified.

It was Akil who suggested to Ramiz that he try out the horse's paces, and Akil who suggested to Sheikh Farid that he allow Juman to accompany Ramiz. Sheikh Farid agreed, but only on the proviso that he go along as chaperone. Celia was ashamed to find herself relieved by this, but it was still with a heavy heart that she waved them off.

She retired to her tent, occupying herself with the embroidery of a caftan which she intended to leave as a present for Ramiz when she left. As the sun rose to its apex she fell asleep, waking in the afternoon to discover that the trio had gone straight to the Bedouin camp, where a new tribe of supplicants had arrived.

'You may join them if you wish,' Akil told her, in a voice which suggested she should not. She took heed of it, eating a lonely supper and retiring early to her divan with her book.

But Ramiz arrived as he had the night before. And, as he had the night before, he made love to her with a fervency and a passion which took them both by surprise all over again.

So it continued the next day and the next, as each new tribe arrived, with Celia spending some time alone, some time at the camp with the children, but avoiding Ramiz in public. Ramiz's spare time was monopolised either by Akil or Juman, but his nights were reserved for Celia.

They made love. They talked. She read to him. He told her of the more interesting cases he had adjudicated that day. She shared with him her ideas for a school camp which could be set up like the alms camp, where Bedouin children could come for at least a smattering of education, even if they did not stay long.

'If you chose one of the bigger oases, where they are likely to stay longer, and made sure the teacher did not mind that one day her class might be five strong, another fifty, then I think it would work,' she said eagerly. 'They are such a huge part of A'Qadiz's population, yet they have virtually no schooling. Yasmina told me one of your sayings: not having the opportunity to test your talents does not mean you do not have them. It's not as if they don't want to learn; it's just that they don't get much opportunity. Their parents have no education either, and cannot teach them.'

With Ramiz's encouragement, she went on to outline in more detail the practicalities of how her 'tent school', as she thought of it, would work.

'You've thought this all through very thoroughly. I'm impressed,' Ramiz said, looking at her with new respect.

'Will it work, do you think?'

'With the right teachers, I don't see why not. But where am to find people willing to take on such a challenge?'

'I would do it,' she said, without thinking.

'Live in a tent teaching Bedouin children? I don't think so. Your father would never permit it.'

'Probably not.'

'What will you do when you go back to England?'

'I don't know.' Celia looked away, biting her lip. 'I don't know. Perhaps I will teach at a charity school there. There is no shortage of children in England needing education, and I seem to have a gift for it.'

'You should have children of your own,' he said, then wished he had not, for the idea of Celia bearing anyone's child but his was unexpectedly painful.

'Ramiz, let us stop this conversation,' she said gently.

'You mean it is none of my business.'

'Ramiz, don't! I do not ask you whether you will marry Juman, but it does not mean I don't think about it. It does not mean I don't feel horribly guilty thinking about it, and what we do here in this tent every night. I don't feel guilty enough to stop, but that is because I know it will end anyway—and soon. I do not ask you because I don't want to know, and because, as you say, it is none of my business—as my life will be none of yours when I leave here.'

His expression darkened, his anger arriving without warning and whipping him into a stormy rage. 'I won't be marrying Juman. She is a child, and she bores me rigid with her endless talk of horses, horses, horses and nothing else. I cannot contemplate taking her or any other woman into my bed when I have you waiting for me. You obsess me! Do you not understand? I cannot get enough of you—yet I must, for you must return to your homeland.'

'Ramiz, it is the same for me.' She gripped his arms, shaking him so that he looked at her. 'Can you not see it is the same for me? I want you. All the time I want you.'

'Celia, I…'

'For heaven's sake, Your Highness, just shut up and kiss me.'

And, for once in his life, Ramiz did exactly as he was commanded.

Chapter Twelve

Lord Henry Armstrong, who had hitherto considered himself in robust health, had been much worn down by the journey across the Mediterranean in the cramped and infested quarters of His Majesty's frigate *Hyperion*, suffering grievously from *mal de mer* exacerbated by some rather vicious fleabites. While the redoubtable Lady Sophia flourished under the conditions, her brother and niece were laid low, forced to remain below decks upon their bunks for much of the voyage. Lady Sophia it was who saw to it that the invalids were provided with what little nourishment their delicate stomachs could tolerate, and it was she who obtained a salve from Captain Mowbray himself, which rid Lord Henry of his unpleasant infestation.

And upon their arrival in Alexandria it was Lady Sophia again who rose to the occasion, conjuring up the transportation which hurtled the travellers onwards so quickly that Lord Henry had no time at all to recover from the pitching of the ground beneath them before being besieged by the bone-jolting experience of an unsprung carriage travelling an unmetalled road with his daughter rather vulgarly urging the driver to 'spring 'em' every time they stopped for a change.

They had arrived at Lord Wincester's residence in Cairo at some God-forsaken hour last night, and now here was Cassie, having made a remarkable recovery, demanding that they resume their journey not twenty-four hours later.

'Absolutely not!' Lord Henry exclaimed. 'I cannot journey another inch without a day's rest.'

'But, Papa, you cannot have considered—'

Lord Henry looked at his daughter with an eye which was considerably jaundiced. He had the tic. He had a splitting headache. In fact there wasn't a bit of him that didn't ache in one way or another. 'You worry too much. What is another day, after all this time?'

Cassie who, after seven hours' rest and a bath had made a remarkable recovery, was back in full Cassandra mode. She wrung her hands. 'Another day of suffering, Papa. Another day of Celia wondering when we will come to rescue her. Another day of gazing through the bars of her prison and *praying* for her release.'

'For God's sake, daughter, you should be on stage! You know, I can't understand how someone who looks as if a puff of wind will blow her away can survive such a journey as we have made with so little visible effect. I congratulate you on your constitution but—*but*, I say—I do not share it. I need another day before I go traipsing off across the desert. Apart from anything else, I must consult with old Wincester. The negotiations that George Cleveden was sent to conclude are extremely important—far too important to make a mull of because I didn't have time to receive a proper briefing. Damned inconvenient of George to get himself killed in the middle of it all, I must say.'

'But, Papa, surely my sister is the more important issue at stake? Aunt Sophia!' Cassandra turned large blue eyes, wide with appeal, upon her aunt. 'I beg you, let us make haste today. Apparently it is only a very short trip to the Red Sea, where we can take a boat to this A'Qadiz. A gentle sail, Lord Wincester says it is.'

'What the devil does old Wincester know about it? He's never been,' Lord Henry exclaimed exasperatedly. 'Instead of treating me to histrionics, you'll make far better use of your time talking to that fellow—whatshisname—Finchley-Burke. He saw Celia only a week or so ago. Now, go away and allow me the dignity of recovering my health in private.'

Recognising the note of finality in his voice, Cassandra was forced to retreat, stopping only to press upon her father some most efficacious powders, before returning to the drawing room with her aunt.

There, Peregrine awaited her nervously, torn between a desire to pay homage at the temple of her beauty and an equally strong desire to avoid her terrifying aunt, whose baleful eye reminded him rather too much of his mother.

'You will accompany us, naturally. We need someone who knows the ropes,' Cassie informed Peregrine, putting her new-found seaman's slang into use. 'You've done the journey before, and you know all about camels and such. In fact compared to everyone else here, including even Lord Wincester, you are quite the expert,' she said, conferring upon the young man one of her most beguiling smiles.

Peregrine blushed. Now that Lord Henry Armstrong, with his reputation for honesty and integrity, was actually here in Cairo, the Consul General was regretting the liberties he had taken in suggesting that the Lady Celia's incarceration in A'Qadiz could be of service to her country. In fact Lord Wincester had forbidden Peregrine from mentioning it, putting Peregrine in a very awkward position indeed. Not even Lady Cassandra's charming countenance and nymph-like figure could tempt him into spending any more time in her presence than necessary, lest he betray himself.

'Thing—thing is, Lady Cassandra,' he stammered, appalled at the very notion of having to keep her, her esteemed papa and formidable aunt company on a trek across the desert, 'thing is, I have to go to India.'

'Mr Finchley-Burke!' Cassandra exclaimed. 'Surely you would not let us down?'

'Eh! No, no, didn't quite—that is—you don't need me. You'll need a guide for the desert, but you'll be able pick one up at the port—don't want me along, keeping you back.' But Peregrine knew he was clutching at straws.

'India will wait, Mr Finchley-Burke. My sister cannot. You, I am sure, will not wish to think of her incarcerated in that place a moment longer than necessary.'

Peregrine's memory of Lady Celia was of a female perfectly content to stay where she was, but he did not quite know how to put that to her sister.

'How did you find my niece, Mr Finchley-Burke?'

Peregrine jumped, for he had quite forgotten Lady Sophia's presence. Now, faced with her gimlet gaze, he quailed. 'Well, it was quite simple, really, once I got to the palace.'

Lady Sophia rolled her eyes. 'No, you nincompoop, I'm referring to her health, her mental state.'

'Oh! Yes! Quite! She actually seemed remarkably well. Very composed young woman, Lady Celia. Seemed to be handling it with real aplomb,' Peregrine said bracingly.

'Ah, that does sound like Celia,' Lady Sophia said placidly.

'Of course it does, Aunt Sophia. Celia is not the type to have hysterics, you know that, but just because she does not show her feelings it does not mean she has none.' Cassandra clasped her hands to her bosom, unwittingly drawing Peregrine's attention to her curves. 'Remember, this man—this Sheikh al-Muhana—has her in his harem. I picture him rather old, with a black beard and a sort of grasping look.'

'As to that,' Sophia said with pursed lips, 'I have been making enquiries, and believe harems are not all decadent places. It may be that he has placed Celia in his harem simply to keep her safe. Do not let your imagination run away with you, Cassandra. I have every confidence in Celia's sense of propriety and her good sense.

You must rid yourself of the notion of her as some sort of concubine.'

'But, Aunt, what if Celia's choice is to submit or surrender her life?' Cassandra asked tragically, once more allowing *One Thousand and One Nights* the upper hand.

'There is no point in wasting our time on idle speculation,' Lady Sophia said acerbically. Realising her niece was genuinely upset, and upon the brink of tears, she softened her expression marginally. 'Really, Cassie, you know your sister well enough. Celia is hardly the type to appeal to a sheikh, for she is not in the least exotic—and even if she did, which I strongly doubt, she is not the type to simply submit. Celia,' Lady Sophia said with authority, 'is not a tactile woman.' She got to her feet. 'We will leave you to your arrangements now,' she said to Peregrine. 'Come, Cassandra, what you need is some rest. Fortunately I have some laudanum in my reticule.'

'Sheikh Farid has requested an audience with you.'

The servants were packing up the camp in preparation for the journey back to Balyrma. 'With me?' Celia closed the lid of her dressing case, and turned towards Ramiz, who was standing in the doorway. 'What can Sheikh Farid wish to say to me?'

'I've been telling him about your idea for a Bedouin school. In amongst that gaggle of little admirers who follow you about wide-eyed, begging for stories, are three of Sheikh Farid's youngest children, and their mothers have been singing your praises.' Ramiz grinned. 'You've made quite an impression on them.'

'But what can I say? You said yourself the problem is finding teachers.'

'*"To him that will, ways are not wanting."* If Sheikh Farid wants a school for his people, teachers can be found. He has not until now believed it is what his people want. It looks as if you may have changed his mind.'

'You will be coming with me, won't you, Ramiz?'

'Yes, but you don't need me to tell you how to behave any more than I need to remind you of the honour Sheikh Farid is conferring upon you. You have a very charming way of making whoever you speak to feel as if they are the most important person in the world. Even me.'

'In your case it is because it is true.' The words were out before she could stop them.

Ramiz stilled.

'I mean,' Celia said lightly, 'in the eyes of your people, of course.'

'Of course,' Ramiz said thoughtfully.

'Does Sheikh Farid wish to see me now?'

'Yes, now. Akil can go ahead with the caravan. Tonight will be our last night in the desert. Tomorrow we will be back in Balyrma.'

'It will be strange, being back in the harem.'

'Celia, you don't regret what has happened? Between us, I mean?'

He looked troubled. *Was it he who had regrets?* She could not bear that. Though she rarely took the initiative, even in the most commonplace of touches, Celia took Ramiz's hand and pressed a kiss onto his palm.

His skin was warm, his taste tantalisingly familiar. 'I will remember it always,' she said, rubbing his hand against her cheek. 'This last week has been magical. I will never regret it. Never.'

'Celia…'

She had a horrible suspicion he was going to apologise. Or, worse, offer her some sort of reparation. 'Please, Ramiz, don't.'

'Don't what?'

'Don't spoil it. As an interlude from reality it has been perfect.'

He pulled his hand away. 'That is still how you see it?'

She looked at him in bewilderment. 'Do not you?'

Ramiz shrugged. 'We will take the camels to Sheikh Farid's camp. That way we will waste less time.'

'Ramiz…'

But he was gone. She stared at the spot in the tent where he had stood. In the last week she'd thought she had come to understand him completely, but today she had no idea what he was thinking—what it was she had said to him to make him look so…what? Angry? A little, but not just that. She pulled an *abeyah* the colour of cinnamon, embroidered with russet and gold, over her caftan, and checked her appearance in the mirror. He had seemed almost disappointed. But why?

Tonight would be their last night in the desert. Their last night together in her tent. When they returned to the palace would it all be at an end? Was that what he meant? That he would not visit her in the harem? Had he had enough of her? Was he letting her down gently?

A horrible sick feeling made her slump down onto the divan. When he'd said it was their last night in the desert, he'd meant it was to be their last night. Ever. There could be no other meaning. Celia blinked rapidly to prevent the hot tears which welled up in her eyes from spilling. She'd known it would end, but she'd hoped it would last until she had to leave. Now she saw he was right. To drag it out, waking each morning wondering if it would be this day or the next when her papa would arrive, would be unendurable.

Her papa would take her home. But home was here, with Ramiz. Without him she might as well be condemned to a nomadic life, just like the Bedouins. Celia sniffed and blew her nose, and chastised herself for the fanciful turn her imagination had taken. She had tonight. She had the memories. Things could be worse, she told herself bracingly, though she wasn't exactly sure how.

The meeting with Sheikh Farid went well. Celia was nervous beforehand, worried she would let Ramiz down. 'It's not possible,' Ramiz had said reassuringly, surprised to find that he meant it. 'I trust you.'

He had meant that too, which was more of a surprise, for the truth was he didn't normally trust anyone completely to act on his behalf, to act without his explicit instructions, to think for themselves—not even Akil. Yet he trusted Celia. He trusted her judgement and he trusted her ability. Sitting by her side, translating only when consulted, he watched with admiration as she set about charming Sheikh Farid as she seemed to charm everyone she spoke to, from the market traders in the souk, to Yasmina, his servants, every child who came within a hundred yards of her, and now this wily old Bedouin, who was already smiling and making jokes after just fifteen minutes in her company—something it had taken *him* many visits to achieve.

Sheikh Farid summoned his wives and younger children. Ramiz recognised the little girl who made a beeline for Celia's lap as the one he'd seen her with the day before. They had been counting out numbers using pieces of straw. Now Celia encouraged the child to show her father what she had learned.

The meeting concluded with a promise on Sheikh Farid's part to give thought to the problem of finding teachers—a giant leap forward as far as Ramiz was concerned.

'You are blessed in your visitor from the West,' Sheikh Farid told Ramiz. 'She has the brains of a man in the body of a beautiful woman. If only you could be persuaded to stay,' he continued, turning towards Celia, 'I would be happy to take you as my next wife. Though I fear that Prince Ramiz here would have something to say to that.' Sheikh Farid smiled sadly. 'I should not grudge him, for I already have six fine wives and this poor man has none, but you must understand I speak as a father. I had hoped my Juman would please the Prince, but I can see she is not to his taste.' The Bedouin touched his hands together and bowed. 'Safe journey, my friends. Peace be with you.'

Celia returned the gesture. '*Wa-alaykum as-salam*, Sheikh Farid. May our paths cross again one day.'

'I will pray for it.'

Celia's farewells to the many Bedouin children who crowded round her, tugging at her *abeyah* for attention, were less formal and more protracted. Ramiz watched almost unnoticed, content to remain in the background, a strange emotion tugging at his heart. It was pride, he thought. He was proud of her, and proud to be in her company. It felt good, this sharing. A taste of what it could be like to have a consort. A partnership.

'She has the brains of a man in the body of a beautiful woman.' Sheikh Farid's words were a high compliment indeed, and Celia deserved it. She was exceptional. She deserved to be recognised in such a way—as herself, on her own terms. It was only in seeing someone else do so that he realised he had long since stopped trying to slot her into any preconceived role himself. She was Celia. Unique. He would never meet anyone like her again.

She finally escaped the clambering embraces of the children and allowed Ramiz to help her up onto the high saddle of her camel. Smiling and waving, the children followed them for about a hundred yards, Sheikh Farid's little daughter being among the last to give up the chase. Celia, touched immeasurably by the affection she had been shown, was dabbing at her eyes with a scrap of lace. Beside her, Ramiz kept his camel to a slow trot to allow her to regain her composure. The reality of her leaving was beginning to dawn on him with cold clarity.

This 'interlude', as she called it, he had intended as his cure. *The only way to eliminate temptation is to yield to it.* Asad's words, which only a few days ago had seemed to be the answer to his prayers. Now they mocked him. He had yielded to temptation, he had abandoned his principles to do so, but far from being sated, he was now addicted. Addicted to Celia's body. Addicted to her company. Addicted to her mind.

He needed her. He craved her. He could not imagine how it would be without her. Loneliness loomed like the vast desert plain stretched out before them in the rising heat of late morning, scorched of life, bleached of colour, dusty and arid.

A messenger had come in the night. The English had arrived at the port. The escort Ramiz had organised to attend them was even now leading the caravan across the desert to Balyrma. By the time they returned to the city tomorrow Celia's father could be waiting to take her home. They had only tonight. Just one more night.

Ramiz could hardly bear to look at the bleakness which was his future. Almost he resented Celia for doing this to him. Until she'd arrived he hadn't even known he was lonely. Until she'd arrived he hadn't needed anyone or anything. Only A'Qadiz mattered. A'Qadiz was his life and his reason for being. Now A'Qadiz without Celia seemed as drained of colour as an English morning in November.

Tonight would be their last together. Tomorrow he would cut her from his life. Why did it feel as if he would be severing a part of himself? He didn't even know what she felt about it all, not really. He hated the way she looked so cool and collected, when he ached with something horribly akin to love. But he could not love her and he would not—any more than she could or would love him.

Tonight was all they had left to them. Tonight must be enough, for there was no more to be had.

When Ramiz joined her in the tent he seemed different. Celia couldn't say how, just that he was. He had been in a strange mood since the morning's visit to Sheikh Farid. Distant, but watchful. Every time she looked at him he was looking at her, his eyes slits of amber, the tiny lines at their edges more pronounced than usual, as if he were frowning, but he did not seem angry. He seemed tense. And now, prowling around her tent in a dark blue caftan, restless as a caged tiger.

Neither of them had eaten much over dinner. They had not spoken much either. Celia was aware—too aware— of the fact that this was the last time. She could feel her heart beating, marking time like a pendulum, swinging inexorably back and forth, back and forth, counting out the seconds and the minutes and the hours.

She was apprehensive, waiting for him to make the first move as he always did when they came together. Excitement lay like a sub-strata beneath the layer of tension. Tonight she wanted it all. She did not care about the risk. She did not care about the possible consequences. She did not care about anything other than knowing, experiencing the completion of their union inside her— something Ramiz had been extremely careful never to allow. She loved him for it, and knew she should be grateful for his self-control. She was, but it left her feeling as if something was missing, something lacking. It left her feeling empty. She wanted him to make complete love to her. Just once.

But she was nervous. And if she hadn't known him better she'd have said Ramiz was nervous too. Something was bothering him, though he denied it when she asked him.

'I've made you a present,' she said, pulling the caftan she had so carefully embroidered out from under a cushion and handing it to him.

Ramiz shook it out and examined it. Dark blue silk, she had copied its pattern from one of his others. The long sleeves were embroidered in shades of blue in the traditional pattern which Yasmina had shown her. The same pattern was repeated around the hem and at the neckline, delicate but unobtrusive, designed to give weight to the garment rather than adornment. The most intricate work was on the motif she had sewn on the left breast. A crescent moon and a falcon—Ramiz's own insignia—but the bird was in full flight, and in its beak it carried a rosebud.

Ramiz gazed at it in silence, tracing the image with his finger.

'Do you like it?'

He laid the caftan down carefully on a divan. 'It is a very evocative image.'

'It's how I think of you. Me. This.'

'Us,' Ramiz said softly, stroking her hair behind her ear so that he could lick into the little crease behind her lobe, inhale the scent of her that lingered there, feel the strength and the fragility of her that seemed to be encapsulated at that precise point, in that combination of soft flesh and delicate bone.

'Us,' she said breathlessly, allowing herself to feel

the word, to think the word, to believe that it could be true just for tonight.

Ramiz pushed back the heavy fall of her hair to flutter kisses onto the nape of her neck, his fingers kneading her shoulders, stroking the wings of her shoulderblades. He pulled her against him, slipping his hands down to her waist, wrapping his arms around her, folding her into him.

She could feel his erection pressing against the base of her spine. She could feel the wall of his chest, his heart beating slow and sure against her back. Her head nestled into his shoulder. She closed her eyes and drank in the scent, the feel, the soft sound of his breath—drank it all in so that she would remember it for ever.

Ramiz turned her round in his arms and kissed her. So tenderly. So softly. Holding her as if she were something precious, his hands on the side of her face, his thumbs caressing her jaw, his eyes warm and golden, with such a look that she felt as if she were melting. She closed her own eyes and surrendered to the moment, which was like no other moment that had passed between them. A long, languorous moment, as if they had all the time in the world just to kiss and kiss and kiss. Gentle kisses, gentle caresses, as if they would soothe rather than arouse, as if they would coax and cajole, a slow burn—so slow that they barely noticed the flames rising.

Her clothes disappeared as if they had melted. His hands were on her breasts, touching her as if he had never touched her there before, his fingers marvelling at the roundness, the smoothness, the creaminess of her skin, the pink puckering of her nipple. His mouth landed like the whisper of a butterfly, sipping and sipping and sipping until she was nectar, trickling hot and sweet in a path downwards from her nipples to her belly to the darker, more sumptuous heat between her thighs.

He was naked. She was naked. Liquid with desire, molten with it, she lay touching and being touched, kissing and being kissed, stroking and being stroked. His shaft throbbed under her caress, but he seemed in no hurry, intent on tending to every curve and dip and swell, every crease and pucker, rolling her onto her stomach to kiss down her spine, the curve of her bottom, the back of her knee, the hollow of her ankle bone, then on to her back, to work his way up again, reaching the softness of her thighs, the damp heat between them, jolting her from floating bliss to jagged desire in an instant.

Celia moaned and clenched back on her climax, catching Ramiz unawares when she wriggled out from under him, rolled him onto his back, placing herself on top of him, leaning over him so that her breasts were crushed into his chest, her nipples taut and hard on his skin, his shaft taut and hard between her legs. She kissed him urgently. She saw the urgency reflected in his face, his eyes dark with it, his skin flushed with it, and then as she kissed him she felt herself lifted, his hands gripping her waist, and he thrust up and was inside her, deep inside her, as he let her fall on top of him at the same time.

She gasped her pleasure, lying still over him. He pushed her gently upright, steadying her by the waist, and the action allowed his shaft to forge deeper. His thrust forged it deeper again, touching something, a spot high inside her, that triggered an instant clenching and pulsing climax, sending her over in a headlong rush so that she was barely conscious of him thrusting inside her still, of the tension of his control etched on his cheekbones, on the rigid muscles of his shoulders, the corded sinews of his arms as he gripped her and thrust, and she lifted and fell in the same rhythm, lifting and falling, feeling him building and thickening as with every thrust he hit that same spot again and she trembled and shuddered.

She could determine the moment when he would push her from him by the way his eyes lost focus. She could see the resolution in him in the way his grip changed. She could feel his climax tightening in the base of his shaft. She could feel him swell, her own muscles gripping and holding, furling and unfurling against him. Ramiz groaned. She fell on top of him, pushing him down as he thrust up, pushing him hard down so that he couldn't move, and with a harsh cry he came, pouring hot and endlessly, high and deep inside her, and it was more, more than she had ever imagined it would be—for it was as if their essences mingled, and for now, in this instant, they truly were one.

They lay melded together for long moments, breathing fast, hearts thumping in wild unison, limbs entangled. Celia's hair trailed over Ramiz's shoulders, over his arms, which were wrapped tight around her waist in an iron grip, pressing her against him as if he would never let her go. She floated on a cloud of ecstasy, glided on a current of the sweetest, warmest air, heavy yet weightless, finally understanding the word *sated*.

Gradually their breathing slowed. Ramiz's hold on her relaxed. She waited, but the anticipated rejection did not come. He smoothed her hair back from her head. He kissed her gently on the mouth. He turned her onto her side and cradled her into him—two crescents fitting perfectly together. He ran his hand possessively down her flank and held her thus until she slept. And when she awoke in the dark of the night, when the lamps had burned out, he was still there. Still holding her.

'Celia.' Ramiz kissed her neck.

She tensed. Now he would leave. Now he would say something. But he didn't. Except her name. 'Celia…' in that husky voice, raw with passion, brushing over her skin like velvet, and he turned her to face him and then he kissed her, and it started over again—except this time Ramiz took control, Ramiz lay on top of her. It came harder and faster, their joint climax, as he thrust with her legs wrapped around him, and he poured himself into her with no need for her urging, his cry one of abandon she had never thought to hear and would never forget.

In the morning when she awoke he was dressed, sitting on the edge of the divan, with his formidable look back in place. She stretched out her hand. 'Don't hate me.'

Ramiz shook her away. 'If I hate it must be myself. A man must take responsibility, since a woman must bear the consequences. It should not have happened.' *It should not, but he could not regret it.* His own intransigence confused him.

'It was my fault.'

'No. The fault was mine. We must trust to the fates that you are not punished for it.'

Celia bit her lip. Punished! He was talking about the possibility of a child, their child, as punishment. She sat up. 'I should get dressed. You wanted to make an early start.'

His mind seethed with words. His heart seethed with emotions. He couldn't understand it—any of it. He couldn't think straight. He wanted to shake her until she told him what she really felt. He wanted to make love to her again, to experience that sweet perfection of their union, a perfection he hadn't known possible until last night.

Ramiz got to his feet, running his hand through his hair. 'A messenger arrived yesterday. Your father is here in A'Qadiz. He arrived at the port two days ago. He will be at Balyrma shortly—perhaps even before us.'

'You knew last night?'

Ramiz nodded curtly. 'This is the end.'

'You knew last night?' Celia repeated stupidly.

Her eyes were like moss damp with dew. Her hair curled like fire over the creaminess of her skin, over the soft mounds of her breasts. She looked like Botticelli's *Venus*. He had never seen anyone so beautiful or so irresistible. Having her, taking her so completely, possessing her, had made it worse, much worse. Knowing did not satisfy. It only made the wanting more painful, for he knew now what he would be missing.

'Why didn't you tell me, Ramiz?'

He had no answer—none he could give which would not force him to confront—what he did not want to confront—so Ramiz shrugged. 'You know now. There are two women with him also. One young, one old.'

'My aunt? The other is probably a maid.'

Another shrug. 'Get dressed. You will find out soon enough.' He turned to go.

'Ramiz?'

'Well?'

'You were saying goodbye, weren't you? I understand. It was perfect while it lasted—our fairytale. I want you to know that.'

He blanched. The words were almost his undoing. A fairytale. That was all it was. Ramiz left the room.

In the main part of the tent he saw the caftan she had embroidered for him. He picked it up. The motif dug like thorns into his heart. He could never wear it. Never. But he folded it carefully and took it with him all the same.

It came to him then, as he strode across the sand to his own tent. He loved her. That was what it was—this craving, this need to be with her. It was because she was part of him.

She was his. He felt it more fiercely than the burning heat of the sun. She was his. He loved her. And soon she would be gone.

Chapter Thirteen

Contrary to Ramiz's expectations, when they arrived at Balyrma there was no sigh of Celia's relatives. In fact dusk was falling and Celia was beginning to think they would not arrive at all that day when the doors of the harem were flung open and, to her astonishment, not just Aunt Sophia but Cassie stood before her, looking extremely dusty, exhausted and bewildered.

'Celia? Is that you?' Cassie was the first to speak, standing transfixed before the exotic-looking creature who bore a distant resemblance to the sister she had come so far to rescue. She hesitated, unaccountably nervous.

'Cassie!' Celia flew across the courtyard to embrace her sister. 'Cassie, I can't believe it's really you. Are you well? I can't tell for all the dust. Cassie, it really is me, I promise.' Celia kissed her sister's cheek. 'And Aunt Sophia. You've come all this way, and so quickly. You must be exhausted. Please come in. Fatima, Adila—here are my aunt and my sister. They will want food.' Celia broke off to issue instructions in Arabic, before ushering Cassie ahead of her to her favourite salon.

'You have learned the language?' Cassie said in amazement.

Celia laughed. 'A little only.'

Cassandra paused at the fountain, trailing her fingers in the water and looking around her at the lemon trees, the tiled pillars, the symmetry of the salons running round the square, one leading into another. So strange, yet Celia looked so at home here. Even the way she walked in her jewelled slippers was different. She seemed to float and ripple.

'You look like Scheherazade in these clothes,' she said, regarding her sister with a mixture of envy and awe. 'So very glamorous. I hardly recognise you.'

Celia made a little twirl. 'Do you like them? They are so much more suited to the heat here, and such lovely colours.'

'Celia, are you—can it be that you have *abandoned* your corsets?' demanded Lady Sophia, looking at her niece's all too obvious curves, revealed by the clinging fabrics. 'I do trust you do not leave your rooms in such a toilette?'

Celia laughed. 'No one wears corsets here, Aunt, it is far too hot.'

'And your hair—is it the custom to wear it down like that?'

'Not outside. Then it is covered by a veil.'

'And you have no stockings. What are these things

under your robe? They look remarkably like pantaloons. Do you tell me it is also common to have one's *undergarments* on display?'

'Dearest Aunt, they are called *sarwal* pantaloons, and, yes, I am afraid it is quite acceptable. Oh, Cassie, Aunt Sophia—I can't tell you how wonderful it is to see you. Please do sit down. Adila will bring you some sherbet. You will like it; it is most refreshing.'

'Where do we sit?'

'On the cushions. Like so.'

Celia floated gracefully onto the carpeted floor. Cassie followed suit, but Lady Sophia took a seat with extreme reluctance. 'Only heathens sit on the floor.'

'Where is Papa, Aunt?'

'He has an audience with the Sheikh.'

'How are the girls? Are they well? Did you get my letters?'

'Yes, they are all very well and send their love. But, Celia—' Cassie looked anxiously at her sister '—are *you* well?'

'Do I not look it?'

'Yes. Very. In fact I don't think I've ever seen you look better. You look—older, but more beautiful,' Cassie said, sounding as confused as she felt. 'Not in the least like our Celia. I have to confess I am a little intimidated by you.' Her laugh tinkled like the cold water of the fountain. 'What do you think, Aunt?'

Lady Sophia pursed her lips. 'Hmm.' She took a cautious sip of the sherbet which Adila had handed to her on a silver tray. 'Do they speak English?' she asked, nodding at the maidservants.

Celia shook her head.

'And this place we are in—is this what is known as the harem?'

Again Celia nodded.

'Where are the other women?' Cassie asked, looking around her as if she expected a flock of scantily clad females to suddenly appear.

'Sheikh al-Muhana is not married. He has no wives,' Celia said with a smile.

Lady Sophia cleared her throat. 'Celia, I must ask you. Has that man committed any—any improprieties with you? You must know that your sister has been most concerned for your—your... I told her not to worry, of course. I told her you would not—but you must put her mind at rest. Tell us plainly, child, have you—have you been forced to—? In short, Celia, this man has not laid a hand upon you, has he?'

Though she tried desperately to stop it, when she was faced with the frank blue eyes of her sister and the worried grey of her aunt, Celia felt a blush steal over her cheeks. 'Sheikh al-Muhana has treated me with the utmost respect,' she replied falteringly. 'He was conscious from the first that I—that my family—that Papa... He has done nothing to compromise the relationship between our two countries,' she finished with a tilt of her chin. 'In fact it was Ramiz—Sheikh al-Muhana—who saved my life when we were attacked by the brigands who killed George.'

Needless to say this statement produced a welter of questions from Cassie. Though Celia tried to gloss over George's role in events, Aunt Sophia's sharp nose scented scandal. 'George Cleveden was reputed to be an excellent shot,' she said. 'I cannot understand how he came not to defend himself.'

'He did not have the opportunity to fire his gun. It was all so sudden.'

'And it was early morning, you say? How came it that you were not in the tent with him?'

'I found the tent claustrophobic and chose to sleep outside.'

'Had you and George quarrelled?'

'No, Aunt Sophia, nothing of that nature. We had not long been married. We were still…well, getting used to each other.'

'Hmm.' Lady Sophia treated Celia to her Sphinx look. 'You should know that your sister and I came all this way in anticipation of having to support you through the trial of your husband's death and your subsequent incarceration here. Cassie in particular has been most upset by the idea of your suffering inopportune advances from this Sheikh al-Muhana.'

Celia pressed her sister's hand. 'Have you been worried about me, Cassie? Poor thing. There was no need as I have been very well looked after, I promise. I am so sorry to have caused you to fret.'

Cassandra examined the intricate silver *passementerie* braiding on the sleeve of Celia's caftan. 'What is it you're not telling us?' She lifted her eyes, meeting her sister's with a puzzled look. 'It's true I've been worried sick about you, and I can't tell you what a relief it is to see you in one piece, looking so well, but—but that's

just it, Celia, I don't understand it. What has happened
to you?'

Celia pulled her sister into a tight hug. 'Cassie, nothing bad, I promise.'

Cassandra sniffed. 'You've always told me everything.'

'Hmm,' said Lady Sophia once more. 'Celia, I believe
Cassandra would be the better for a wash and change of
clothes.'

'Of course she would.' Celia clapped her hands to
summon the maids. 'Cassie, go with Fatima and Adila.
You will be amazed by the bathing chamber, and they
will give you some of my clothes to try if you wish. Then
you will see that they are just clothes, and I really am
your sister. Go on—you will feel much better.'

Cassandra left. 'Well,' Lady Sophia said when they
were alone, 'since it is obviously not George Cleveden
who is responsible for that glow you have about you,
young woman, I presume it is this sheikh. You will tell
me, please, now that your sister's blushes have been
spared, what exactly is going on here.'

Lord Henry Armstrong's meeting with Ramiz was
conducted on much more formal terms, in the splendid
surroundings of the throne room. Ramiz, clad in his
royal robes of state, sat on the dais, with Akil standing
in attendance. To Peregrine's relief two low stools had
been placed in front of the throne, and to these Ramiz
graciously waved his visitors.

'I think we have met before, Your Highness,' Lord

Henry said, sitting cautiously down, having made his bow, 'though I can't recall where.'

'Lisbon, about four years ago,' Ramiz replied. 'Until my brother was tragically killed in battle I spent much of my time abroad as my father's emissary, and my brother's too.'

'Thought I recognised you,' Lord Henry said with satisfaction. 'Don't often forget a face, though I'm not quite so good with names. Well, now, tragic business this, but no point in dwelling on it, so we might as well get straight to the point. George Cleveden came here with the objective of agreeing rights of passage through A'Qadiz's port. I've been authorised to conclude those negotiations.'

'I am sure we can reach terms agreeable to us both, Lord Armstrong,' Ramiz said smoothly. 'I know how very important the route is to your East India Company.'

A lesser diplomat would have expressed surprise, but Lord Henry's experience stood him in excellent stead. Like a good gambler, he knew when he had been trumped. 'Quite so,' he said. 'Three months is a considerable advantage over two years. What is it you seek from us in return?'

'We will discuss the details tomorrow, but let me just say it pleases me to be able to conclude a pact which I believe will be to the long-term advantage of both our countries. Tonight I am sure you wish to rest after your journey. The desert can be unkind to those unfamiliar with it. And you will obviously wish to see your daughter.'

'No rush on that. Celia and Cassie will have their heads together, happy to wait until our business is concluded.'

Peregrine frowned. His instructions from the Consul General were clear. The Lady Celia was to be questioned prior to the treaty for any pertinent information. Acutely uncomfortable as he was with the damnable position in which Lord Wincester had placed him, he was even more terrified of disobeying the explicit orders of such an influential man. He tugged on Lord Henry's sleeve. 'My Lord, would it not be wise for us to speak to Lady Celia now?' Peregrine said with a significant look. 'Find out how she is, what she has been up to, et cetera. She'll be anxious to tell you all about her adventure, if you get my drift.'

'Dammit, man, I said it can wait,' Lord Henry said, frowning.

'But, My Lord—' Peregrine persisted awkwardly.

'I said not now,' Lord Henry said furiously. He turned towards Ramiz. 'You will forgive my assistant. He is rather tired,' he said, drawing Peregrine a censorious look.

Ramiz clapped his hands together and the doors at the far end of the throne room were flung open. 'Indeed—as I am sure you are too, Lord Armstrong. My servants will escort you to your quarters, and to the men's *hammam* baths. I will join you later for dinner.' He nodded his dismissal. 'Akil, a word, if you please.' Waiting until Lord Henry and Peregrine were safely out of earshot, Ramiz got to his feet and cast his jewelled headdress onto the throne. 'Get that idiot assistant on his own.

There is something going on and I want to know what it is.'

'And the treaty?'

'As we agreed. Lord Armstrong knows his position is not strong. Give a little to massage his ego, and he will not argue with the main points. Are Lady Celia's sister and aunt with her in the harem?'

Akil nodded. 'If things go well, Lady Celia can leave tomorrow.'

'Why do you dislike her so much?'

Akil hesitated. 'It's not that I don't like her. Under different circumstances I would like her very well. But she does not belong here, Ramiz.'

'You saw how Sheikh Farid took to her. And his wives.'

'And many other people—my own wife included. The Lady Celia is undoubtedly charming.'

'But?'

Akil shrugged. 'You know what I think. Do not let us quarrel over it. It is not just that she doesn't belong here, Ramiz, her family would no more accept it than your own people. In the eyes of the likes of Lord Armstrong we are heathens. It wouldn't surprise me to find that he suspects his daughter has been kept in your harem as a concubine,' he said with a smile.

'If he thought that he would hardly have been so polite just now,' Ramiz snapped.

'He is a statesman first, a father second. He will get the treaty signed to advance the British cause, and then he will worry about his daughter. Mark my words, Ramiz, he says nothing for the moment, but that does not mean he will remain silent. We must hope the Lady Celia has nothing to complain of.'

Ramiz cursed. '*You* must rather hope for your own sake that *I* have nothing to complain of. Find out what Finchley-Burke was so cagey about and report back to me before dinner. And bring Yasmina to the palace tomorrow, Celia will wish to say her farewells.'

'She *is* going, then?'

Ramiz ran his hand through his hair. 'Would it be so impossible to imagine her staying?'

Akil shook his head and made for the door. 'You don't really want me to answer that,' he said, and left.

For a long time afterwards Ramiz stared absently into space. The problem was not that it was impossible to imagine Celia staying; it was that it was impossible to imagine her leaving. He did not know how it had come about, but she had become indispensable to him. He, Ramiz al-Muhana, Prince of A'Qadiz, did not want to contemplate the rest of his life without her. Now he wondered if he had to. If Sheikh Farid accepted her, why not others? As his consort, with the fulfilment she would bring to his life, would she not more than make up for any potential backlash which failure to marry to one of his neighbours' daughters would inevitably bring?

After last night he was as certain as a man could be without hearing the words that she loved him. Last night she had made love to him, as he had made love to her. Last night had not been about the pleasures of the flesh—it had been something more fundamental, almost religious. The worship of a lover by a lover. The desire to create one being from two separate halves. The need to celebrate that union with the planting of a seed. How much he had derided that idea until now. He wanted Celia by his side. He wanted her to be his and only his. He wanted children—not as the means of cementing the succession, but as the fruit of their love.

It would be asking much of her. To stay here in A'Qadiz, to surrender her family, to exchange her loyalties from one country to another, to commit herself not just to him but to his kingdom, a place steeped in custom and traditions alien to her. It was not something she could do half-heartedly either, if she was to be accepted. There would be changes, and with Celia by his side some of those changes would come more quickly than he had planned, but some things would never change. As his princess she must not just pay lip-service to their traditions, she must embrace them. It was much to ask. Perhaps too much.

Ramiz forced himself to imagine life without her. His mind refused to co-operate. She was his—had always been destined to be his. Tomorrow, in the clear light of day and before her family, he would claim her.

Filled with determination, and a lightness of heart which it took him some time to realise was a foretaste of happiness, Ramiz retired to his chambers to change. He wondered how Celia's reunion with her sister was going. He wondered what she was saying of him, if she was confiding anything about him. No, she would not. His Celia—for already he was thinking of her thus— was fiercely loyal. She would tell nothing which might compromise his relationship with her father. Nothing which would put his treatment of her in anything other than a favourable light. She loved him. He was almost sure of it.

The urge to seek her out and declare himself was strong, but duty forbade it. As Ramiz finished bathing and donned a clean robe in preparation for dinner, Akil arrived, looking sombre.

Dismissing the servants, Ramiz turned to his friend. 'Well?'

'I spoke to Finchley-Burke as you suggested, Highness.'

'You call me Highness. It must be bad news,' Ramiz said with an ironic smile. 'Spit it out.'

'Ramiz, you must understand if I was not absolutely sure of this…'

Ramiz's smile faded. 'What is it?'

'The Lady Celia.'

'What of her?'

'She has been spying on you.'

'Don't be foolish.'

'Perhaps spying is the wrong word. She has been collecting information about our country.'

'A natural curiosity, Akil.'

'No, Ramiz. I'm sorry, but it's more than that. They left her here deliberately, with instructions to make use of your attraction for her.'

'You are being ridiculous.'

'I'm not, I assure you. Oh, nothing improper was asked of her. According to Finchley-Burke it was all neatly veiled—her duty to her country, the memory of her dead husband…you know the kind of thing.'

'You are saying that Celia was instructed to extract

information from me that might prove useful to the British government by—? No, I can't believe it.'

'Ramiz, I'm sorry.' Akil put a hand on his friend's shoulder but it was shaken off. He took a step back, but met Ramiz's eyes unflinchingly. 'I *am* sorry, but you must ask yourself why else would a woman of her birth have allowed you such liberties? Come on, Ramiz, it's not as if she put up much resistance, is it?'

Ramiz moved so quickly that his fist made sharp contact with Akil's jaw before he had a chance to defend himself. Akil staggered back against the wall, frightened by the blaze of anger he was faced with.

Ramiz took a hasty step towards him, his fists clenched, but stopped short inches away. 'My hands are shamed by contact with you. You deserve to be whipped.'

'Whip me, then, but it won't change the truth.' Akil spoke with difficulty, for his jaw was swelling fast. There was blood on his tongue. 'She has used you. It is as well we found out before tomorrow, for you can be sure her father would have found an opportunity to allow her to brief him. She has used you, Ramiz, we are well rid of her.'

'Get out! *Get out of here!*'

'Ramiz...'

'*Now!*'

Akil bowed, still clutching his jaw, and fled. Alone, Ramiz slumped down on his divan, his head in his hands. There must be an explanation. But Akil would never lie to him. He knew that for a certainty. There was no reason either for Finchley-Burke to concoct such a story if it was not true. He would not demean himself by asking the junior diplomat to repeat it. Celia would answer to him personally.

Lady Sophia, having much food for thought, graciously agreed to permit Fatima to help her bathe, after much encouragement from Celia. 'Please, Aunt, I promise you will find it a most amenable experience.' Celia had also been fulsome in her descriptions of A'Qadiz, and her recent trip to the desert in Sheikh al-Muhana's caravan, but despite being pressed had said little of the Sheikh himself—even less of her relationship with him.

Cautiously lowering herself into the scented water of the tiled bath, Lady Sophia realised that it was Celia's very reticence which gave her most grounds for concern. The girl was smitten, it was obvious. She would consult Henry in the morning, for the sooner Celia was removed from this sheikh's beguiling presence the better.

Left alone together with Cassie, Celia gave in to her sister's plea to be allowed to try on her exotic outfits. She was sitting on her favourite cushion, watching Cassandra parade before her, laughing and telling her she looked rather like the Queen of Sheba, when the crash of a wooden door slamming with force onto tiled walls made the smile die on her face and had her leaping to her feet.

Celia reached the doorway in time to see Ramiz stride across the courtyard. His face was set and white with fury. 'What's wrong? Is it my father?'

'Traitor!' He stood before her wild-eyed, his chest heaving.

'Ramiz! What on earth is the matter?'

'I trusted you! Dear heavens, I trusted you. I who trust no one. And you betrayed me.'

Anger glittered from his eyes, mere slits of gold under heavy lids. His mouth was drawn into a thin line. Celia clutched a hand to her breast. 'Ramiz, I have not betrayed you. I would never—what has happened? Please tell me.'

'You lied to me,' he snarled.

'I did not lie to you,' Celia responded indignantly. 'I would never lie to you. You're frightening me, Ramiz.'

'I doubt it,' he flashed. 'I doubt anything frightens *you*, Lady Celia, consummate actress as you are. I should have known. Akil was right. I should have guessed from the start that such a delicate English rose would not subject herself to the brutal caresses of a heathen like myself without reason. Do they *know*, my lovely Celia?' he hissed, nodding contemptuously at Lady Sophia and Cassie, paused on the brink of intervention in the doorway of the main salon. 'Have you told them the price you paid for whatever pathetic little snippets of information you have garnered for them?'

As realisation dawned Celia began to feel faint. 'Mr Finchley-Burke,' she said, her voice no more than a whisper.

'Precisely. He is here with your father. You didn't expect that, did you?'

Horribly conscious of the presence of her aunt and

her sister, Celia shook her head miserably and moved a little further down the courtyard. 'Ramiz, it's true. Mr Finchley-Burke asked me to—to keep my eyes and ears open. Those were his words. It is also true that I thought about it—but only for a few moments. I was just relieved to have an excuse to stay here, Ramiz. I never intended—I would never use—especially not now, after…'

'I don't believe you.'

'Ramiz, please.' Celia took a step towards him, her hands held out in supplication, but he shrank away from her as if she were poison. She swallowed hard. Tears would be humiliating. 'It's the truth. Even if I did consider it at first…'

'So you admit that much?'

Celia hung her head. 'I thought if I could salvage something from George's death… But it was a thought only—a fleeting one. I never really intended—I know I never would have. And that was before you and I…'

'There *is* no you and I. Not now.'

'*Ramiz!* Ramiz, you can't seriously believe that I would have made love with you for any other reason than—' She broke off, realising that what she had been about to say was exactly what she had sworn never to say. That she loved him. Looking at him in anguish, she could think of nothing *except* that she loved him.

Now he did touch her, pulling her into his arms, pushing her hair back from her face, forcing her to meet his hard gaze. 'So why did you, Celia? Why did you allow me such liberties? Why did you give *me* what you gave no other man?'

'You know why,' she whispered. 'I couldn't stop myself.'

'How can I believe that when you obviously had no such difficulty in denying your husband?'

'George has nothing to do with this.'

'But he has everything to do with it. Was it not for the sake of his memory that you did all this?'

'Ramiz, have I ever asked you anything remotely sensitive when it comes to A'Qadiz? Have I prodded you for information? Have I ever attempted to cajole secrets from you? You know I have not!'

But he was beyond reasoning. 'You have done worse than that. You have forced me to betray my honour. You gave yourself to me. You threw yourself at me in the hope that I would succumb and I did. I do not doubt for a moment that your intention is to cry ravishment now, thus allowing your father the moral upper hand, which he will have no hesitation in using to his advantage.'

Celia stared at him in absolute astonishment. 'I truly thought you knew me. I thought you understood me. I thought I understood you too. But I don't. I would die rather than do such a thing.'

'I didn't expect you to admit it. I just wanted you to know that I'd found out. It is I who would die rather than allow you to take further advantage of me. There will be no treaty. Never. Now get out of my sight.'

He threw her from him contemptuously. Celia staggered. 'Ramiz, please don't do this. Please.'

'I am done with you. All of you. You will leave Balyrma tomorrow. I will have an escort to see you out of my kingdom. I don't want to see or hear from you ever again.'

The harem door clanged shut behind him and he was gone. As Celia crumpled to the floor, covering her face with her hands, Lady Sophia and Cassandra rushed towards her, helping her to her feet and back to her salon, seating her on her divan and wrapping her in a velvet throw.

'It's all right, Celia,' Cassie said, holding her tight and casting a bewildered look at her aunt.

Almost oblivious of their presence, Celia huddled under the soft caress of the velvet. It would never be all right. Nothing she could say would make any difference. Ramiz despised her. It was over.

Chapter Fourteen

'Let me in! Open up at once, I say.'

Celia raised a weary head from her pillow and listened.

'Open up! Dammit, my daughters are in there. Will you open the door?'

'Papa?' Celia stumbled from her divan to the courtyard, to find Cassie and Aunt Sophia staring in consternation at the closed door of the harem. 'Is that Father I can hear?'

'We can't get the door open,' Cassie said. 'There's no handle on this side.'

'Open up,' Celia called to the guards in Arabic. 'It is my father.'

The door swung open, revealing an irate Lord Henry with a red-faced Peregrine beside him. The eunuch guards had drawn their scimitars and were barring the way. 'For goodness' sake, Celia, tell these men to let us through,' Lord Henry said testily.

'This is a harem, Papa. Sheikh al-Muhana is the only man who is permitted to come here. Why did you not just send for me?'

'Couldn't get anyone to understand a damned word I was saying.'

'But where is Ramiz?'

'If you mean the Prince, I have no idea. Didn't turn up for dinner with us last night—haven't seen him this morning. Took us the best part of the last hour to track you down here. I've never seen so many corridors and courtyards in my life. This place is like a maze.'

Celia spoke softly to the turbaned guards, gesturing to her father. Reluctantly, they sheathed their scimitars. 'I've told them to leave the doors open and promised we will remain in full view in the courtyard,' she said, gesturing her father in. Peregrine, who looked as if he would prefer to stay on the other side of the door, entered with some reluctance.

Lord Henry looked about with interest. 'Well, so this is the harem. Where are all the other women?'

'There aren't any. Prince Ramiz is not married. What has happened, Papa? You look upset.'

'Well, and so I bloody well should be,' Lord Henry said, casting a contemptuous look at Peregrine. 'Come here, Celia, let me look at you.'

Lord Henry inspected his daughter, who was dressed in a green caftan of lawn cotton, with her copper tresses flowing down her back, in some state of disorder from sleep. Perfectly well aware that the trauma of the scene with Ramiz and her consequent disturbed night showed in the dark shadows under her eyes, Celia put her arms round her father's neck, avoiding his scrutiny. 'It is lovely to see you, Papa. I'm sorry you've had to come all this way.'

'Aye, well, providential as it turns out. Or at least,' he said, glowering once more in Peregrine's direction, 'I thought it was until this damned fool told me what he and that idiot Wincester had cooked up.'

'Lord Armstrong, I assure you I was just the messenger,' said Peregrine. 'Wouldn't dream of— Would never—' He broke off to look beseechingly at Celia. 'I beg of you, Lady Celia, to inform your father of what passed between us.'

'Let us sit down,' Celia said wearily, clapping her hands to summon Adila and Fatima, and asking them to arrange divans in the courtyard for her guests, much to Peregrine, Lady Sophia and Lord Henry's relief. Celia and Cassie, who was dressed in one of Celia's outfits, though she retained her corsets, sat on cushions, leaning against the fountain.

Once coffee was served, and the maidservants had retired, Celia took a deep breath and recounted her original interview with Peregrine. 'I assure you, Papa, he was most circumspect in his request, and most painfully embarrassed by it too. I admit, I did consider the possibility of disclosing any information which I obtained here—not by subterfuge but simply because I *was* here—but after Peregrine left I decided I could not. Lord Wincester may consider my first loyalty is to my country, but while I am a guest of Sheikh al-Muhana, my country is A'Qadiz, and I would not insult him by betraying him. If I did, would I not be betraying my country rather than serving it?'

'Quite right, quite right,' Lord Henry said. 'Well said, daughter—exactly as I would have told old Wincester myself, if I had been consulted. Call me old-fashioned but diplomacy is an honourable vocation. I'll have no truck with stooping to nefarious methods. Britain can fight her corner without resorting to that.'

'Yes, Papa. I only wish I had said as much to Mr Finchley-Burke at the time,' Celia admitted, shame-faced.

'And why did you not, may I ask?'

She coloured, but met her father's gaze. 'I wanted to stay here. I was glad of the excuse not to leave. I didn't say as much to Mr Finchley-Burke, but I think he guessed.' She turned to Peregrine. 'Did you not?'

He shrugged in agreement.

'But why?' Lord Henry looked at his daughter afresh, seeming to notice for the first time her loose hair and traditional dress. His eyes narrowed. 'Why are you dressed like that?' He cast a worried glance at his sister. 'Sophia?'

Lady Sophia, looking unusually disconcerted, in turn cast a warning glance at Peregrine. 'Perhaps if you are finished with Mr Finchley-Burke, Henry…?'

Immensely relieved, Peregrine rose from his seat, but Lord Henry detained him. 'He made this mess— damned fool confessed all to that Akil chap last night— so he can stay where he is until we've agreed how to patch things up. Which I won't be able to do until I know all the facts.' Lord Henry got to his feet, dipping his hand into the fountain as if to test the temperature, and sat back down again. 'Out with it,' he said, looking at Sophia. 'What is going on?'

'Papa, there is nothing going on,' Celia said hurriedly. 'Only that I—that Ramiz and I—that Sheikh al-Muhana and I...'

'Celia thinks herself in love with the man,' Sophia said testily. 'That is why she stayed.'

'In love! With a sheikh! Are you out of your mind, Celia?' Lord Henry leapt to his feet once more, looming over his eldest daughter. 'I hope—I do most sincerely hope—that you have not lost all sense of propriety as to have been spending time alone with this man.' He eyed his daughter's guilty countenance with astonishment.

'I am afraid, Henry, that after the scene Cassandra and I witnessed last night there can be no doubt at all that she has,' Lady Sophia said grimly.

'Eh? What scene?' Lord Henry demanded, now looking thoroughly bewildered.

'Sheikh al-Muhana came here last night, presumably as soon as he had discovered the Consul General's little subterfuge,' Lady Sophia explained, with one of her gimlet stares which made poor Peregrine quake. 'While Celia chose to keep the detail of what passed between them private, it was obvious from the—the manner in which they spoke that Prince Ramiz and your daughter are no strangers to one another's company.'

'Dear heavens.' Lord Henry staggered back into his chair. 'What on earth are we to do? The treaty,' he said, staring at Celia in horror. 'That treaty—you have no idea how important it is. A long-term commitment like the one we're aiming for is crucial. Fun-da-mental,' he said, banging his fist on his knee, 'is that we trust one another. Now I find that the Prince thinks my daughter has been spying at our government's instigation, and not only that she has been behaving like some sort of—of...'

'Papa!'

'Father!'

'Henry!'

'I say, sir...'

Lord Henry glared at the four shocked faces surrounding him. 'Well, how the hell do you think it looks?' he demanded furiously. 'Must I spell it out for you?'

'No, Henry,' Lady Sophia said hastily. 'I don't think that is necessary.'

Lord Henry mopped his brow with a large kerchief and sighed heavily. His Lordship was not a man prone to fits of ill temper. Indeed, his success as a diplomat was in large part due to his ability to remain level-headed in the most trying of circumstances, but an arduous trip by sea and sand, the incompetence displayed by everyone involved in this sorry matter, and now the scandalous and highly uncharacteristic behaviour of his eldest daughter had sent him over the edge. 'What were you thinking, Celia?' he said, his voice heavy with disappointment.

Celia, who by now was feeling about one inch tall, bit her lip. 'I wasn't thinking, Papa, that is the problem,' she said stiffly. She got to her feet with as much dignity as she could muster, shaking out her caftan and pushing her hair back from her face. 'Ramiz is an honourable man, and one who values the welfare of A'Qadiz over everything else. I am sure, with a few concessions on your part to compensate him for the misunderstanding, he will still be prepared to come to an agreement over the use of the Red Sea port. It will do your cause no harm to inform him that the matter has been a cause of estrangement between you and I, for upon that subject I think you will find you and he are in complete accord.'

'On the contrary, Lady Celia, I would be most upset to discover that I was the cause of your estrangement from your family. I know how much they mean to you.'

All eyes turned to where Ramiz stood, framed by the doorway. A night alone under the stars in the desert had done much to cool his temper, and with an element of calm had also come rationality. It was true Celia had never made any attempt to extract information of any sort from him, but more fundamentally he felt in his bones that she would not lie to him.

In his determination to be rid of her, Akil had exaggerated. With the discovery of his love still young, and Celia's feelings for him as yet undeclared, the situation had punctured Ramiz in his most vulnerable spot, but with the dawn had come renewed certainty. He loved her. He was sure of it, though he had never loved before—and never would again. He loved her. She was his other half, and as his other half could no more do anything untrue than he could.

Ramiz had returned to the palace filled with hope. Making immediately for the harem, he had come upon the open door, through which he had witnessed most of the courtyard scene. He had not stopped to wash or change. His cloak and headdress were dusty, his face showed a blue-black stubble, and there were shadows under his eyes. Ignoring all but Celia, he now strode into the room.

'I must speak with you,' he said urgently, taking her by the arm.

'You will unhand my niece at once, sir,' Lady Sophia said brusquely. 'You have done quite enough damage already.'

Confronted with a sharp-eyed woman bearing a remarkable resemblance to a camel dressed in grey silk, sweeping down upon him like a galleon in full sail, Ramiz stood his ground and kept his hold on Celia. 'Lady Sophia, I presume?' he said haughtily.

'And you, I take it, are Sheikh al-Muhana. I do not offer my hand, sir, nor do I make my bow, for you do not merit such courtesy. Unhand my niece, sir. She has suffered quite enough of your attentions.'

Ramiz's eyes narrowed. He took a step towards Lady Sophia, who flinched but did not give ground, then halted abruptly, snapping out a command in his own language. The two eunuchs came immediately into the courtyard, their swords drawn. Before they could protest, everyone except Ramiz and Celia had been ushered with varying degrees of force from the room. The harem door banged shut.

'Ramiz, what…?'

'I'm sorry.'

'What?'

'I'm sorry.'

'I've never heard you say that before,' Celia said, with a fragile half-smile.

Ramiz took her hand between his, holding it in a warm clasp. His face was stripped of its mask, leaving him exposed, raw, and there was something more there—something she recognised but had never dreamed to see, had never even allowed herself to hope for. It looked like love.

Celia caught her breath. 'Ramiz?'

'Celia, listen to me. I heard what you said to your father just now, but you have to believe I came here to ask you to forgive me for doubting you before I heard the words. What I heard just confirmed what I knew. What I should have realised last night—' He broke off and ran his hand through his hair, pushing his headdress to the floor. 'I wasn't thinking straight. I'd only just realized—only just begun to wonder if it was possible—then when Akil told me—I simply lost control. But there's one thing I'm sure of—will always be sure of. I love you. Without you my life would be a wilderness. I love you so much, Celia, say you love me and I will be the happiest man on earth. If you will just—'

'Ramiz, I love you. I love you. I love you.' Celia threw herself into his arms.

'Celia, say it again!'

'I love you, Ramiz.' She beamed at him. 'I love you.'

Finally he kissed her, his mouth devouring hers, the day's growth of stubble on his chin rasping against her tender skin, his hands pressing her so close she could scarcely breathe. She kissed him back with equal fervour, whispering his name over and over in between kisses, relishing the feel of him hard against her, the familiar scent of him, the wildly exhilarating excitement of him, and underpinning it all the simple rightness of it.

They kissed and murmured love, and kissed and repeated each other's name in wonder, and kissed again until, breathless and transformed, they sat together entwined in one another's arms on the floor of the courtyard, becoming dimly aware of an altercation on the other side of the door which seemed to have been going on for some time.

'My father,' Celia said. 'He probably thinks you're ravishing me.'

'If he would go away and leave us alone I would,' Ramiz replied with a grin. 'I did not like the way he spoke to you, or of me,' he said, his tone becoming serious. 'And your aunt too. They do not relish your choice of husband.'

'Husband?'

Ramiz laughed, a loud, deep and very masculine laugh of sheer joy. 'My love, light of my eyes, you cannot be imagining I mean anything else. You are the wings of my heart. I must tether you to me somehow.'

'But, Ramiz, what about tradition? I'm not a princess, and in the eyes of your people I'm not pure. Yasmina said…'

'Celia, what *I* know and what *I* think is all that matters. You *are* a princess—you are my princess. I will be a far better ruler with you by my side than alone. It is you who has taught me that, you who has made me realise that in order to be the man I ought to be I must have you with me.' Ramiz took her hand and bent down on his knee before her. 'Marry me, my lovely Celia, marry me. Because I love you, and because you love me, bestow upon me the honour of calling yourself my wife, and I will do you the honour of being your husband for ever, for even death will not part us. Marry me, and make me the happiest man on this earth and beyond.'

'Ramiz, that is the most beautiful thing I have ever heard.'

'Yes, darling Celia, but it was a question.'

'Yes.' Celia smiled and laughed and cried all at once. 'Yes.' She threw herself into his arms, toppling them both back onto the cushions. 'Yes, yes, yes,' she said, punctuating each affirmative with a kiss.

A loud thump outside the door startled them both. 'I think we'd better face your father before my guards are forced to use their scimitars on him,' Ramiz said.

It was not to be expected that either Celia's parent or her aunt would accept her marriage without protest. Ramiz listened with remarkable patience while first Lord Henry and then Lady Sophia asserted that such an alliance would end in disaster, would make Celia miserable, and would be the downfall of her sisters, who would be quite lost without her.

Celia countered by pointing out that her marriage to the ruler of a kingdom rich in natural resources with a port of immense strategic importance could hardly be deemed a misalliance. 'In fact,' she asserted, 'you should be honoured to have Prince Ramiz as a son-in-law, Papa, for association with him can only enhance your own career prospects—provided you can persuade him to forgive your rudeness.'

Lord Henry was much struck by his daughter's good sense. From that moment forward his affability towards Ramiz was marked. Indeed, in a lesser man such extreme cordiality might well have been branded obsequiousness.

Lady Sophia, whose objections were, to be fair, based upon her real affection for her niece, took rather more persuading. At Celia's behest Ramiz left the matter most reluctantly in her hands, concentrating his own efforts on discussions with Lord Henry on settlements, dowries and the all-important treaty.

'You talk as if I will be living here in isolation from the world,' Celia said to Lady Sophia as they walked in the palace gardens later that momentous day, 'but I hope you don't mean to deprive me of the company of either yourself or my sisters. I will be expecting all of you to stay here with us for extended visits—starting with Cassie, if she wishes,' she said, smiling at her sister. 'Though she may not wish to postpone her Season.'

Cassie clapped her hands together in excitement. 'What is a Season compared to this? Say I may stay, Aunt. I can come out next year, and anyway,' she said mischievously, knowing perfectly well what her aunt thought of Lord Henry's intended, 'I don't want to steal Bella Frobisher's thunder by having my come-out ball in the same season as her wedding.'

As the day progressed, and Lady Sophia graciously permitted Ramiz to take her on a tour of the royal palace and its famed stables, her stance visibly mellowed. The following morning, a visit to Yasmina cemented the seal of approval. Yasmina's mother was visiting—a formidable woman of Lady Sophia's stamp. The two ladies spent a most amenable few hours together, with Yasmina translating, at the end of which Lady Sophia was able to declare herself happy with her niece's proposed marriage, and even prepared to remain in A'Qadiz in order to attend the nuptials.

'Ramiz came to call this morning,' Yasmina said to Celia over a glass of tea. 'Such an honour—our neighbours will be talking about it for ever.'

'He and Akil are reconciled, then?'

Yasmina nodded happily. 'He knows Akil only acted for the best. He loves Ramiz like a brother.' She pressed Celia's hand. 'I have never seen Ramiz so happy. You will forgive me if I spoke out of turn when we first met?'

'Yasmina, I trust you will always say what you think. Your friendship means a lot to me, I would hate it if you started treating me differently when I am Ramiz's wife.'

'Not just a wife, you will be a princess.'

'I will still be Celia, and it is as Celia that I ask you to be frank with me, Yasmina. What will the people really think about our marriage? Ramiz says that what makes him happy will make his people happy, but I know it's not that simple.'

Yasmina took a sip of tea. 'I will not lie to you. There will be some who will find it difficult to accept simply because it is a break with tradition. But Ramiz has come to symbolise change for A'Qadiz, and a Western bride will not be such a huge surprise as it would have been two years ago when Asad ruled.'

'You said that because I was married before—'

'"A prince's seed must be the only seed planted in your garden,"' Yasmina quoted. 'I remember. But it has been, hasn't it? The man you were married to was a husband in name only. You need not be embarrassed. I told you, I have the gift.'

Celia shook her head, blushing. 'No. Ramiz was the first—has been the only…'

'Then, with your permission, that is what I will say. People will listen to me as Akil's only wife,' Yasmina said proudly, 'and it is natural to talk of such things. You need not worry. I will drop the word in a few ears, and you will see. Now, we must go and talk to your aunt and my mother, and Akil's mother too. We have a wedding to plan.'

It took four long weeks to orchestrate. Four long weeks during which it seemed to Celia that she hardly saw Ramiz, what with the need for him to personally invite all the ruling families of all his neighbours, and the need for her to receive endless visits from the wives of Ramiz's most esteemed subjects, to say nothing of the terrifying amount of clothes which Yasmina declared necessary for a princess, and the equally terrifying regime of buffing and plucking and pampering and beautifying to which Celia was subjected.

At Ramiz's insistence, Celia and Cassie rode out every day, with only a discreet escort, signifying to the people of A'Qadiz the start of a new regime of freedom, and signifying to his beloved Celia and her sister the trust he had in their ability to treat such freedom with discretion.

Aunt Sophia left with Lord Henry for Cairo, promising to return in time for the week-long celebrations. Having heard her confess that her one remaining reservation was that the wedding would not be a 'real' one, Ramiz suggested that he would be happy for an English priest to participate if she wished. Suitably reassured, she informed him that she would not insult him by demanding any such thing.

Abstention from intimacy of any sort was part of the tradition surrounding the celebrations. This Ramiz and Celia managed with extreme difficulty, but were assisted by Ramiz's frequent absences, Cassie and Yasmina's perpetual attendance upon Celia, and the fact that the palace harem was suddenly overrun with female visitors.

By the time the week of her nuptials finally arrived Celia was beginning to think it never would, so slowly had the days passed despite the frenzied activity.

The formal betrothal, which took place in a packed throne room, was the first ceremony. Celia, dressed in richly embroidered silks and heavily veiled, was presented to Ramiz by her father. The ring, a fantastic emerald set in a star-shaped cluster of diamonds, was placed on her right hand.

Next came a round of pre-wedding visits and feasts, with the women and men strictly segregated. Lord Henry accompanied Ramiz on the most important of these, returning after each one more exuberant as the extent of his future son-in-law's wealth and influence was revealed.

The night before the wedding was spent by Celia in the harem, where her hands and feet were painted with intricate designs of henna like the ones she had seen on Sheikh Farid's wives. Ramiz's formal wedding gift was delivered—a casket of jewels which it took two men to carry, including an emerald necklace, bracelets and anklets to complement her ring, each beautifully cut stone set in a star of diamonds.

Finally it was the wedding day. Dressed in gold, veiled and jewelled, and almost sick with anticipation, Celia stood before her sister and her aunt.

Cassie, in a traditional Arabic dress of cornflower-blue silk the colour of her eyes, hugged Celia tight. 'I'm so happy for you.'

'And I too.' Lady Sophia, splendid in purple, her grey curls covered by a matching turban in which feathers waved majestically, gave her a peck on the cheek. 'Good luck, child.'

Ramiz was waiting for Celia at the doorway of the harem, which she crossed for the last time, for they would share rooms in a newly decorated part of the palace—another tradition he had broken, having insisted that they would not spend another night apart. He was dressed in white trimmed with gold, the pristine simplicity of the tunic and cloak showing to perfection his lean muscled body, the headdress with its gold *igal* highlighting the clean lines of his face, the glow in his copper eyes which focused entirely on his bride.

They progressed under a scarlet canopy through the city, a band of musicians preceding them, family and close friends taking up the rear. Crowds sang and prayed, strewing their path with orange flowers and rose petals. Children clapped their hands and screamed with delight, jostling with each other for the silver coins which were thrown for them to gather. And through it all Celia was conscious only of the man by her side, of the nearness of him, of the scent of him, of the perfection of him.

Ramiz. Her Ramiz. Soon to be her husband.

The wedding ceremony itself took place in an open tent in the desert on the edge of the city, strategically placed on a hillside to accommodate the massive crowd. The bride and groom sat side by side on two low stools on a velvet-covered dais, while first Lord Henry spoke, in the hesitant Arabic in which Akil had coached him, before formally handing over his daughter. The *zaffa*, Sheikh Farid himself, declared the couple man and wife. Ramiz removed Celia's ring from her right hand and placed it on her left. Then he helped her to her feet and removed her veil. She was dimly aware of applause. Dimly aware of Cassie crying and of Aunt Sophia sniffing loudly. What she was most aware of was Ramiz. Her husband.

'I love you,' he whispered, for her ears alone, his voice sending a shiver of awareness through her. 'My wife.'

'I love you,' she said, looking up at him with that love writ large across her face. 'My husband.'

The applause became a roar as Ramiz kissed her. The music started, and she and Ramiz performed their first dance together—she nervously, he with aplomb. They sat together as the feast got underway, receiving congratulations, but as dusk fell and the first of the stars appeared Celia thought only of the night to come. They left, covered in rose petals, on horseback—a perfect black stallion for Ramiz, a grey mare for Celia, the wedding gift of Sheikh Farid. Their journey through the desert was magical and brief, silent with promise as the horses picked their way through the sand until the dark shadow of palm trees marked their arrival at an oasis.

A single tent. A fire already burning outside it. An ellipse of water lapping gently at the shelving sand. The stars like silver saucers. The new moon suspended in the velvet sky.

'*Hilal*,' Celia whispered to her husband, as they stood hand in hand looking up at it. 'New beginnings.'

Ramiz smiled tenderly. 'New beginnings. Come with me. I have a surprise for you—a gift.'

'Darling husband, you have done nothing but shower me with gifts since our marriage.'

'And I will continue to shower you with gifts for the rest of your life, since you are the greatest gift of all. Come with me.'

Ramiz led her over to the tent. As they grew nearer Celia could make out a strange contraption. It had a round base from which a wooden pole rose to support an irregular shape. It looked a bit like a very odd sundial. As they got closer Celia realised that the bulky shape was made of cloth. It was some sort of covering. She looked at Ramiz in puzzlement. He put a finger to his lips before carefully removing the cloth. There, on a perch, sat a hooded bird of prey, white and silver with black wing-tips. 'A falcon!'

'*Your* falcon, my beloved.'

'Oh, Ramiz, he's beautiful.'

Ramiz removed the hood from the bird and, taking Celia's hand, pulled a leather gauntlet over it. 'Keep very still.' She hardly dared breathe as he placed the bird carefully on her arm. 'The wings of my heart,' he said to her, 'my gift to you.' He jerked her arm and the bird flew high, its magnificent wingspan outlined against the crescent moon. 'Now, hold out your arm again, and whistle like this,' Ramiz told her, and Celia watched breathlessly as the bird glided back, landing delicately on her gauntlet. 'Like the falcon I fly, and like the falcon I will always return to you,' Ramiz said, putting the hood back on the bird.

He led her into the tent. 'I hope these are happy tears,' he whispered, gently kissing Celia's eyelids.

'I didn't know I could be so happy,' Celia replied, twining her arms around his neck. 'I didn't think it was possible. Love me, Ramiz. Make love to me.'

'I intend to, my darling. Tonight. Tomorrow. And tomorrow. And tomorrow, and…'

But he had to stop talking to kiss her. And to kiss her. And to kiss her. Until their kisses burned and the abstinence of the last few weeks fuelled the flame of their passion, and their love made that passion burn brighter than ever—brighter even than the stars in the desert sky which glittered above their tent. They made love frantically, tenderly, joyously, with an abandon new to them both, whispering and murmuring their love, shouting it out to the silent desert in a climax which shook them to the core, and which Celia knew, with unshakeable certainty, truly was the new beginning heralded by the crescent moon.

A new life together beckoning her.

And a new life growing inside her.

* * * * *

Historical Note

While I've tried very hard for historical accuracy, I've taken a few liberties with timings and some events referred to in the story which I hope you'll forgive me for.

In 1818, Mehmet Ali had already wrested control of Egypt from the Ottoman Sultan, and the major powers, primarily the British and the French, were maintaining a local presence in the hope of rich pickings when the Ottoman Empire collapsed. The British Consul General was Henry Salt, a renowned Egyptologist who did, like my fictional Consul General, regard the relics of ancient Egypt as there for the taking, but there the similarity between my bumbling diplomat and the real one ends.

Obviously, A'Qadiz is an invented kingdom. In my imagination it sits in what is now Saudi Arabia with a coastline a couple of days' sail away from Sharm-el-

Sheikh, which would be an ideal port for the "fast" route to India via the Red Sea. This route did play a significant role in reducing the overall journey from two years to three months, but it was about fifteen years after the story is set that this came into use, and not until 1880s that the Suez Canal made it commercially viable.

In real life, it could take up to three months to get from England to Arabia, depending upon the weather, the type of ship and the number of stopovers, though at a push it could perhaps have been done in about three weeks. Since I needed Celia's family to come to her rescue, this proved to be a bit of an issue. I speeded up the process by giving them access to the Royal Navy, but there is no doubt that I've stretched credibility a bit by expecting a letter to get from Cairo to London, and Celia's family to get to Arabia when they receive it all in the space of about six to seven weeks.

Richard Burton's (bowdlerized) translation of *One Thousand and One Nights* is the most well-known, but it was not published until 1885. The French edition was published in 1717 however, and this is the one Celia has read.

COMING NEXT MONTH FROM

HARLEQUIN®
HISTORICAL

Available July 26, 2011

- **THE GUNFIGHTER AND THE HEIRESS**
  by **Carol Finch**
  (Western)

- **PRACTICAL WIDOW TO PASSIONATE MISTRESS**
  by **Louise Allen**
  (Regency)
  (First in *The Transformation of the Shelley Sisters* trilogy)

- **THE GOVERNESS AND THE SHEIKH**
  by **Marguerite Kaye**
  (Regency)
  (Second in *Princes of the Desert* duet)

- **SEDUCED BY HER HIGHLAND WARRIOR**
  by **Michelle Willingham**
  (Medieval)
  (Second in *The MacKinloch Clan* family saga)

REQUEST YOUR FREE BOOKS!

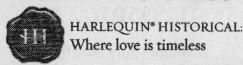

HARLEQUIN® HISTORICAL:
Where love is timeless

2 FREE NOVELS PLUS 2 FREE GIFTS!

YES! Please send me 2 FREE Harlequin® Historical novels and my 2 FREE gifts (gifts are worth about $10). After receiving them, if I don't wish to receive any more books, I can return the shipping statement marked "cancel." If I don't cancel, I will receive 6 brand-new novels every month and be billed just $5.19 per book in the U.S. or $5.74 per book in Canada. That's a savings of at least 17% off the cover price! It's quite a bargain! Shipping and handling is just 50¢ per book in the U.S. and 75¢ per book in Canada.* I understand that accepting the 2 free books and gifts places me under no obligation to buy anything. I can always return a shipment and cancel at any time. Even if I never buy another book, the two free books and gifts are mine to keep forever.

246/349 HDN FEQQ

Name _____ (PLEASE PRINT) _____

Address _____ Apt. # _____

City _____ State/Prov. _____ Zip/Postal Code _____

Signature (if under 18, a parent or guardian must sign) _____

Mail to the **Reader Service:**
IN U.S.A.: P.O. Box 1867, Buffalo, NY 14240-1867
IN CANADA: P.O. Box 609, Fort Erie, Ontario L2A 5X3

Not valid for current subscribers to Harlequin Historical books.

Want to try two free books from another line?
Call 1-800-873-8635 or visit www.ReaderService.com.

* Terms and prices subject to change without notice. Prices do not include applicable taxes. Sales tax applicable in N.Y. Canadian residents will be charged applicable taxes. Offer not valid in Quebec. This offer is limited to one order per household. All orders subject to credit approval. Credit or debit balances in a customer's account(s) may be offset by any other outstanding balance owed by or to the customer. Please allow 4 to 6 weeks for delivery. Offer available while quantities last.

Your Privacy—The Reader Service is committed to protecting your privacy. Our Privacy Policy is available online at www.ReaderService.com or upon request from the Reader Service.

We make a portion of our mailing list available to reputable third parties that offer products we believe may interest you. If you prefer that we not exchange your name with third parties, or if you wish to clarify or modify your communication preferences, please visit us at www.ReaderService.com/consumerschoice or write to us at Reader Service Preference Service, P.O. Box 9062, Buffalo, NY 14269. Include your complete name and address.

*Once bitten, twice shy. That's Gabby Wade's motto—
especially when it comes to Adamson men.
And the moment she meets Jon Adamson her theory
is confirmed. But with each encounter a little something
sparks between them, making her wonder if she's been
too hasty to dismiss this one!*

*Enjoy this sneak peek from ONE GOOD REASON
by Sarah Mayberry, available August 2011
from Harlequin® Superromance®.*

Gabby Wade's heartbeat thumped in her ears as she marched
to her office. She wanted to pretend it was because of her
brisk pace returning from the file room, but she wasn't that
good a liar.

Her heart was beating like a tom-tom because Jon Adamson had touched her. In a very male, very possessive way.
She could still feel the heat of his big hand burning through
the seat of her khakis as he'd steadied her on the ladder.

It had taken every ounce of self-control to tell him to
unhand her. What she'd really wanted was to grab him by
his shirt and, well, explore all those urges his touch had
instantly brought to life.

While she might not like him, she was wise enough to
understand that it wasn't always about liking the other person. Sometimes it was about pure animal attraction.

Refusing to think about it, she turned to work. When
she'd typed in the wrong figures three times, Gabby admitted she was too tired and too distracted. Time to call it a
day.

As she was leaving, she spied Jon at his workbench in
the shop. His head was propped on his hand as he studied
blueprints. It wasn't until she got closer that she saw his

eyes were shut.

He looked oddly boyish. There was something innocent and unguarded in his expression. She felt a weakening in her resistance to him.

"Jon." She put her hand on his shoulder, intending to shake him awake. Instead, it rested there like a caress.

His eyes snapped open.

"You were asleep."

"No, I was, uh, visualizing something on this design." He gestured to the blueprint in front of him then rubbed his eyes.

That gesture dealt a bigger blow to her resistance. She realized it wasn't only animal attraction pulling them together. She took a step backward as if to get away from the knowledge.

She cleared her throat. "I'm heading off now."

He gave her a smile, and she could see his exhaustion.

"Yeah, I should, too." He stood and stretched. The hem of his T-shirt rose as he arched his back and she caught a flash of hard male belly. She looked away, but it was too late. Her mind had committed the image to permanent memory.

And suddenly she knew, for good or bad, she'd never look at Jon the same way again.

Find out what happens next in ONE GOOD REASON, available August 2011 from Harlequin® Superromance®!

Celebrating

Blaze **10** *years of*
red-hot reads

Featuring a special August author lineup of
six fan-favorite authors who have written
for Blaze™ from the beginning!

The Original Sexy Six:

Vicki Lewis Thompson
Tori Carrington
Kimberly Raye
Debbi Rawlins
Julie Leto
Jo Leigh

Pick up all six Blaze™
Special Collectors' Edition titles!

August 2011

Plus visit
HarlequinInsideRomance.com
and click on the Series Excitement Tab
for exclusive Blaze™ 10th Anniversary content!

www.Harlequin.com

Harlequin *Presents*

USA TODAY *bestselling author*

Lynne Graham

introduces her new Epic Duet

THE VOLAKIS VOW
A marriage made of secrets...

Tally Spencer, an ordinary girl with no experience of relationships... Sander Volakis, an impossibly rich and handsome Greek entrepreneur. Sander is expecting to love her and leave her, but for Tally this is love at first sight. Little does he know that Tally is expecting his baby...and blackmailing him to marry her!

PART ONE:
THE MARRIAGE BETRAYAL
Available August 2011

PART TWO:
BRIDE FOR REAL
Available September 2011

Available only from Harlequin Presents®.